THE RE-REMEMBERED

A COLLECTION OF STORIES

DWIGHT L. WILSON

RUNNING
Wild
PRESS

Published in North America and Europe by Running Wild Press. Visit Running
Wild Press at www.runningwildpress.com Educators, librarians, book clubs (as
well as the eternally curious), go to www.runningwildpress.com.

ISBN (pbk) 978-1-955062-46-6
ISBN (ebook) 978-1-947041-98-1

WIDER UNITED STATES TIMELINE

Year	Chapter Titles	Elsewhere in America
1814	Displaced	British burn Washington, D.C.
1824	The House Servant	The United States Bureau of Indian Affairs established
1827	The Cousin	Freedom's Journal, first Black owned newspaper published
1829	Presidential Audience	Andrew Jackson begins as President of the United States
1832	Bone Interpreters	Black Hawk War Ends
1832	Back in the Day	First Wagon Train (Bonneville's) crosses Rocky Mountains
1835	Uppity	Unsuccessful attempt to assassinate President Jackson
1839	The Little Cabin	The first portrait in America is taken
1842	The Well-Tanned Ghost	Slave revolt in the Cherokee nation.
1844	Grandfather's Mouse	The Great Flood of 1844 hits the rivers Missouri and Mississippi
1847	Peace in the Valley	United States win several key battles in the Mexican War
1847	Between Us	John C. Fremont become first governor of newly annexed California
1848	Wild Flowers	California Gold Rush begins
1849	Accepting Grace	Los Angeles and San Francisco are incorporated as cities
1849	Words	Census shows that more than 10% of those classified as Negro are blended
1850	Time	Fugitive Slave Act made law
1852	Let There Be Light	Uncle Tom's Cabin published
1853	The Tour Guide	The United States annexes from Mexico much of what becomes our Southwest
1853	Turning	Yellow Fever kills nearly 8,000 in New Orleans
1855	The Shawl	Bleeding Kansas battles begin between anti and pro slavery factions
1856	The Kissing Game	Pro slavery forces burn Lawrence, Kansas
1859	Brown's Brigade	Pike Peak's Gold Rush in Colorado and Comstock Lode in Utah begin

INTRODUCTION

I am one who like Frederick Douglass escaped from slavery. In bondage I dared dream that once bondage was behind me, I would be known as Sarah Freedom. Indeed, so reads my forged free paper, a despicable passport that I must carry in the land of my birth. I mention these facts because Esi, my mother, often encouraged us to hold onto the ancestors' hands. In her imitable words, "Re-rememory is what makes a people a people."

The stories found on these pages are reconstructed from either my own life or were told to me by others in my circle. I share them as this tortured country is on the brink of war started by those whose idea of justice is keeping my people in perpetual slavery. Even those of us with "free papers" are downtrodden and without basic human rights. We have been told that even in war our men will not be allowed to fight in fear they might kill a white man.

1
DISPLACED

I have witnessed loved ones and others beaten to within an inch of their lives by slave masters. I have heard that at a nearby plantation two men and one female younger than I failed to survive savage beatings. The patterns ripped into the backs of relatives and friends resembled chopping blocks. Yet, I was destabilized by Caesar's description of his efforts following the Alliance of Indian resistors' loss at The Battle of the Thames. He left the killing fields to protect the children and Indian women who were camped in a stand of beech trees less than a mile from the battleground. Etiquette said these non-combatants should be spared, but General Harrison and those under his command often thought nothing of burning their possessions and killing even babies. Many children remembered earlier atrocities. Despite their training, they screamed as mothers and elders scrambled to gather them to a safe place whose existence was more dream than reality. When I heard that a few frightened women threw their babies into the river rather than risk seeing their heads smashed, tiny scalps taken as trophies, and skins flayed for riding whips, my heart broke on their behalf. Were they not also as much my people as the slaves whose lives were constantly at risk?

"We left in a hurry taking the horses of every warrior we knew was dead," said Caesar, my dear Shawnee friend. "If there was any question, we left the others in case they should need them in the retreat."

"What if they fell into the hands of the white soldiers?" I asked.

"In trying to save a horse should I lose a nephew?" asked Caesar.

Caesar said that while guarding their flight south he killed two of the enemy, but this time the pursuit was by few and the whites had little heart for the assignment. The soldiers returned to the looting. For miles the refugees on their own land could see billows of black smoke covering the sun.

The remnant of Tecumseh's forces had retreated across the Detroit River and were almost into Ohio before Caesar learned his father had been killed. Another warrior had reported that he had heard a phrase from the older man's death song, but in Caesar's mind, everything except the secret burial of Tecumseh seemed to be in a fog. "Losing my father and a brother made my mother beyond consolation," said Caesar. "She was not alone. This was no time for proper grieving. Even removed from the battlefield we were worried that white settlers would be emboldened by our great loss and try to pick us off one by one. We had Creek and Cherokee relatives in the south. Taking all them folk through Kentucky and Tennessee, areas we had already lost, without a great many warriors and no food with us, was asking for militias to massacre us while calling us thieves."

The one hope he could think of was to deliver Cocheta, his mother and others to Wapakoneta where Shawnees led by Black Foot lived in relative safety. Black Foot's Shawnees had either been neutral or fought against Tecumseh's resistors.

Most of the young warriors who did not join the patriots admired the war chief and wanted his cause to succeed but were afraid the odds against them were too great. My brother Robin had hung on every word our mother had spoken about the homeland. He recalled how the Akan had been destroyed because some tribes had cooperated with white slavers. Had it not been so, our parents would not have been kidnapped in Fante-land.

After a few weeks in Wapakoneta, Caesar told his mother he expected to be on the run for what remained of his life. She understood the choices before him and said, "I never gave birth to a warrior with the dream he would become a farmer."

"I left for the south."

In time, his mother adjusted to the point that she was made peace chief of the Wapakoneta women. Caesar said, "At no point had someone in our line risen so high."

"Ain't you a chief?" asked Robin.

"Chief of what?" said Caesar. "If I called myself a war chief who is there to answer a call to battle?"

I said, "You are my chief."

He smiled. A trace of sadness crossed his face and left as quickly as a needle pulling thread passes through cloth.

Monni, Caesar's wife, did not miss his reaction being called a chief. "And do I not answer your call into battle as we help free the slaves?"

Here was a woman only a few shades darker but with more red tinting to her skin. She might help me learn what it means to be a full partner in life.

* * *

3

On the way south, Caesar stopped with Clark and Mary Crispin Ferguson, parents of four children. The baby was seven months old and one day would be my husband. The Fergusons were Quaker friends who lived in Waynesville near the creek named for his great grandfather. When they told their version of this story, never once did they mention Caesar so much as smiling.

"Thee looks downcast, Stalking Panther," said the 29 year old, blond-haired, Mary Crispin, speaking in Shawnee and using his true name.

She had spoken in Shawnee because Caesar was accompanied by a stranger and she knew protocol demanded respect on land some Shawnee continued to claim as their own.

"You can use your own language," said Caesar. He extended a package of salt wrapped in a cloth. "Shouting Bear's mother is Creek but his father was Irish. He also speaks your language."

Dinner consisted of beef alamode, beef mince pies, string beans, and pared white clingstone peaches in a heavy syrup. Mary Crispin's husband, Clark said, "Richard Mentor Johnson lead his Kentuckians west of Waynesville. They were primarily in pursuit of Tecumseh, but their hope was to invade Canada and take it for the United States. A cousin who refused to fight was used to repair guns and lend his brute strength to help pull cannons through The Black Swamp. There he came down with malaria. When well enough to move, he remembered he had kin in Waynesville."

"Do I know this man?" asked Caesar. "He sounds like a deserter."

"My grandmother was a Wickliffe. David Wickliffe doesn't see himself as a deserter," said Clark.

"We have seen the Kentuckians kill deserters."

"Surely, they would not have executed David," said Mary Crispin.

The men knew the answer but said nothing. Instead, Caesar considered the main dish. "Mary, this beef reminds me of buffalo. If it didn't have all this stuff in it—"

"The 'stuff', is merely bread, suet, onions, cloves species, and egg."

"I didn't mean no offense," said Caesar. "It's just been long years since I had buffalo."

"I thank thee for what I assume by the light in thy eyes is a compliment. I too tasted buffalo once shortly after we came to Ohio."

"I guess you whites liked it so much y'all hunted 'em out," said Caesar.

The room grew silent until Caesar looked at the young Ferguson children who were eating mince pies. "Them little things the little ones is eating seems like good eating too."

The children had been taught to keep speech at a minimum when adults. The older ones nodded and smiled confirming his suggestion that the pies were tasty. Mary Crispin rose and silently handed Charles to Clark while she went to the stove in the kitchen area of the great room.

Clark kissed Charles's forehead and said, "My cousin was as much forced into the army by the Kentuckians as ever was an American sailor by the British navy."

Mary Crispin returned with fresh water, sat the pitcher down and while taking the child back from Clark said, "David spoke of much that disturbed me. He said there were reports that the scouts came across more than a few wandering Indian families and bragged that they stripped the fields and storage bins, killed as many as possible because they were at war not seeking prisoners. They did the same with several Shawnee,

Lenape, and Potawatomi villages, leaving the people without crops."

"They did the same when they come upon Ottawas further north," said Caesar. "I guess you see why when we lost at the Thames, we had to get our loved ones away."

"Whites are uncivilized," said Caesar's friend, Shouting Bear, speaking for the first time.

From what I have learned, various tribes who once lived east, have seen their villages attacked and butchered. Some tribes have wholly disappeared. On other occasions people in threes and fours have escaped with no place to go. Sometimes they have united trying to make new families with the vague hope that one day they could form a village. The ever-pressing whites have forced these people to be no more than vagabonds living an unstable life and needing benevolence simply to survive.

"We have seen the remains of some of them folk you mentioned," said Caesar. "We buried them because those who murdered them did not."

"Oh, for the want of Light!" said Mary Crispin barely stopping herself from crying.

"Unless I am mistaken," said Caesar to Clark, "there were Ross County Quakers fighting against us too."

"I have heard I had relatives in the army but all Fergusons are not Quakers," said Clark in an embarrassed voice.

"If Quaker is the same as Christian," said Shouting Bear, "all Quakers ain't Christian either. In fact, from what my Pa taught me, all Christians ain't Christians. He used to say, 'Only the Great Spirit can create by word. People must act'."

"Far be it from me to argue with a guest's absent father," said Mary Crispin before redirecting

the discussion, "Caesar, as thy great grandfather's blacksmith skills were needed by the Shawnee, our cousin's skills were needed by the Kentuckians."

"My great grandfather was not impressed," said Caesar. "He was freed by the Shawnees."

"I meant no offense."

"I am not offended. I am frustrated," said Caesar. "Where is this David Wickliffe? Is he hiding at the sight of 'a savage'?"

"My cousin went home to his wife and children."

"Perhaps like Daniel Boone he'll remove to Missouri and push the Osages even further west," said Caesar.

"Boone, was another Quaker who turned on us in Kentucky," said Shouting Bear.

Mary Crispin, whose family knew Boone's when they were still practiced Quakerism, exchanged glances with Clark. The couple was surprised by how well Shouting Bear was informed. There was a lengthy silence before Clark said, "Antoine Chene has become a scout and spy for the Army fighting you."

"Chene grew up with us," said Caesar. "He calls himself 'Anthony' these days. His mother was a Shawnee, father a Frenchman, and his wife is Tecumseh's aunt. When the British closed the gates on our warriors at Fallen Timbers, Tecumseh predicted Chene would be a turncoat that would end up hurting us more than the British would. I think of Chene as a catch-penny with no more honor than a merchant who sells a keg of whiskey to a child."

"General Harrison laughs at us. He travels with a Seneca bodyguard and has paid other devoted spies, Shawnee, Lenape, Seneca, Mingo, Wyandotte..." said Shouting Bear.

"Add those to whites who in the past pretended to be friends," said Caesar, "and it becomes clear why our chance of victory at the Thames was so small."

"Yet thee trusts the British?" asked Mary Crispin.

"I can count the grown whites I trust on one hand," said

Caesar with more than a touch of rage. He calmed himself, "If you raise these children right I would have to use two hands."

"This is a sad world," said Clark.

"You two have proved yourselves friends."

"Thank thee," said Clark. "I know the names of other Shawnee scouts, sent by Black Hoof to help the Americans."

"I trust you but I don't understand you," said Caesar. "Are you not an American?"

"I am a Quaker who wants peace. Failing that, I want people to be loyal to their own interests when those interests have right on their side."

"We captured many Shawnee traitors. We even were forced to kill some," said Caesar. "The traitors all put their lives at risk more than they know. The Kentuckians hate all of us. In fact, one Kentuckian shot and almost killed Black Hoof." After a pause, Caesar said, "Thank you. I know you are willing to give me the names of other turncoats, but I probably already know them and this war is over. We learned the hard way that there were more Shawnees fighting against us than with us at the Thames. I saw some of them at Wapakoneta when I brought my mother to live among them. Without the help of warriors, such as Shouting Bear, from other tribes we would not have had a chance."

"I heard that most Indian nations chose neutrality," said Clark.

"How can you be neutral when someone is attacking your friends?" said Caesar. "Even a child understands that to sit when friends are being attacked is to help the attackers."

"Ain't that right son?" said Caesar as he looked at the oldest child, six year old Samuel.

Samuel looked first at his father then his mother. Neither coached him so he looked at his empty plate, hiding his thoughts.

Before the room grew too tense Caesar asked, "Could I have a few more of them peaches?"

Mary Crispin passed the bowl.

"I am a convinced Quaker, a convert," said Clark. "But before I see women and children murdered, I'll fight with you."

"That's good to know," said Shouting Bear.

With thousands of Kentuckians involved in the War of 1812 and their families and friends resentful of those from whom they had stolen the land, Caesar used paths less traveled. Caesar and Shouting Bear followed mostly forest trails through Kentucky, once Shawnee land, but at the time the most hostile state to Indians in the union. In times of active combat, the Warrior's Trail forged first by buffalo and then by the Shawnees and other tribes would have been the fastest. After several days' ride he arrived at the home of Creek relatives living in land now claimed by the state of Georgia. Instead of finding a place of peace where he could ponder his future, to his consternation he found the village preparing for war not only with Andrew Jackson, a man he had long despised, but also with the Cherokees.

Caesar's mother was born a great granddaughter to Tiffee, a powerful woman among the Creek. He parted the many ducks and geese that surrounded her three-room home and found the "Great Lady" sitting at the dinner table with a bowl of venison, rice, black-eyed peas, swamp cabbage, fried bread and melons on the side.

He described Tiffee as about my color and height, 5' but a little bigger in body. She rose in her colorful loose blouse over a nearly floor length brown skirt and opened her arms. He kissed the solid gold comb that held the lengthy ribbons and said, "Mother I am home."

She held him back a little and replied, "I see that my great great grandson, The Stalking Panther, has become a man." He smiled until she saw something in his eyes. "So it is true, Tecumseh has lost?"

"He is dead as is my father, brother, and most who fought with us."

"What of Shouting Bear?"

"He returned. I suppose he is playing chunkey with the other warriors as we speak."

"We know that game," said Robin suddenly. "Me and Dan was learned to play by Zephyrine;s boy Tra. Cherokees love it."

"We taught them how to play it. My great great grandmother insisted I eat. She said, 'You look much thinner than when you were here with Tecumseh'."

He accepted a place at the table. She ladled food into a bowl. What of the Cherokees? I heard before you returned north, their war chief, the Ridge, threatened to kill you. Did any of the young Cherokee warriors go with you?"

"It was Tecumseh he threatened but I doubt he was serious. A few Cherokees fought with us in the north."

"The central word was few," said Tiffee. "We Creek have fought Cherokees all of my life. You know you cannot trust that people."

"My cousin Lanyi is trustworthy."

"Unlike you, I have no Cherokee cousins. You are a man torn in many directions." When Caesar did not say anything, she added, "When all is said and done each of our nations must stand against the white interlopers or we will be swallowed like small fish stuck on the same stick, roasted in a common fire, and eaten by a common mouth that spits out our bones onto the common earth."

"You sound like Tecumseh."

"No. He sounds like me. I am the elder."

"You have counsel for me?"

"When have you known me to be silent? Those who want syrup must tap the maple. Many warriors in this village fought with Tecumseh. Other than Shouting Bear, those who survived are with the Red Sticks being led by Menawa. Word coming back says they have already fought Jackson's men many times. If you are quiet you can hear them calling for help." She went silent. The winter wind's voice seemed to pick up.

He stood and said, "I too go, Mother."

She motioned for him to wipe his upper lift and then shooed him out the door. "May the syrup prove rich."

* * *

Tiffee's prayers went unanswered. At the Battle of Horseshoe Bend, Jackson, with the help of Cherokees and White Stick Creeks, had a force nearly four times larger than those with the Red Stick Creeks. Caesar and Shouting Bear joined the Red Sticks who were nearly annihilated. Caesar was fortunate to get away with his life. He left the bloody field with a badly wounded Shouting Bear.

"Where do we go now?" asked Shouting Bear.

"Our world is coming apart," said Caesar, "and you ask me to be a prophet."

"I ask you to help me not die."

The Red Sticks who had escaped were being hunted like wild game. In a state of confusion, the two friends headed north and east which necessitated going through the heart of the land the whites had yet to appropriate from the Cherokees. From Horseshoe Bend they walked for a day and a half before they could take horses from a Georgia squatter. Skirting Head of

Coosa, the Cherokee capital, a day later, Caesar spied a familiar set of horse prints. "Could it be?" he said aloud.

"I don't understand," said Shouting Bear.

"I believe my cousin Lanyi is close by."

"He is a Cherokee."

"Yes, but as you remember, he fought beside us up north in the alliance."

"After Horseshoe Bend I don't speak to any Cherokees."

Sure enough, in a clearing surrounded by pine trees, it was Lanyi who the next morning came out of the small cabin's door to relieve himself. Caesar left Shouting Bear and sneaked up on his cousin. Caesar waited until Lanyi had pulled down his pants. He let out a tremendous Creek war yell, and threw a hatchet into the nearest tree. Lanyi tripped over his pants. Trying hard to pull them up, he rolled right and then quickly left hoping to dodge bullets, arrows or spears. For the first time in months Caesar laughed. He was barely able to say, "Pull up your pants, cousin, or the pine cones may relieve you of the next generation!"

While Lanyi hastily re-dressed, Caesar said in Cherokee, "Why were you not at Horseshoe Bend fighting beside Jackson?"

"Have you aged so much that you have forgotten that I was with you when we lost at The Battle of the Thames? I will never again fight against The People."

"When you disappeared after Tecumseh's burial," said Caesar. "I thought you may have been killed in Canada."

"Not this warrior. I continued fighting until it was hopeless. Where were you at the end? We could have used you."

"There were women and children to protect."

"Your words. My point. I saw no reason to think the white man would stop with destroying the Shawnee," said Lanyi. "I fought with Tecumseh's vision in mind."

"What of those other Cherokees who came north with you?"

"Of the six of us only my cousin, Fetches the Drum, lived and he would have been better off dead—three wounds in his torso, a lost nose. His body wounds were terrible. Those inside were even worse."

"Say more," said Shouting Bear using sign language, who had been warily watching Lanyi.

"Fetches the Drum had nightmares of the men killed beside him, including his father. Four or five warriors were killed when a cannonball tore through them. He tried to commit suicide at least twice before we made it across the Ohio River. On the way home he would suddenly begin crying even on the most beautiful day. Once we arrived home, he tried to kill his wife and mother—"

"Where is he now?" said Caesar.

"He left with The Ridge and the other warriors. Unless I am mistaken, he managed to get himself killed in war. That's what he wanted most."

"Perhaps I would have been better off had I died on the battle field," said Shouting Bear to Caesar.

Caesar translated for Lanyi. The Cherokee looked closely at Shouting Bear and then reached out to examine his wounded arm. "I am no healer but I doubt you can keep that arm."

Caesar served as interpreter and added, "Gangrene. He thinks you have gangrene."

Shouting Bear's face turned ashen.

"I-yo ka!" called Lanyi in a loud voice to his wife. "We need your help."

Lanyi was over 6' tall but Caeser described I-yo-ka as just a few inches taller than my 5' and her skin considerably lighter from not being as much in the sun. After I had become a professional seamstress I asked about her dress. Caesar closed his eyes, perhaps conjuring up an image of his cousin's wife and told me it was basically red but there was a white band on the lower half, the sleeve cuffs and the shoulders with diamonds centered by peace symbols. Despite my prompting, he could not recall the color of the symbols, "Dark", was all he could recall.

Caesar and Lanyi held Shouting Bear down so that I-yo-ka could remove his arm to the elbow. To his credit, he did not scream.

"I am impressed that she did not flinch," said Shouting Bear when he came to from blacking out.

"Neither did you," said I-yo-ka in Creek. "That a Creek man can match a Cherokee woman is a thing of wonder."

Caesar and Lanyi laughed. "She was born Creek," said Lanyi, conceding the language to the visitor. "I bought her from slavery and she lives as a Creek."

"A lost arm and a found funny woman," said Shouting Bear trying to smile. "What a day to be alive."

"Speaking of losing," said Caesar. "I have lost two great battles in a row."

"You're not much of a gambler," said Lanyi returning to Cherokee. "We won at River Raisin and Detroit and your spirit was not down."

The point was well taken, but Caesar knew that all of Shawnee-land was lost and probably the totality of Creek-land would soon follow. "Will you go to Missouri where the other Shawnee have been driven?" asked Shouting Bear.

"You're welcome to stay with us," said Lanyi.

"I have just killed two Cherokee warriors and Jackson acts as though he owns the Cherokee nation." He paused. "I will go back to my great grandmother's village. Perhaps she has an idea how a man can live without syrup."

2

THE HOUSE SERVANT

They approached Fruits of the Spirit Plantation on a road lined with willow trees and wide enough for two carriages to easily pass each other. Perhaps a half mile up the road sat the brick, two-columned, fifteen room big house. It was on a tiny rise overlooking the Hazel river, three fields, two of tobacco and a third planted in corn. The slave quarters were a quarter mile away to the east. The shack used by our family was across from one that was a twin. It was used by the only other true family on the plantation. Just to the north, facing each other, were the large dormitory for male slaves and the smaller one for female slaves. Neither of the dwellings used by slaves had more than one room.

The row of slave quarter houses was interspersed with maple trees. Although hidden from the view of the big house, not far away from the slave quarters, the Hazel River flowed from the Shenandoah Valley on toward the sea. On our side was a grove of "witness" sycamore trees. These the slaves used to record significant events like who was sweet on whom and to mark births, deaths and sellings away. Before Nat Turner's rebellion everyone knew that some slaves could write. Even though writing was not illegal while I lived on Fruits of the Spirit, our marks were deliberately cryptic hoping that snooping whites could not decipher what lay in the hearts of the oppressed.

On a warm May day in 1824 former President of the United States, Thomas Jefferson, was driven to Fruits of the Spirit. Along with the driver was his body servant and a woman named Sally Heming. No questions were asked. No explanations given by her master for her presence. Sally was a comely, fair-skinned woman who wore her hair straight down her back. Without explanation our foreman informed us that on the Sunday of Jefferson's visit, the bulk of the slaves were not to attend church. For most of us, our attendance of Reverend Stringfellow's church was more pageantry than worship. It gave the slave masters the opportunity to measure whose collection was growing, failing, strong or sickly. It was also a time for breeding. Many of the couples quietly went into the woods to mate. I never heard of an escape at this time. The patrollers heavily policed the environs and the unwritten law proscribed that anyone caught any place other than the woods or inside the church would receive imaginable torture. The story has it that during my infancy a couple left the woods. They were found a mile north. She received 20 lashes while he received 40 and both were doused with a bucket of hot pig fat. Whether or not it was true, some fled north at other times, but it had the singular effect of chasing thoughts of lovers stealing during church services.

My mother brought her three surviving daughters over to Eula's, Mama's best friend. Susannah, Fannie and I played or talked with Eula's daughters. Mama sang while breaking snap beans for the day's big meal. Eula's daughter Mae was a house servant who gained social status with the slaves by telling secrets. In a short visit, she told us that Sally's room was attached to Jefferson's.

"You gotta do better than that, daughter," said Eula, breaking off mid-song. "Any fool knows she ain't sleeping amongst us, not with all them fancy duds she be wearing."

"Do 'any fool know' where she is sleeping, Mama?" asked Mae.

"Is you talking smart?" said Eula. "I will slap the black off you and when you wake up, dead might not seem such a bad idea."

Mama just sighed, but once more my two sisters and I rejoiced that Esi was a "salt-water" woman who had not been so long in America that she had succumbed to beating her children. Eula knew of at least five generations of her family who had been slaves. She was also half Cherokee, but from what I have learned, they too did not use violence against their own. I have no idea who convinced Eula that corporal punishment was a virtue, but I saw her take a switch to a son who in my eyes was full grown.

"I'm sorry, Mama," said Mae. "I forgot myself."

"You sure did," said Eula. "It must be something in them table scraps done addled your mind. Find yourself and tell me some news worth more than a piece of chicken leavings."

Mae related a story well worth remembering. What I'm sharing is as near as I can remember it. Of course, the late Patience Starbuck, an avid reader and as close to an aunt as I have known, once said, "All history is fiction, written from a man's eyes to fit the shape of his imagination."

In hope of counterbalancing the drift toward fiction, even before I met Patience, intuition led me to check Mae's story with my brother Dan who had been called in from the fields and given the honor of alternating with both Mae who fanned our master and Eve, another Fruits of the Spirit slave who fanned the former President. Dan verified the parts he had personally witnessed. For my part, because I am a woman with no reason to reshape this garment to fit a slender figure, I am trusting the voracity of what I am offering,

* * *

Jefferson and Nathan Prescott, our slave master, were on the big house porch being fanned as Dan sat on the grass below the porch shining the master's and guest's shoes. He was at the ready both to relieve the perspiring women and to fetch something should the white men require a drink or food.

Jefferson told Prescott that the famous general Lafayette was scheduled to arrive in November. When he asked Prescott if he had ever met him, the host admitted, "I never had the pleasure. Mr. President."

"Ah, then I insist you come to Monticello for dinner and fine wine when he arrives. It may not be as fine as the deviled crab and roast saddle of lamb, crème Brule that I dined on before leaving but it will surely be sumptuous."

"My palette is not as refined as yours, sir, but I assure you my cooks will treat you well."

After a pause, Jefferson said, "It is said that you are teaching Latin to that slave of yours who makes my shoes and those of so many others of our class."

"Phyllis Wheatley learned in Massachusetts. Am I wrong?"

"I am told she also knew Greek," said Jefferson. "In a free country who am I to question what a fellow planter does with his property? I would suppose that if I can learn Sanskrit, which is infinitely more difficult to learn than elementary Latin, a talented nigra can try his tongue at "Vini and vidi."

"I dare say he has advanced beyond the basics. But yes, I do not expose him to certain incendiary teachings." In teaching him English, I have cultivated—if I may share the analogy—a page from your book. I have constructed a Bible with selected passages. However, my 'book' is for my own edification."

"I would doubt this special slave edifies you."

"He does not. Kenneth continues to speak when spoken to and learns only what is taught. There is no suggestion that he think about more than conjugations and endings—no beginnings."

After the two men had laughed heartily, Jefferson said, "Speak more about these lessons of the Caesars."

"I have made available a few well-edited books for Kenneth to take home. A few of his children have even chosen to avail themselves of what I call 'guided learning'. Their eyes only meet that which reinforces their state as meek, docile, obedient, subservient, inferior beings a good deal less than we who are 'only a little less than the angels'."

Jefferson chuckled before saying, "Your caution is well advised. Although I have said that every generation should have a revolution, I was not including slaves. Over the years, many a correspondent, as well as good friends, have warned that there must be a limit to how many slaves can safely be held and given advice concerning humane discipline."

"My slaves are unarmed and more docile than most. None has ever received more than 39 stripes in a single discipline, and then rarely. The specter of being sold south to Mississippi is useful. More importantly, our local militia is well trained and our patrollers among the best in Virginia. After a few unfortunate instances, the latter are screened to keep out the meaner sort of white trash."

Jefferson paused before saying, "Nathan, the only way to prevent those who labor for your happiness from rebelling is to respect them as more than servants. Respect is a practice that stretches beyond lashes."

"I have spent my entire life working at respecting Nigras. However, how can I maintain my course in an economic downturn? I might have to sell a few to the Carolinas or Georgia if not to Mississippi."

"Taking a heavy loss might be manageable but would certainly be unwise," said Jefferson. After a pause he added. "Back in 1796 I had to sell a dozen of my servants to the highest bidder. Even then, I showed them respect. In my presence, no slave dealers were allowed to touch them in forbidden places or call them other than their Christian name."

Prescott raised his hand and Mae cleared her throat. Dan hurried to the porch.

"To the ice house and bring fresh ice for the bucket. However, did you let it melt! Then have Nadine make me fresh mint juleps and see how supper is coming."

Dan hurried off to the cooks and then to the icehouse.

"On the subject of how slaves support our comfort," said Prescott, "I am seeking to expand Fruits of the Spirit. I have heard that you mortgaged 150 of your servants. May I be so bold as to ask if you were happy with the results?"

"It is no secret," said Jefferson. "The downturn of 1819 brought many of us to the brink. Monticello would not be Monticello had I not taken drastic steps as many before me have done. How many servants are in your possession?"

"I have but eighty," said Prescott although the three nearby slaves were aware of only 76 on Fruits of the Spirit and one other with his mistress on nearby property.

"That number should raise a great bounty. Do you need a letter of introduction to my financier?"

"Any letter from one so esteemed can do nothing but raise my value in a man's eyes."

"It sounds as though you are well on the road!" .

"That is a bit further than I have traveled," said Prescott chuckling, "but I do have a friend who knows James Swan in Boston."

"I know him better although you might consider our fellow Virginian, William Short."

"He and I have had some minor conflicts over William and Mary."

"James can be vindictive. By all, James is your man. Because of our business partnerships Yankees are more blessing. Do not quote me in the wrong circles. James is crafty. You must be equally so."

* * *

Mae said, "For breakfast they had them little braised partridges on toast eggs and bacon. For lunch cottage cheese with catsup, meatloaf, Madeira and fruit for dinner they had three different wines, ham and..."

"Ain't you got no sense, Mae?" interrupted Eula. "I want to know news not foods. What about that Sally woman?"

"I don't understand."

"If you don't, gal, you is a bigger fool than I thought you were."

At times, against their will, both Eula and Mama had been appropriated by Prescott. Everyone knew this. No one spoke of it. In fact, they both were so silent concerning the slave masters' despised practices that the world might believe they had not been its victims.

"I was told on pain of lashing not to say nothing about what wasn't meant for my eyes," said Mae.

"Let me help you," said Eula. "You ain't volunteering nothing. You is obeying your Mama. I'm the one who first taught you what lashing is. You understand?"

"Yes ma'am."

"Did the President use that door to the attached bedroom?"

"No ma'am."

"Did the door open and somebody go from one side to the other?"

Mae hesitated before reluctantly answering, "Yes' mam." Quickly she added, "I didn't see nothing. She could have been warming his feet."

"It's so hot catfish is sweating." Eula laughed. "You is a good house servant, daughter. Go on about your business. It's not for the Mama to get the child in hot water."

Mama said, "Eula, I'd tell you but you already know you was wrong to wring that outta Mae."

Eula laughed. "I know you ain't telling me how to raise my own child, Esi. You also know that by and by Mae was gonna forget she was warned and tell about them two all up and down the quarters."

The two friends laughed heartily. Their eyes told a different story. Perhaps their own abuse by Prescott made them feel more empathy for Sally than they could even express to each other.

3

THE COUSIN

Because Charles Ferguson had been allowed to travel with them to further his knowledge of the world, Caesar and Monni, our rescuers, brought me and my brothers Robin and Dan to Warren County, Ohio. As was Culpeper, our home county in Virginia, Warren County was mainly farm country. Waynesville, the nearest village to Caesars Creek, where the Quaker Fergusons had their farm, must have elicited mixed emotions for Caesar. His Creek was named after his great grandfather who the Shawnees had rescued from slavery. He in turn saved a drowning white boy, earning the settlers' admiration. However, Waynesville was named after Mad Anthony Wayne whose victory at the 1794 Battle of Fallen Timbers had broken the Shawnees' strength in Ohio and ultimately led to their crushing defeat twenty years later at the Battle of the Thames.

In 1827, my brothers and I were fugitives. Besides Caesar, Monni and Charles, we had neither friend nor acquaintance in Ohio. Thus, we had our own medley of emotions: excitement, apprehension and pain for the family left behind. The Fergusons offered us warm sanctuary. The next week my restless brothers broached the subject of all our tomorrows. I was well aware that heretofore our lives had offered few choices. It seemed enticing to at last be able to ask, "Where is heaven?" But instead of saying, "Where you lead I will follow", I reminded my brothers that in Virginia we had been treated well by the Hoges. It was my belief that without their assistance we would still be enslaved. They were good Quakers. Perhaps the Fergusons were as well. Why not give ourselves a little time to enjoy the moment with these people.

"Gal," said my senior brother, Robin, after a long pause, "I'm just doing this to shut up your mouth. We done heard there's more safehouses up the line and Caesar is willing to take us higher north."

"Shouldn't we head East?" asked Dan. "Now that we're not with them, maybe Daddy has enough money to buy out Miss Anne. You know Philadelphia is where he dreamed of."

I said, "It could be ten thousand mountains and twenty thousand slave catchers between here and a place we have never seen."

"You always pick the highest numbers you can think of," said Robin.

"If we keep moving, and we get caught it will be your fault. "

The first thread of the argument ended with me winning yet another victory. Well timed manipulation is often the only power the youngest and weakest has.

* * *

I am told that between the time the Crispin and Ferguson families arrived in Ohio in 1800 and the year 1827 when we arrived full of hope, the white population had grown twentyfold, much of it because of Tecumseh's defeat in 1814 and the capitulation of the majority of the Ohio nations to surrendering their autonomy. A few months later, David Wickliffe relocated from Kentucky to Waynesville. By 1827 nearly all of Ohio's Indians had been displaced west. When I learned that he had been a small part of that sad history, I was not pleased with his presence but in no place to suggest he move on.

"Why cometh thee to Ohio, cousin?" asked Clark.

"Thievery is not in our heritage." When Clark did not instantly come to David's preferred conclusion he added. "What can the descendant of the man who first translated the Bible into English do in Kentucky when he knows his people have stolen the land from the original owners and it is being worked by people his ancestors stole from their country?"

"I can't answer that question. "

"If he has a conscience, he can disassociate himself with evil that men do."

"I would suppose thee will be moving back to England," said Mary Crispin. "Surely we have also dispossessed the Ohio Indians."

"The Indians are one and the same: Shawnees," said David, "but this is a slave-free state. One sin is better than two and I have never visited England which as I recall you Crispins joined William the Conqueror in stealing from the original English."

"As with thee, David, I have never been to England and know nothing of that supposed tie."

He looked pityingly at me as though I were proof of his earlier guilt by association. I continued helping Elizabeth set the table and saw no reason to say anything.

* * *

For dinner I helped Mary Crispin and her daughter Elizabeth prepare mashed squash with butter and cream, boiled asparagus and green beans, stuffed roasted pigeons and a Virginia how cake that Mary Pool Hoge had taught me just before our escape.

David recounted his part in the War of 1812 during the meal. I later learned he had shared a portion of the story years before. His voice changed as though it was the highlight of his life.

"As we moved through Indian territory, occasionally we were attacked. Most men were steady but some lost their mind. Others soiled themselves like babies. There was no stopping. We had to make the frontier safe."

I wanted to ask, "Safe for whom," but I was not yet sure of our place in this new world.

"The man next to me took an arrow through his head. I was besplattered with blood, muscle and bits of bone. I panicked, running in circles, zig zagging wildly. Colonel Johnson himself dismounted and slapped me three...four times. I gathered myself, ashamed but alive."

"You were stealing from the tribes. They had a right to attack," said Clark.

"I guess you haven't turned all the way Quaker," said David. "Had you been unarmed and under attack I wonder if you would have argued for their rights, Mary Crispin."

"What rights we grant others and what rights we grant ourselves are often different," said Clark.

"Whatever that means, I agree," said David, "In our soldiers' minds they were fighting for the freedom of their families."

"How did thee manage the march before thee deserted?" asked Mary Crispin.

"That's why the Good Lord made whiskey."

"What about black soldiers?" I asked. "Were any among you?"

"There were black warriors with the Indians but the blacks with us were all slaves, helping with everything except nursing us with milk. They cooked, cleaned up, helped the doctors, buried the dead, attended the officers who owned them. Your father fought in the Revolution. Did he not tell you no American army travels without darkies to do the grunt work?"

"They couldn't fight?" asked my brother Dan.

"I saw one pick up his master's rifle when the captain was tomahawked in an ambush," said David.

"You mean he was out there with fighting all round and he didn't have no gun?" asked Robin.

"By choice, I had no gun. As for slaves they are not trusted with weapons," said David. "They might shoot the master. As it was, three ran away while we were on the trail."

"I would run too," said Charles.

David ignored the statement and said to Clark, "My neighbors would like you as little as they regard me, cousin. They say that Quakers on the frontier are happy to assume Indian lands and let their neighbors bear the risks taken in defending their property. What say you?"

"I can no sooner speak for all Quakers than thee can for all Presbyterians, but I for one would rather die at his hands than kill one of my red brothers and sisters. I see disputants talking through ways to share the Light's bounty as being a higher calling than seizing all the eye can see and claiming all the mind can imagine. The land we are on we paid for."

"Ours in Kentucky did not come free," said David. I wondered if David had hidden behind his mother's birth as a Quaker to avoid combat.

"But who did you Kentuckians pay?" asked Mary Crispin.

27

"The Shawnee or land speculators like Washington, Jefferson and Franklin?"

I could see that although David Wickliffe had left Kentucky because of his discomfort, the Ferguson home in the Quaker enclave of Waynesville might not be sufficiently hospitable for him to settle nearby.

Later, in our room in the small cabin that Mary Crispin and Clark had built before the family outgrew it, I said, "I do not like that David's attitude."

"Until we have our own, we have to listen to all kinds of attitudes that stink like a pig sty." He paused a moment before adding, "What about Clark? He was almost as bad. Only a white man thinks he can go round granting rights like he was Daddy's God."

His point was obvious. I turned over and went to sleep.

* * *

Clark, who had been a hunter before marrying, had killed a deer. With the venison, Mary Crispin had prepared the same vegetables as the previous night but added peach pies as dessert. The deer was more delectable than any meat I had tasted. "Beats pig feet any day," said Dan.

"Almost as good as pork chops," said Robin.

"I saw you licking your lips and that deer juice running down the sides," said Dan.

It was our turn to clean up after the meal. Banter is fine but Robin was a great teaser who abhorred turn-about, "Please," I said. "Let's agree to keep our thoughts to ourselves until we are alone."

"The day you keep our thoughts to yourself is the day I'll sprout wings!" said Robin. Thankfully, although without proper acknowledgement, he accepted my advice.

We joined the others when our chores were completed. The chairs were arrayed in a half-circle. Although we had only heard bits and pieces, David had been holding court for some time. I entered as he those gathered in the heart of the great room that recently a neighbor had returned to his parents' home after living 14 years as a captive. He had been a pack boy when captured on the way to the Thames but was a full-grown man and his English had almost deserted him. I tried my new found freedom by excusing myself and asking why the man had not escaped earlier and was told he was afraid that in passing near unknown Indian villages he might be killed. When I questioned the voracity of this statement, Wickliffe said that after his malaria bout, he too had feared what might happen if he had come upon an Indian village.

"All of the savages despise us."

"They are people, not savages," said Mary Crispin quickly.

"Cousin," said Clark, "my children are in the room. I do not wish them using unacceptable language."

David gave a cursory apology and continued. "The man had confessed that he had come to love the people. He had even married and had children."

"Then why did he leave them at all?" I asked.

"The federal government is insisting the tribe be removed to the far regions of the world and he would rather return to Kentucky."

"What of his wife and children?"

He was reluctant to answer but Mary Crispin gestured subtly with a change in her head's posture that he should answer my well-considered question. "He knew his wife and two sons would be unwanted among his own people."

"This wife and children were his own people," I said.

David had no words to my statement. Disgusted with the

inhumanity of it all I excused myself again saying I had to clean the small cabin where we resided.

That night when we were alone Robin said, "I was proud of you for getting' in that fool's face." His assessment was a bit of a stretch but I said nothing. "I heard that David man making the same old excuses for doing wrong."

"Daddy would not have acted that way," said Dan.

I felt angry but neither of my brothers had given me anything to argue over.

Over the next evening's dinner, we dined on small remnants of the previous day's deer plus a chicken soup whose recipe included dumplings, celery, onions and substantial chunks of both white and dark meat. Mary Crispin was more finicky about extracting bones than was Mary Pool Hoge when she prepared a similar dish. We also had what Mary Crispin called Maryland biscuits along with corn on the cob fresh from the harvest with which my brothers. David told us about the infamous Kentuckian, Richard Johnson whose wife at the time was a colored woman named Julia Chinn. He reported that Julia ran Johnson's household with much the same grace and authority and respect as the white wife or mistress in other southern households. "They even openly have children together."

Such news traveled faster among slaves than it apparently did among some whites. The Fergusons were ignorant of this story but it was well known even among those enslaved in Virginia that in 1825, Julia had acted as Johnson's official hostess during the Marquis de Lafayette's visit to Blue Spring Farm, the Johnson home. David did add a piece that I had not heard. "A crowd of 5000 attended a barbecue in Lafayette's honor. Julia circulated scandalously among them. Johnson has publicly stated that they have been married. Some say both a white and a colored minister performed the ceremony. I was not present, but I do know that although miscegenistic marriages are legally forbidden, they celebrate one."

"Then it works?" Charles Ferguson asked. He spoke one of the few times any of the Ferguson's children were heard speaking to anyone besides each other during the visitor's discourses. He was the Ferguson boy who with the Shawnee couple when we were rescued.

Both of my brothers stared daggers at him but soon let the matter drop, or so I thought until years later Charles told me they had threatened his life if he so much as touched me. By that time, both Robin and Dan had gone north. I had not taken the absurd idea seriously enough to even remember it. Blended marriages were forbidden in Ohio and Charles moved me not at all.

When we were alone and discussing the day, my brothers laughed about how slow the Fergusons worked the fields and how it was necessary for them to slow from their habitual pace. I referred to their work as "slothful." Robin frowned. He wanted as little to do with mastering English as possible. He would not even allow us to teach him to read and write. I read by candlelight on my side of the room when Robin said to Dan, "It was tasty but she had too damn many carrots in that soup."

Dan rarely contradicted our older brother but this time he said, "Come on, man. When was the last time we sat down at a table and had meat other than some squirrel or rabbit? Three days in a row we have eaten not only like white folks but with white folks."

"What table did we have at Fruits of the Spirit? Other than the Hoges house we ain't never ate like we eating here. I just ain't no carrot man. That's rabbit food."

* * *

David Wickliffe was only with us for a week when he decided it was time to move on and begin his new life.

"Clark, I would love to have my wife and four children up here as soon as possible but not to sleep in a tent or a cave. Would you mind if I took those two young colored fellows to help me raise a cabin?"

"They left slavery behind, cousin," said Clark. "Their time is their own. Ask them thyself."

I doubt that he will ever know what his words meant to Robin and Dan. They went with Wickliffe in advance of Clark and his older sons who joined their relative and my brothers after they had gotten far enough ahead in both the family fields and Mary Crispin's brothers, to justify an interruption. Unlike the Fergusons and John Crispin my brothers were paid for their labor. They would learn later that the practice was to donate one's labor but so close to their enslavement it did not occur to them to volunteer their services.

4

PRESIDENTIAL AUDIENCE

When Andrew Jackson was elected in March of 1829 Patience Starbuck, our near neighbor, was irate. Once more she and other women had not been permitted to vote. Most women accepted the disregard as natural but she had grown up on Nantucket where women were held with much more esteem, often running a wealthy family's business while a whaling husband was away for up to three years. Equally galling was the fact that Jackson had long ignored her correspondence.

A few days after the election results were announced, four of us were seated in the great room of the Ferguson house. Mary Crispin nursed her youngest child, while her husband Clark had come in for his mid-afternoon break, and Patience was visiting. I had filled cups with coffee or tea and been invited by Mary Crispin to, "Sit a while before thee returns to sewing," a trade the renowned seamstress was teaching me.

"It would be bad enough if a gentleman were to stonewall me," said Patience, "but for an uncouth fellow like him to pretend that as well as being deceitful and ambitious, he cannot even read and write, strains my heart!"

"Do not disparage the man's being," said Mary Crispin Ferguson, her best friend. "There are no higher and lowers among us."

"I was not suggesting that he is of lower worth, only that he is not so high as to ignore my being."

"Thee knows," said Mary Crispin, "he may barely know his letters. It is said that he will spell the same word three times in the same correspondence."

Instead of laughing with the others in the room Patience said, "He can spell 'yes' or 'no' in any combination he pleases just so he writes, 'Patience Starbuck, I am here to serve this country'. If that is a bridge to far for him to reach, have his secretary read over the missive before it is posted."

Mary Crispin's husband Clark said, "He would swear on the Bible that says 'thou shalt not swear' that everything he does is for the good of the country."

"Please don't tell me that thee voted for him!" said Patience and Mary Crispin in one voice.

"Perhaps the only charm in the vote is that I need not tell anyone how I voted for any candidate."

"Thee is one of them!" said Patience.

"Yes, I am a man who enjoys his privacy," said Clark.

Mary Crispin turned from a vain attempt to stare down her husband who looked at something imaginary in the distance. When she saw her friend's face she said, "Patience, I know by thy bearing, that thee has chosen a course."

"Peace chiefs from various tribes have journeyed to Washington to argue their case. Why shouldn't I?"

Mary Crispin said, "None of them were successful."

"They were not citizens. I am."

"But thee is a citizen who neither can vote nor has a husband who thee might persuade to vote," said Clark.

"For all Jackson knows I might have 100,000 male cousins, 10,000 brothers and 1,000 lovers. Clark, would thee do me a kindness and refill my cup?"

Clark was laughing when he said, "Yes, your highness." I was sitting quietly in the circle and rose to serve, but he smiled, shook his head.

Meanwhile Mary Crispin said, "If thee has a superabundance of such males, thee keeps all but the Nantucket cousins well hidden!"

When they had each stopped laughing and Clark had refilled the coffee cup, he said, "Speaking of hidden, how might thee hide thy biting tongue?"

"Of all that I keep covered, my tongue is rarely included. I just want to get in the door and speak eye to eye with a general turned President who thinks he is Washington's second coming."

I silently weighed their conversation when Patience turned to me. "How would thee like to attend me, Sarah?"

It was one thing to ask a friend's husband to serve a late coffee and quite another to ask a fugitive to go to Washington. I was two years removed from slavery, but due to enterprising Patience, I was in possession of a forged free paper signed by a helpful judge. By their countenances the Fergusons were granting me leave to speak my heart.

"It is my dream to see more of the world."

* * *

From the carriage that met us at the docks to take us to the home of our Folger hosts, I could see that unlike the sketches I had seen of Parisian streets, Washington City was a muddy, unpaved mess. Wide avenues began and ended nowhere. Patience had visited Boston and lived in both New York and Philadelphia. She assured me the city compared unfavorably to "The City of Brotherly Love," my father's dream destination. According to Patience, Washington avenues indicated aspirations to become much more than was presently possible.

"Should the riches from slaveocracy and theft of Indian lands proceed as proposed it is believed that one day this embarrassment for a city will outshine Rome, a city I have yet to see other than in books."

In fairness, there were huge government buildings that were much grander than anything I have seen since. I have yet to visit Philadelphia but I have come to know Cincinnati very well. Although both Washington and Cincinnati had free-running pigs, there were not as many as Robin and Dan had told me roamed the environs of "The Queen City." The vast majority of Washington houses were made of whitened wood with green blinds on the outside and curiously, paired curtains, one white and one red. Everywhere I looked white men chewed and spit tobacco in streams and blacks who appeared slaves shuttled about performing menial tasks or sweated profusely while constructing new buildings or extending a road to what looked like nowhere.

Someone I took as an urban slave approached us selling fruit. It was all I could do to stop myself from saying, "I am not like you. I am free." For all I knew she could have been legally free. Even had my free paper been honestly won, I was exactly as were all other colored people, an unwanted soul in a pretentious country prepared to work us to death but not accept us as siblings. Perhaps the merchant read unearned scorn in my face or simply saw one young colored woman in a plain black dress and one white one in the finest purple silk. The times made it clear which one was in control. She went to Patience's side and was paid double the asking price for two apples.

While in bondage, somehow, I had thought that the capital of the democratic world was slave free. It would be years before I would learn that several of my siblings had been sold in that very city after I had fled slavery.

We stopped at a corner to avoid the huge carriage of four overstuffed personages whose driver was proceeding with total disregard for our vehicle. Our driver explained that he knew the passengers to be senators. In the event of an accident he would be assumed guilty. In Washington it was assumed that to be black was to be a slave and free or enslaved he could not testify in court against a white person.

"I could have testified," said Patience. He knew better than to expect such support from a white person. He rudely showed me his own free paper. He might have been asking me to comment but I refused to even look at it. In fact, I gave him no hint of how he might judge me, limiting my speech with him to greetings and farewells and always placing a ma'am in the sentences when I was required to speak with Patience. On her part, she played every bit the slave mistress, talking either rudely or with disdain to the two of us. Had she not informed me even before we left that it would make our lives easier if she did not appear to be Yankee-minded. Thankfully she did not affect a southern accent. It was difficult enough readjusting to being publicly treated with condescension equal to what Miss Anne, mistress of Fruits of the Spirit always treated us.

We passed the St. Charles Hotel where our driver said slaves were held in the basement before being auctioned off. Then we passed what he referred to as "The Yellow House," a slave market with scores of distraught children, women and men waiting to learn their fate. I felt a strong guilt for I was one of the fortunate few blacks who had never been sold. It was well that I was traveling incognito as a slave. Just when I thought that the carriage might be passed the open display of misery, we came upon two parallel chained coffles, one with as many as 75 ragged and worn slaves entering the city to be spruced up before being sold. Several children and a few adults wept. I also silently wept.

At one point, I was mystified to see a line of eight slaves being ushered in chains just before turning into a convent as two nuns watched with folded hands. A whip carrying driver struck a lagging grandmother so hard on the back that only the presence of two fast moving men prevented her falling into the horse offal. A nun said, "To the driver, "Young man, this is not Christian charity."

When the grandmother was struck Patience had involuntarily let out a muffled scream. Reminding herself that she was acting a role of a woman impervious to black suffering, she quickly regrouped and said, "Is this the most efficacious route to my cousins?"

Her adjective made me wonder if our carriage driver had deliberately placed the oppression of the free-world city's on display. I immediately gained respect for him.

"We are almost there, ma'am," he said simply.

When we left the carriage, I treated him better than I had earlier. "I want to thank you for your service, sir."

Through this simple kindness he may have guessed that I was a free person. All he did was wink at me. He turned to Patience, tipped his tap hand and discreetly kept his hand to his side until she extracted two gold coins from the reticule that Mary Crispin had designed in to match the dress.

The driver received two additional gold coins when he placed our trunks on the Folgers' porch. He rang the bell, waited for the door to be answered and turned to leave.

"Boy," said Mahlon, the host, "here is a coin for thy trouble."

* * *

We pulled onto the grounds of the White House. Mostly black men worked on the north portico. As is our people's habit, I searched to see if any were men I knew who had been sold away from Fruits of the Spirit or one of the other plantations that attended Reverend Stringfellow's church or the district corn shuckings. Ironically, I recognized one handsome fellow who had been sweet on one of my older sisters but dared not call out. He in turn was being watched carefully by a white, whip carrying foreman and did not look our way.

Patience's cousin, Mahlon drove his personal carriage. He delivered us at the front door and said to me, "Sarah, thee seemed curious at the appearance of the workers. After the British burned the President's home, this new White House was primarily built by thy people." He seemed to think this would surprise me but as one who had been reared on a Virginia plantation a few days ride to the south, I was well aware of who did most of the hard labor. If I had not known previously, the gentleman who had taken us on the circuitous trip from the dock had disabused my illusions. "President Jackson is also served by slaves, as were most of his predecessors from Washington descending down to 'Old Hickory'."

I wondered what I was supposed to do with such information, but Mahlon did not explain himself. Instead he said to Patience, "Thee seems more pensive than I remember thee."

"Cousin, thee left Nantucket even before I did. We haven't seen each other since I was a brash girl."

"I would suggest thee be true to thy name with the President. It is said that brash women are not his choice of companion."

His words seemed to energize Patience."If I were given to being a companion for a tyrant, I might honor my name. Please, meet us at the corner in an hour and a half, cousin."

Mahlon smiled and nodded. We left the carriage unassisted and he urged his two horses forward.

At the door to the White House a guard said to Patience, "No Nigras permitted here."

"What may I ask is thee?" said Patience. He did not respond. Patience peered into the nearest room and saw colored servants in the background, "and are the servants—or should I say 'slaves'-whites in brown paint?" He met her sarcasm with silence. "Is it possible that thee may be mistaken?"

"Ma'am, I don't make nary rule here or anyplace outside of my household." Disgusted she said, "Sarah, I dare not send thee back to my cousins' home alone. Mahlon says potential kidnappers roam these streets as much as in Cincinnati." I had yet to learn how to recognize obvious kidnappers. Reflexively, I inched closer to her. She turned to the doorman. "A fifteen-year-old colored girl in these wilds might be as exposed as a single sheep in a den of wolves. Is there nearby a trustworthy owner of a conveyance who can escort my servant back to my Folger cousins' home?"

I was grateful that she used the word "servant" which was southern-euphemism for "slave" but in my case was true. She was paying me for my servous at a rate even higher than she had paid our public driver. Her relatives had been sufficiently friendly that even though I obviously would not have the opportunity to view a president up close, I was not unduly disturbed with the turn of events.

The doorman surprised us with a smile. "Somewhere I've

got a daughter about her age. I'd be happy to keep a eye on this child dressed like a Quaker."

I wore Quaker garb although I certainly was not one. Mary Crispin had thought, for safety's sake, it would be wise to masquerade. Instead of correcting a man who used the very accent with which I had grown up, I silently assented to put myself under his watchful protection. It had been some time since I had last conversed with a colored man who I assumed was my father's peer. I admitted to myself both that I missed Daddy and had he been the butler he would have made the same offer.

"Where shall I stand, sir?"

"It's been many a month since I been called 'sir' outside of my home." Pointing a few feet away, he said, "For now, under that tree over yonder would do just fine.

* * *

"Li'l Miss, Ma'am," began the doorman when we were alone.

"Sarah is my name and yours, sir?"

"Mr. Hicks. You heard me tell your misses I got a daughter about your age. She be 5-6 shades darker and go by the name of Mindy. I ain't seen her since Master sold her away back in '22 so I can't tell you how tall she is or how much she done rounded out. Like I said, I'm a Hicks but she could be going by the name FitzHugh. They the ones had papers on us at the time."

"Why did you not keep FitzHugh to flag her should she come looking?"

"Hicks is a name me and her mama talked about after a Quaker preacher named Hicks come to our plantation when me and her mama was children. He didn't listen but that Hicks man told Master slaves should be free. I don't know that Mindy ever heard us whispering about what we'd do if the Jubilee ever came. She could be wearing FitzHugh like that flag. But we hated them folk with a passion and who you know done found some lost relative once they got sold off?"

"I understand," I said. Then I broke a rule my parents had explained was sacrosanct and asked about his own condition. "Did your master free you after Elias Hicks suggested it?"

"How'd you know the man was named Elias?" he asked excitedly. "You done met him too?"

"No, but my mistress knows him and has told me how much he means to her."

"That woman in that bright green dress is a Quaker too?" he said perplexed. "I seen a heap more Quakers than Elias Hicks but wasn't one of them dressed like her!"

"She is her own woman, Mr. Hicks." He pondered my words and I added. "Yes, she is a Quaker. No, I am not a Quaker. I am a free servant."

He overlooked my prideful statement. "I pushed myself to once more cross the line. "You, sir, were you freed?"

"Do chickens have teeth? The low-down snake may have studied Hicks advice for years. Then he sold everybody on the plantation to the highest bidder. Ain't a one of my kinfolk together as I speak. Even my wife is a Hicks. Last I seen her she was moving toward them cotton fields. Georgia? Alabama? Mississippi? Who knows? I heard Master living somewhere up north running merchant boats to buy from his used-to-be neighbors. About my Mindy...you done seen a Mindy by the last name FitzHugh or Hicks?"

I hadn't forgotten his original question. I explained how before coming to Washington I had kept near to my safehouse. The only colored people I had seen lived in a radius of 10 or so miles. Then I took my turn at the sad dance vainly asking about my own lost relatives.

Unfortunately, a self-important man arrived at the door. He

saw us chatting doorway to tree before I noticed his approach. "What is the meaning of this indolent behavior?"

A maid named Miss Fina rushed over to my oak. Wearing the mask, she said, "Child, ain't I done told you to just take a short outhouse break?" She bowed to the newcomer then thrust a dust rag in my hands. "Clean them there pictures in the hall 'til they shine like August sun!"

I spent the remainder of my time waiting for Patience, dusting huge portraits of the Founding Fathers and wishing Mr. Hicks could take the chance to say at least another word to me. Did he fear going back to nearby fields or being sold as far away as Mississippi? Did either of us even know what possibilities the powerful had at their evil disposal?

Bolder than Mr. Hicks, from time to time Miss Fina came close and asked me about more than a dozen of her lost friends and neighbors. As with Mr. Hicks, I was unable to help. She too was unable to help me locate any of my lost relatives. However, she did explain the nuns and slaves that I had seen earlier.

"They just church folk owning slaves. You name 'em and I done seen white church folk buying, keeping and selling us. That's how I came here. The Society of the Sacred Soul sold me to the President's secretary. He got top dollar. I got more drudgery and less time to pray. The worst work they ever gave me was to scrub the convent floor every day on my knees. You know, 'cleanliness is next to Godliness'."

* * *

Patience was directed to where the A.J. Donelson, the President's secretary waited. Considering the considerable number of letters that she had sent Jackson since his massacre of the Red Stick Creeks in 1813, she had expected as long as a two-hour visit and was willing to let Mahlon wait until she had completed her work. Donelson informed her that the president was busy and could afford her but thirty minutes.

"This is an outrage!"

"This is the nation's capital ma'am," said Donelson. "The president has important business that calls for his attention."

A different black servant escorted Patience to the president's office. The servant opened the door, refilled Jackson's whiskey glass from the cantor on an exquisite table just inside the room, closed the door, and went on duty just outside the room.

Jackson was dressed in black clothing except for a white shirt. His unkempt hair showed reddish strains but was graying. He continued looking over a paper, drew a bold black diagonal line through it, took a small sip from the whiskey glass, stood and said, "Forgive my rudeness in greeting you. The work is endless.

Patience was taken aback by a man who westerners seemed to think was a giant being about 6'1 and thinner than a rail, surely not even 140 pounds of gaunt flesh. Awkwardly she said, "My condolences to you for your wife's recent death."

Jackson's countenance changed briefly. He sighed and returned his face more to what Patience had expected from a general known for his bloodthirsty ways."I cannot adequately speak of Rachel's loss, so shall we will focus post haste on the reason for your trip from the western frontier?"

She sat first and inhaled to regain her focus after his startling appearance.

With deliberateness he said, "Despite all civilized people realizing as soon as the first white man set foot in the new world the savages forfeited the land, considering the many letters you have written on behalf of them I suppose you wish to once more plead their case. I trust it is for the good of the people."

"I announced as much in my latest letter. The only one, I might add that you have seen fit to answer since the first."

"I assure you I read each, but I am a man of action who duty requires me to be occupied with material matters. A.J. wrote, I signed."

She was surprised by his candor, casting some doubt on the deceiver she perceived him to be. She recited in order all of the Indian removals from her chosen home state of Ohio. Later she told me that at times it felt as though she were a Biblical prophet recounting in reverse the long Exodus from Egypt to the Promised Land.

She moved on to recounting what Caesar, our African-Shawnee friend, had told her had happened out west where they had been forced to oust their cousins. She was graphic in their struggles, speaking of deaths along the way and after arriving, unacceptable land, late annuity payments and other breeches of treaties always written to disadvantage the rightful owners of the land. Jackson was unmoved.

"In your letters--my secretary has often kindly referred to them as 'nearly tomes'--you have often mentioned that you are Nantucket born. May I ask why you failed to mention how and why your Quaker forbears removed the Indians from that esteemed island?" She had underestimated his mind, as northerners so often do to those of us born in the south. Pressing what he saw as a new advantaged Jackson overplayed his hand, "You Yankees must learn that you are a pattern for our behavior."

"If this is so, why have you chosen to discontinue following our lead and gone backward, deep into the wilderness?"

He appeared momentarily stunned, but smiled and said softly, "In all your gentle bluster you ignore I adopted a Creek boy."

"I know that beforehand you orphaned him while

massacring his whole village. Then you stole the land that rightfully was his."

Jackson took out his pocket watch, glanced at it and said, "I will not try to explain the meaning of treaties or nation-building to a woman. You clearly do not understand the world cannot be ruled without the shedding of blood. I must say that so long a journey must have been made for more than savages."

"I suppose your characterization of good people as savages is why you betrayed even the Creeks and Cherokees who fought beside you and allowed the Shawnee, Delaware and Wyandotte who allied with northern American armies to have their land stolen and then be removed west."

"Possession of endless rolling prairies, crisscrossed by pure streams, miles from the frontier, should bring them great joy."

"If their joy was your goal I might say more. Instead I look at the long list of broken treaties—by the way I understand how to read treaties. I also understand coercion. However, on this trip, given the paltry moments your secretary allotted me, I will move to the next topic."

"The hour glass grows empty."

"Half-hour glass," Jackson smiled graciously. "I have long written to you about slavery."

"Forgive me, Miss, but the Constitution is clear concerning the Nigras' place in America. They were born to be bottom dwellers. You are right to have spent most of your time on the redskins."

"Your enthusiasm for doing the wrong thing is breath taking."

"I am sworn to administer our government for the good of the chosen people and, as I have proven many times, I will defend it to the death."

There was a knock before the door opened. A.J. Donaldson entered. Jackson signaled him to speak. "Mr. President,

Governor Forsyth has arrived from Georgia for his consultation."

Jackson stood and said, "Thank you for your time, Miss Starbuck."

Patience also stood. "No surprise that with time too you have shorted me. I hope one day you will learn that what is morally wrong cannot be politically righted."

"A word of advice before you leave, Miss Starbuck. You should not be so tempestuous in your correspondence or in your person. All of us whites are on the same side. God has offered hard evidence that it is the correct side."

"Evidence?"

"Since you are in the capitol, pay a call on the British, Dutch, and Spanish ambassadors. They introduced a system that we but follow, a bit more successfully, but as the opposite of trailblazers." She was stunned at his suggestions. "And since you are obviously a traveler, do the same with Northern governors. Their states also followed the lead through the wildernesses of this great nation. The source, madame. Go to the source."

She recuperated. You sit in the president's chair and are the source of this my fractured country. You admit the evil of others yet continue in it. Forbidden fruit known to be poisonous is only consumed by fools."

Patience said the president flushed so red that had she been a man he might have challenged her to a duel right on the White House grounds.

5
BONE INTERPRETERS

Caesar was an African rooted Shawnee who, together with his wife Monni, had rescued my brothers and me from slavery. Around campfires and in subsequent years, he told us stories of the old days when it seemed The People ruled the world. Each of his stories had lessons embedded but I believe he also told them to keep alive the knowledge that before the whites appropriated Shawnee land, he had not always been homeless. Nearly all that I am sharing I learned from Caesar or Monni.

Caesar's mother's name was Cocheta. Whites translated it as "The Stranger." She was born a Creek but had lived among the Shawnee most of her life. As a young woman she had witnessed her husband and other Algonquins crush the separate American armies of General Harmar and General St. Clair. The pride people of color had in those victories circulated among slaves as far south as the plantation where I was enslaved in Virginia. The victories had occurred respectively on October 22 and November 4, Indian Summer days when whites intended to destroy recently gathered Native American harvests and starve The People during the winter. If we people of color had been in power, we would have made the days holidays.

The fortunes of war reversed. Whites stormed and burnt Shawnee villages where Cocheta lived on three separate occasions. Each time, Cocheta and her friends picked up the pieces and retreated. Following the rebels' great loss at the Battle of the Thames in 1814, Caesar settled his mother in Wapakoneta where Shawnees who fought with the Americans were constrained to a small reservation under the leadership of chief Black Hoof. In Wapakoneta, Cocheta lived among warriors who had helped kill Tecumseh as well as one son and her husband.

She eventually left Wapakoneta and settled first in the Shawnee village of Hog Creek and next in the nearby Shawnee village in Lewistown. Everywhere she relocated one-time friends who had chosen Americans over Tecumseh's vision of a united Indian confederacy outnumbered those who had rebelled. She would have returned south but her birth family was Red Stick Creek and General Jackson had allied with the Cherokees to nearly annihilate them. She took stock finding that most of the people she knew were dead and that it would not be long before the survivors would be removed west. In anguish she resigned herself to having only a few more choices than slaves.

In 1826 Caesar and his wife Monni accompanied his alienated mother to Crooked Creek in faraway Arkansas. When they reached their destination Cocheta moved into a village made up of several refugee eastern woodland tribes. The displaced people worked hard to make their new life livable. Predictably, white pioneers soon demanded they be removed elsewhere.

"I have never been to the great waters beyond the horizon,"

she told a dying friend. "What's more I would rather join you in death than be kicked that far away."

* * *

In the fall of 1832, Caesar had just returned from our trip to rescue my brother Robin. His first act was to change from the driver's uniform he had worn while pretending to be Patience Starbuck's slave and into buckskins. He and his wife Monni were planning another trip beyond the Ohio River to rescue the enslaved. The couple paused long enough for a meal of bacon dumplings, Caseknife beans pumpkin pudding and ginger-bread. At the time I was still away.

Mary Crispin, my mother-in-law, reported she had said to the Shawnee couple, "One week later and Clark would have slaughtered a hog. I hope this simple meal suits."

"Your husband need not be concerned with our mouths," said Caesar. "I'm happy just to be back from wearing a foolish looking suit."

"We are grateful for your hospitality," said Monni who had been reared by Quakers following the massacre of her family.

Most of the conversation focused on a narrow escape from slave catchers and the wounding of my two brothers. Robin, the oldest, was at the table with his leg heavily bandaged. I was back in Cincinnati, where the ambush had taken place, with Dan who appeared more seriously wounded and recuperating.

The Fergusons waited until the visitors were finished eating. Then Mary Crispin said to Caesar, "Thy mother is back from the west and is living as a servant of John Johnston's family."

Caesar was speechless. There was a rumor that John Johnston had fired the rifle that had killed Caesar's father. On the side of the field where Caesar's father fell, Johnston was only one of scores of whites, at least a dozen Indians, and four or five armed blacks in the American army. Caesar had not assigned his father's killing to Johnston but hated him for being an agent of the Federal Government.

"I have heard the Johnstons are good people."

"Not from me," said Caesar growing agitated. "He is not even beyond using whiskey to confuse the People he pretends to represent.

"My family was friends with Rachel Robinson Johnston's Quaker family back in the Delaware Valley," said Mary Crispin. "Rachel and I are the same age and enjoy each other's company. She visited here while you were away and said she is happy with thy mother's work."

"That don't explain why my mama is working for the man who calls himself 'the best Indian Agent in America'. Every one of them is a thief. How many feathers do you get for being a good thief."

"He is questioned by both sides. Others have called him an 'Indian Lover'," said Mary Crispin.

"They call you the same and 'Nigger Lover' too, but in no way does he compare with you," said Caesar. "It takes more than being hated to be good."

"I will concede that point," said Clark, "but any woman as tiny as Rachel who has 14 living children can use as much help as comes her way."

"Y'all keep missing the point," said Caesar looking at Monni.

"We must leave now," said Monni to the Fergusons.

"That mean you ain't got no idea when we going see you again?" said my brother Robin.

"That's how life works," said Caesar, "whether or not we recognize it."

* * *

The tall Johnston had enjoyed the distinction of being the Indian agent not only for the Shawnee but also Miami, Lenape, Wyandotte, Seneca and Potawatomie. His frequent publicly stated justification for helping to remove the people of these nations was that if they attempted to remain in their traditional homes, they would be exterminated by white settlers aided by the American army. Was he couching his own people as blood thirsty leeches or contemptively suggesting the Indians were inordinately weak, was a question Tecumseh frequently had posed his followers. Despite the passing of two decades, Caesar had not decided Johnston's motives. He that regardless of the situation, Johnston had always presented himself as morally superior.

On the way to Piqua, Caesar and Monni discussed the Shawnee Trail of Tears that they had made with his mother and those under the leadership of Tecumseh's surviving brother, Tenkswatawa, the Prophet.

"I will always remember Mother's face when we arrived to help her leave Ohio," said Monni. "The relief in it warms my heart to this day."

"What I remember most," said Caesar, "was when she reminded me why she had named me Stalking Panther."

His mother had seen him as a youth who always watched over those he loved. Others might sit back and wait for assistance to arrive or, like vultures, prey on the dying. Not this beloved son. She knew as soon as he learned that hundreds of his people were being sent west, he would appear to see if his mother was among them and how he might make himself useful.

The trip took them through countless places where the villages of various Indian tribes had stood. Each had been appropriated by whites, leaving only the ghosts of days gone by, more than once, strewn piles of bleached human bones and Indian names. Those named included Indiana's Kokomo, Pottawattamie Park and Shipshewana; in Illinois, Itaska, Algonquin and Cahokia; and in Ohio, Chillicothe, Wapakoneta and Piqua.

Caesar had wondered if graves had also been desecrated. "They stripped us clean and kept our names. A whole world lost. "

On the Shawnee Trail of Tears, they passed crude windowless, single-room cabins surrounded by fields of corn and laughing white children. Again, he wondered. Had their father killed some of his people or was the family simply among the tens of thousands of squatters who referred to the Indians as savages?

Laden with produce from the last Ohio harvest, for a few days, people had spoken of hope. When the supply of vegetables dwindled, white settlers were happy to exchange fresh corn for extra furs and keepsakes and mementos that now seemed burdensome to carry. Enough deer and wild turkeys were in the area to keep bellies full of flesh. The refugees were without cash and being shadowed by whiskey sellers who lured the weak to exchange anything of value for what never brought more than temporary relief and occasionally led to fights, even killings. What the people desired most were horses, blankets and bearskins. Along with summer's end, hordes of mosquitoes disappeared. Unfortunately, so did the wild game that was hunted out by pioneers who were themselves trying to outrun the frontier line.

In early autumn, while he was on a scout ahead of the refugees, Caesar saw a camp meeting. On the outskirts, hard drinking men held a shooting contest. Although only one of his great grandfathers had been black, believing it was safer, he identified himself as a "colored man" instead of a Shawnee. When insulted, he said nothing when repeatedly called a "damned nigger." He was allowed to put his horse up as collateral and join the shooting contests. He rode away with two deer and a cow after winning three separate contests. The fresh meat would help greatly for the next few days.

Through October and November, rain fell seemingly every day. Lack of fodder cost scores of horses their lives. People joined the remaining horses in dying. With streams high and roads clogged with mud, the normal burial rites could not be practiced. Worse yet, a whiskey-seller reported to the captain of the county militia that sick Indians were coming their way. The captain rode out with a posse. Caesar as interpreter when the captain said, "We got it on good authority you redskins got the ague, cholera, and the typhoid."

Caesar saw no use in arguing. He accepted the instructions to detour away from the next four villages. It cost several extra days on the marked road that had been established by Indians following the now disappeared buffalo. Fortunately, the detour also allowed them to travel through two forests that were as yet virtually untouched by the whites. The fresh meat may have saved several lives.

At the first feast in months, Cocheta said, "We are the ones who choose to survive."

Monni wondered if the woman who died in the last stream had simply given up, allowing herself to drown.

Although their fortunes seemed improved, it was only temporary. By January about a quarter of the original refugees had died. Again, the living hungered and grew ill. The clothing of the majority had become so ragged that nightly mending was almost useless.

Monni got off her horse to soothe a crying orphan and said to Caesar, "Only the massacre of my family when I was a child back in Virginia was worse for me, and that happened in a manner of a few minutes. This journey is slow torture."

The couple talked about everything in life except what had been done to her as a child that prevented having babies and what he had witnessed at the Battles of the Thames in Canada and Horseshoe Bend in Alabama. They had drifted into a pact that guided their response when one had a nightmare. The one less tortured woke the spouse, held on spoon style while softly calling the lover's name until a becalmed sleep enveloped both.

When he told me this story he said, "Never try to compare your tragedy with another's. You can only feel your own sorrow. Kokumethena, the Grandmother, wants us to be compassionate."

After the People crossed the Mississippi, Cocheta said to Caesar, "Go back my son. We have now forded the biggest river. We are nearly at the end." Caesar had protested that she was not yet safe in her new home, but she said, "This is no place for a warrior. Your father was descended from slaves. Your time would be better spent helping the ones in total bondage escape to something better."

Her peripatetic son and daughter-in-law promised to visit her every few years and she did her best to accommodate herself to being a stateless woman. She realized that Caesar and Monni were equally unmoored.

True to their word, Caesar and Monni had visited his mother twice in the six years since beginning the removal west. Cocheta had exercised the mother prerogative and changed her mind, resettling in Ohio.

The couple arrived at what once was a Shawnee village. John Johnston had transformed the grounds into a farm whose grounds resembled a Virginia estate and house a Philadelphia manse.

"I do not remember this place said Caesar. I have been here many times before the whites stole it. If not for the few trees he has not cut down, I might not guess where we are."

"The whites call what he has done 'improvements'," said Monni.

"They also call this their land. Their theft, with the help of some of our people, will never sit well with me."

"Nor should it," said Monni.

They rode their horses past the apple orchards the Johnstons had planted, pig pens and barn, arriving at a three-story brick house. Caesar the way toward the front door when Monni caught his arm. "I smell cooking in the rear. Mother is probably there."

They tied their horses and discovered that Monni was correct. Cocheta was busy cooking in the lower level kitchen of the Johnston house. She was dressed in her traditional buckskin clothing with fringes hanging from both the lower half of the dress and the cape like top garment extending from the shoulders. Caesar and Monni less conspicuous linsey-woolsey and calico garb to reduce the chance that they might draw unwanted attention and be forced to defend their presence on the road.

Caesar greeted his mother then said, "Why did you come here, Mother? With Tecumseh we turned away from all things white."

"Let us compare clothing."

"I am not speaking of clothing."

"I thought not. I am here because when we were without hope and the warriors of the seven tribes considered war, it was Johnston who saw to it the murderers of our people were hung. He avenged us after my dear friend Windsinger was butchered like a hog and the other eight at Fall Creek were killed. I know you disagreed when Johnston insisted the chiefs witness the executions. Others saw it as a good thing. In my mind, he respects us. I need respect more than I need love."

"I too loved Windsinger," said Caesar, "and appreciate that Johnston made certain that there were hangings. He is also fluent in every language spoken in Ohio and can communicate with those spoken in Indiana and Michigan. Such skills are good but not enough. He more than balances his good with being a great friend of General Harrison, a man sworn to annihilating us. I expect an Indian Agent to be perfect, someone I can follow because he is so loyal to my interests. I do not want to worry about him misleading me. Instead, he is a White Agent."

"Surely," said Cocheta, "you do not believe he stole our allotment from us as we know the others did?"

"That is not the point."

"Your father taught you the arts of war, hunting, interpreting, and smithing. Who taught you the art of analyzing?"

"I analyze what I see: my mother is living with the enemy."

Cocheta who was busy preparing a beef roast dinner for the Johnston family, looked up from her work. "I considered everything: living under Black Hoof's leadership...planting turnips and cabbages, watching over hogs—things my mother's mothers never ate—going west where, as here in Ohio and back in Georgia, whole clans and villages have left the face of Mother Earth. I am still dressing and worshipping in the old way, even if I must honor the traditional festivals by myself or find others who are living in Ohio without permission. I am enabled to follow these old ways because through Colonel Johnston I am permitted."

"Permitted?" asked Monni, trying gently to suggest her mother-in-law reconsider her chosen path.

DWIGHT L. WILSON

Cocheta overlooked Monni's words. "I no longer had the possibility of living among a people that I could call my own. In the west we were being dominated by the Cherokee who proved themselves enemies both to the Creek nation of my ancestors and the Shawnees who have been my people most of my life. I admit that I wanted more than respect. I wanted sweetness. Where were the markers to help me distinguish a sugar maple from an oak, a hive from an ant hill?

"I knew the whites love Colonel Johnston and would not steal what he calls his own. Finally, where we stand is sacred ground to my chosen people. This is the best place to spend my last years."

"Why did you not marry Blue Heron?" asked Caesar.

"What good could come from marrying a man who after the Battle of the Thames could not remember his own daughter's name?"

She went back to basting and turning the beef quarter on the rotisserie.

"Once that would have been buffalo," said Caesar.

Cocheta silently stepped away from the beef to churn milk.

"Milk is not even agreeable with your stomach," said Caesar.

"Neither is arguing, but I have been known to do it with those I love," she said with a smile.

Caesar almost laughed at her turn of phrase. Catching himself he said, "Do you also clean their chamber pots?"

"Be respectful, son. They clean their own pots. I am a helper. I am not the slave your great great grandmother was."

"Mother," said Monni, "may I ask how you came here and how long you have been here?"

"There is no place on land that I have traveled without knowing how to find my way back and I have been in this house

58

since shortly after your last visit. You left one day. I left exactly one moon later."

"If you knew where you were heading why did you not tell us when we came for a visit?" asked Caesar.

"I was an adult before you were born. When I know where and when I am going it is enough."

"So, Johnston has had more of my mother than I have since the days of my youth?"

"Contain your anger," said Cocheta. "Have I not always taught you to beware of making a powerful white man an enemy. Even the weakest can stab you in the back in more ways than the new moon sky has stars, and you may never know how your strong body became scattered ashes."

"All that I have left of value is you and Monni. What can any white man take from me, Mother?"

"I am not a white man. I only know who holds the power."

Wearing a long-sleeved white shirt and dark trousers, but without a hat or a coat in his own home, John Johnston came into the room. "Had I known you were here, Caesar, I would have worn my Taylor of Dayton's bombazette." Caesar was not in the mood for light talk. "Welcome to Upper Piqua."

"You welcome us?" said Caesar.

"I had heard that you were here, Caesar. If it is for peaceful reasons, you and Monni are both welcome."

"The war is over," said Caesar continuing in the Shawnee he had been using in conversation with his mother. "You speak Shawnee why don't you speak in our tongue?"

"As you acknowledged the war is over. I am in my own house and know very well that you also know English," said Johnston. "This is no longer Shawnee land."

Continuing in Shawnee, Caesar said, "You have stolen our land, kept Piqua, our name for it, added the word 'Upper' as though you are somehow superior, and thrown away our language!"

"To the victors go the prize," said Johnston. "I have often thought about meeting you again. I want to say I was friends with your uncle and his sons. I had hoped you too would be a good Indian."

"I loved my uncle but we disagreed and you should have known that. Every time you saw me, I was with Tecumseh and he was with Black Hoof."

"Yes, you were a renegade."

"You call those who side with you who invaded, 'good' and we patriots who fought to keep our land 'renegades'."

"To the victors go the designations as well, you have already said as much." After a silence, Johnston smiled and said, "Will you stay for dinner?"

Before Caesar could refuse, Monni squeezed his hand and answered the question. "Yes, if we can talk away from your family afterwards."

* * *

"You are welcome at my table," said Rachel Johnston, a petite, dark haired woman, more than a foot shorter than her husband. She dressed in a simple white cotton dress and held a babe in arms. She gestured grandly at a table filled with roasted beef, corn on the cob, a traditional Shawnee pole bean dish, squash, stewed apples, freshly churned milk and cushaw squash pie. "Husband, would you say grace."

Johnston said a short prayer and bit into his first piece of corn, lightly spraying Caesar, who to his left. He did not seem to notice as Rachel introduced first the baby and then the remaining twelve children by name ending with the eldest who was visiting and seated opposite his father. "I am told that you are beloved Cocheta's son. Your name sir and madame?"

Caesar and Monni introduced themselves. Introductions ended and Rachel said, "This beautiful cushaw pie is a shared entity. Cocheta taught me how to flavor the cushaws and I taught her how to make the crust. Please save room for it as dessert."

Johnston sprayed Caesar again, but noticed this time. "Pardon me, Caesar. I am simply a rough Scots-Irishman more used to potatoes than corn." Without waiting for forgiveness, he continued, "Although no longer a Quaker here on the frontier, Rachel is a part of the old ways. Good etiquette in all things. Her parents did not approve of a Scots-Irishman marrying her, but agreed when I suggested I would let the bonny lass reign in the house and follow her dictates."

He smiled at his wife who returned with an even broader smile before saying, "Actually we eloped and my father's disapproval was because he refused to convert to being a nonviolent Quaker. Now that the wars are over, John is so given to jesting."

"Happily you did not refer to me as a jester."

She leaned over and touched his cheek lightly. "For this meal only, I abdicate my rights to rule and permit my giant of a husband, Colonel Johnston, to rule the conversation."

John did not maintain the light-hearted momentum his wife had attempted to establish. The meal passed politely but in near silence with none of the Shawnees uttering a single word. Initially Cocheta was assisted by the young daughter of Johnston's Quaker secretary. Once the food was in place, Caesar was relieved to see both women naturally sat at the table with the family instead of in some corner or back room.

When Caesar had finished his meal Rachel said in Shawnee, "If it pleases you, Stalking Panther, you may be excused."

Surprised that she knew that much of his mother tongue, Caesar smiled and nodded his head.

The men stood to retire to the small library. Without invitation, Cocheta and Monni joined them.

Confident that the other understood the exchanges, the two strong willed men kept the conversation in their first tongues.

"There were those who wanted you to be the peace chief at Black Hoof's death," said Johnston.

"I am not surprised that you know opinions among my people," said Caesar, "but I have chosen to pursue peace in ways that those who refused to join Tecumseh cannot understand. Tell me, what do you pursue, Johnston?"

"We have known each other since my family's migration to these parts decades ago. From my years in Ft. Wayne I have not changed. But if there is some confusion, as host, I am happy to clarify matters."

"You speak of migration and we see invasion. Even worse, Johnston, you have been instrumental in the removals of the rightful owners of this land."

"Yes, as Indian Agent, I had to negotiate the treaties as ordered by my superiors and facilitate the removals."

"You feel more like a White Agent. All you have done is to advance their interests."

"The federal government pays my salary but I am a free man who is not owed by any party."

"Is it true that you personally recruited our own warriors to fight against Tecumseh's alliance?"

"It is true," Johnston said without blinking an eye. "Tecumseh might well have won had he arrived fifty years earlier. You know better than I that warriors need to fight. Most like also to win. Tecumseh knew his victory chances were small, yet you followed him. Why? And don't say because of your father. We both know men like General Richard Butler's son, Tamanatha by the Shawnee woman, who not only fought against their father and brothers, but killed them."

"Your arrogance grows too strong, Colonel...I believe that is what your wife called you. Just because you have lived among us does not make you one of us. If you had been one of us you would not have aided in the theft of our world."

"I was serving as the principal American interpreter when your father held the same position for the Shawnee. I have done the same when he was absent and you were present acting for the Shawnee. You are almost as articulate as a white man. Have you ever known me to misinterpret?"

"Colonel, it was you who mentioned peace chiefs. You were supposed to act in the same capacity as a peace chief. Instead of as an advocate for invaders. You should have been loving and protecting us. You played with words. I am not accusing you of misinterpreting what was being said by those who outranked you. I am declaring that you knew those words were lies. Your truth-telling reputation outside of making treaties was being used to mislead us. Unlike the interpreters Jackson has appointed who speak not a word of Shawnee, Wyandotte or Miami, during each treaty you correctly interpreted the words you heard, but you knew that even as they were spoken, the Americans were insatiable. We owned a deer and you asked for one section after another until we were left with just a single muddied hoof. Then the Americans took even that, leaving us to content ourselves with the scent of what you were eating in our faces. Yet you ask me to honor you because you were an 'innocent' interpreter for a band of liars?"

"Whatever happened in the past, now I am protecting your mother."

"The Shawnee nation was more than a lone woman!"

"You are speaking with bitterness and anger. I, on the other hand, speak calmly with Christian civility and love."

Caesar laughed wryly. "If I had helped kill your father, brother, leader, and the woman you intended to marry, how would you speak to me? As for Christian civility, does Your Bible advocate savaging the lives of others?"

Caesar waited in vain for Johnston to reply. "One last question: do you have any regrets?"

"That is not fair."

"Fair? I who have always been loyal have lost nearly everything. You who have papers on what should have been mine, ask for fairness."

Johnston sighed. "Yes, I have a regret. More than once I put obedience to man ahead of obedience to Christ. I cannot return lost yesterdays. How do we make the best of tomorrows?"

Caesar was unprepared for this change in direction. He parlayed the blow with, "Do not steal my mother."

Before Johnston could protest, Cocheta threw up her hand. "He has not 'stolen' me son. He has offered me more sanctuary than I found elsewhere."

"She speaks truly," said Johnston, surprising the room by switching to Shawnee.

"Unlike many," said Caesar, sustaining the Shawnee, "my mother always speaks truly...without and within the meanings."

"Perhaps I have overstepped in words and deeds," said Johnston sigh again. "What next? Will you take your mother with you?"

"I am devoted to my mother. You have heard her. She has made her choice."

Cocheta walked to Caesar. He opened his arms and they embraced. She whispered, "Farewell for now, my son. Continue the stalk."

Monni stepped closer. Cocheta gestured also to embrace her daughter-in-law. "The men have had their say but I am not a stone, centered in a field. Mother, I never met your husband, but I have been told his bones rest uneasily in a field somewhere outside of a Canadian battlefield. When we married, Caesar helped me find my family's bones."

Cocheta understood the implications. "My son," she said to Caesar, "will you take me to bring back your father's bones. We can place them next to where his own father's remains are buried outside of Wapakoneta."

"After I gave you sanctuary," said Johnston in English, "you would leave this great house?"

"If a short journey is considered a leaving, there is much to say about your interpretation," said Cocheta.

I have always marveled at Caesar's description of his mother's strength. I assumed she was an inspiration to both him and Monni. Without ever meeting her, I knew she was an inspiration for me.

6
COLONEL ROBIN

Quietly, Clark Ferguson worked hard to befriend my big brother, Robin. The blond, slender, medium height, middle-aged, Scots-Irish Quaker could see that Robin was a different man from the untrusting youth he had been before being kidnapped by Bacon Tate and his gang of slave catchers. Certainly, his appearance had changed little. He was still a few inches taller than Charles, freckled and with curly red-hair. His African roots were clear, but something in his bearing differed from the man he had known three years prior.

When my father-in-law broached the subject to Charles, my husband reported he said, "Father, he has been through Hell and lived to tell the story as a free man. Any man alive would be changed."

"If I had to weigh the value of thy advice, son, it would be little more than a corn husk. I will see for myself what I might learn.

My husband reported that the two talked after a third meal of simple Three Sisters Soup with added chicken and Maryland biscuits one evening when Robin told a tale that he had heard while enslaved in Georgia. At the time, I was with our brother Dan in Cincinnati where he had been shot in the back. Thus, this is more my husband's tale, enhanced but a bit after he relayed it to me.

* * *

A certain North Carolina slave holder called Master Ward was so secure in his slaves' behavior that, on the Sunday when the whites received communion, rather than have them denied "the Holy Host" he allowed itinerate preachers to deliver sermons outside of the church. True, they were surrounded by the regular overseer and a farmer hired for the day. Both white men were armed and watchful. One such Sunday, a slave called Uncle Billy whose grandfather had been bonded to a Quaker family before their general emancipation, acted on what he had heard of early Quakers. He interrupted a foolish sermon.

The visiting preacher had just summarized his main point of slaves being obedient to masters when Uncle Billy stood up from the assembly and said, "Mr. Preacher man, is we going to be free in Heaven?"

The preacher was stunned silent at Uncle Billy's impertinence. "In case you got wax in your ears," Uncle Billy raised his voice, "Is God gonna free us in heaven or do you expect us to serve y'all night and day until even Heaven come to a end?"

The preacher wiped his forehead with a spittle-laden handkerchief, started stuttering, finally concluding, "I ain't God."

Uncle Billy sat down. "Glad you done figured that out!"

Charles said, even his parents and siblings laughed heartily at Robin's tale. When the room quieted Robin told them, "Uncle Billy took 99 lashes," for his impertinence. Not long afterwards he died. The master pronounced the death by natural causes but charged his overseer a week's pay for cruelty to an animal.

Mary Crispin escorted the younger children to bed where she would read to them what she believed was a more age appropriate story.

With men only present, Robin said, "Truth is, don't none of us see religion the way slave masters want it to be seen. By and by we see the ones on the bottom rising to the top. Once we get there, won't be no white folk ruling nothing worth having, no place for overseers, whips or even the best slave holders."

Clark said, "Have we not treated thee well?"

"Y'all ain't white folk no longer," said Robin. "Y'all's 'nigger lovers'. Somewhere in between white and black and you sure ain't slave holders. To tell the truth, Clark your family and a very few other is the only folk I've known born white and still worth trusting. It might be a few others hiding in the weeds. Only their actions and the Good Lord will tell."

After an awkward silence Charles asked, "Then thee has become religious?"

"I'm trying," said Robin. "I done prayed that me and my daughter will get free and now that we is, I want to give y'all's Lord a better chance than I've had most of my life."

"How far would thee say thee has come toward that worthy goal?" asked Clark.

Robin was unable to measure the distance to a place he had never visited; however, he could explain the furthest he had been from being a Christian. Before I share what Charles and my father-in-law reported, it would be helpful to give some background. The year before the three of us escaped was 1826, we were in the midst of the worst drought in Virginia history. Our rations had been severely lowered but some nearby slaves nearly starved. Every slave I knew was in tatters because the masters could not maintain their own overabundant outfits and simultaneously grant us our semi-annual new outfits at Christmas and Easter.

It was the custom of slaves to boast of our masters' wealth when we came together at Reverend Stringfellow's church or for corn shuckings. In many cases we tried to convince ourselves that we need not worry about being sold off to raise new funds for masters in danger of bankruptcy. Because times harder, young men increasingly voiced their anger. Many made out of white hearing promises about running away or worse. I understood their rage. Some of the most belligerent men had wives, sisters or mothers who had been ravaged by the overlords. On two separate plantations young males grew so restless that overseers used unusual tortures. On the first, other slaves were ordered to strip a teenager in front of the other slaves. The teenager was held down by the four strongest men, one of which was his uncle. His own mother was ordered to scrape off all parts of his body or submit to unimaginable brutalization by the masters' sons. His brother was ordered to rub his bare body with straw and salt it. All the while, the poor boy screamed and more. He was staked by shackles and kept in place until noon the next day. On the second plantation, a father of six was extended by a rope around his hands and for a day and a night hovered above a large nail. How he managed both to soil himself and receive punctures only a few times each was more miraculous than Jesus feeding thousands with a few loaves and fishes.

Foolishly such behaviors were thought to distract from extreme hunger and make all slaves more docile.

Robin spread the word that he was in favor of a rebellion. "Ain't we got no rights?" he asked to our brother Dan.

"None that they have to honor." .

Robin thought through a plan of action and chose leaders

on all the plantations that were sent to occupy the balcony of Reverend Stringfellow's church. These "captains" as he called them, would be told the fullness of his plans when the time was right. Naturally word spread that a rebellion was being planned. Every suspected spy in Culpeper County was threatened with castration or its equivalent should the masters learn before revenge was won.

"Help me," said Clark, "thee speaks of others being abused but surely thee was not abused."

Robin slowly pulled off his shirt and displayed a back that showed ten times more stripes than I can imagine on a tiger. He quickly put it back on. "Y'all talk about freedom and liberty and such and ain't nary one of you been a slave. I called myself Colonel Robin and I was going grab some of that freedom and liberty and a whole lot more of revenge."

Because he wanted things to fall apart for the whites, Robin suggested his captains disrupt their own plantations anyway they chose. Here and there people pretended to be sick; at one plantation twelve slaves went on a five day refusal to work. At others, taking meat, milk and trinkets that the masters considered theirs increased. Tools were broken. One particularly outraged man broke the leg of a perfectly good mule. When the word spread about the poor mule, several prime horses were released around the county. Nearly all were returned safely to their plantations.

"Didn't the whites suspect anything?" asked Clark.

"Hadn't nothing new happened," said Robin. "Just more of it. It was nearing the time when I was going unleash Nyame's fury. I had word spread, 'Colonel Robin says, step it up!'"

Two county bridges collapsed "from too much weight" on the same day. One master broke his neck and other his shoulder but others were only shaken. "Miraculously" their drivers were able to jump clear and only secure a few bruises. The following day the homes of four masters and three patrollers were set on fire.

"Why the patrollers?" asked Charles.

"Them boys should've been fighting beside us instead of helping the very ones who had them trying to make a living against slave labor."

"Wouldn't that make them hate you more?"

"Nobody got caught. Besides can you tell me what would make 'em love us? While the masters slept, they was out all night spitting on anybody they saw trying to visit a wife or sweetheart, catching runaways, beating 'em and bringing 'em back ambushing' women who went to the outhouse."

Mary Crispin had returned from putting her young ones to be. "Two wrongs don't make a right."

"That's a good point," said Robin. "They'd done more wrongs than there's stars in the cry. What we did to them hardly evened the score."

"Oh, Robin," Mary Crispin said shaking her head. "It is amazing the poor fabric that hate sews."

"What we was doing was all about love. Love for self, love for our kin, love for our people."

"You planned all that by yourself?" asked Clark.

"I done told you, there was a man and a woman captain on a dozen plantations. They didn't need me planning to show 'em how we was being treated. Think about this: one of the captains on Master Davis's plantation was his cook. Folk used to say he was such a good-hearted man his slaves loved him more than they loved Jesus. His wife didn't drink coffee and slaves wasn't allowed to. That cook captain put poison in Davis's coffee and he dropped dead. The whole county knew with his morning coffee he ate six or seven biscuits smothered in red-eye gravy. He was so well loved they thought he musta swallowed a piece of biscuit the wrong way. We might none of us been to school but we knew how to kill a white man if we wanted to. I was one colonel. It must've been fifty-eleven captains."

* * *

"So, here's the skeleton of my part of the plan to bring the harvest once the ground was cultivated," said Robin. "As I heard a Georgia preacher say, 'You may have to put some meat on it to make these dry bones walk.' There must've been near about a hundred of us we could truly trust to do the deed. The signal was going to be the first day after the next full moon when the Fruits of the Spirit crew I was with was close enough to the crew on one of the sides of our plantation, I'd sing back to back Wade in the Water and Make These Dry Bones Live. It was just two other plantations touching ours on the 40 acres we was working the month we was looking to rebel. From them two one man was going run that night to tell somebody on the other six plantations. In case he got stopped, the first man was going run the opposite way and make his circle ending back where the second man started. You follow me?"

"I think so," said Clark.

"Were you going to fight with your fists and farm tools?" asked Charles.

"Against shotguns?" asked Robin surprised at the question. "Since first the notion for a rebellion come in my mind, we had been stealing knives and guns, bullets and whatever could send a white man to Hell."

"Surely thee did not expect all of you to survive," said Clark.

"What's worse than slavery? If some of us died sooner, the rest was going die later. Why not die like men and women who was worth being re-remembered?"

"The word is 'remembered'," said Mary Crispin.

"No it ain't," said Robin. "We was already re-remembering we was born to be warriors. It was for others to remember us."

"I see," said Mary Crispin.

"My friends on every plantation that attended Stringfellow's church used to call me 'Wild Robin'. After we attacked Fruits of the Spirit, I'd show 'em just how wild I was. We would kill Stringfellow for all his lies, circle back and Colonel Robin would lead my family to Philadelphia.

"What of thy father?" There was a heavy silence. "Would he have followed a son?"

"Daddy wanted nothing more than freedom. That's what he lived for, worked day and night for."

"Then he knew what you were planning?" asked Charles. "I thought thee said he was a Christian."

"Ain't been none finer but he wasn't no Quaker. The ones he learned his Christian from was men who used violence and terror just like Quakers use breathing and when he learned about my plan he got silent then says, some man named Joshua was a Christian and he fought the battle of Jericho."

"That is not how I was taught the story," said Mary Crispin.

"Would you men have killed women and children?" asked Clark.

"The council had a argument over that. Some said the women and children was benefitting from our work like the menfolk. Others pointed out the mamas was raising male children to grow up to be like they daddies. I hated Miss Anne almost as much as Master Prescott, but Dan got me to promise to save her. That's when I told the captains, 'Don't kill a woman, girl child any age and no boy child that couldn't beat my little sister Sarah in a fair fight."

I was outraged when Charles reported this to me. Why did I have to be the standard of who was worthy to live?

Plantations throughout the area were on edge waiting for the word to attack. Then Nathan Prescott died suddenly. I was with Robin when he learned of the master's death. He released a yell so loud I thought of the lions of Africa. The one thing Robin had not considered was what to do with his blood lust if the most despised man of all was removed. For the next several days others tried to rekindle Robin's fire. I too did not want to die a slave. In fact, all of my sisters and even Mama were members of the plot. Just when I thought Robin was rallying, Miss Anne declared that Prescott's would send Robin, Dan, and me away.

There was a silence in the Ferguson home that Robin broke. "Y'all don't know how many times I've cussed myself out for running out of steam when Prescott died. I come to see all the time the heart of the matter was wanting' to strangle Prescott."

After a deep silence Mary Crispin said, "Thee must forgive thyself, Robin. There is much of God in thee. The Still Small Voice" might have spoken to thee. Release the self-flagellation and thee will find peace."

"Ain't no peace for a black man. I'll use what my daddy taught me to answer that question Clark asked back a while about how I done changed. I never listened much to Daddy's Bible quoting, but the day I got down to Georgia after they kidnapped me from Ohio, Mama Matilda gave a before sunrise sermon. She said, 'Jehovah who comforteth us in all our tribulation, that we may be able to comfort them which are in any trouble.' My re-memory said, 'Back in the day, Daddy was always saying that'."

"Then," said Mary Crispin, "it was thoughts of thy loving father that carried thee through to freedom."

"In my way of thinking, it was Daddy and everybody else

on this earth that loved me that carried me through to wherever I am."

"We love thee," said Mary Crispin.

Robin, the hardest man I had known before we had rescued him from Georgia slavery smiled and said, "I guess that mean y'all helped carry me through too."

When Charles related this story, Robin for months had been dead of a blood clot. I sat with the 're-rememory' of my beloved brother. Then wept again.

7

UPPITY

Mother lost two children in the 1819 influenza epidemic and others in miscarriages. mentioned the others except when dating another event, "Back in the spring of 100 when I lost..." Among those who survived, older than me in our family were two overbearing brothers who were both woman chasers and two beautiful sisters neither of whom chose to study Latin or English with our father. Along with my sisters, my younger brother, Luther was left behind when Robin, Dan, and I escaped. Luther had been my joy, a willing student of Latin and English and usually prepared to accept my reasonable direction. He was a married preacher when we were united after 25 years apart. Except for loving me dearly, he had changed greatly. This is my retelling of one of his many adventures.

* * *

Seminole is a word meaning runaways. Runaway slaves from Georgia, Alabama, and South Carolina were the first Seminoles. The Black Seminoles were recognized decades before their red allies, who were at the time, still primarily members of the Creek nation. Many decades later several Creek villages would leave the main nation, move south from Georgia and Alabama and accept a few hundred Chickasaw and Choctaw migrants who for various reasons were displeased with life with their main nation. Regardless of their origin, most Red Seminoles white encroachment. The Red Seminoles joined other native peoples who had lived in Florida for centuries. Initially European-rooted people were naturally welcomed into the Seminoles. Many had already intermarried with Creeks, some rising to the position of chief. When, in time, it became obvious that the whites wanted Florida for themselves, the united Seminoles decided that white fixation on skin color and chattel slavery made them corrupted and unwelcomed as spouses.

Almost from the beginning, Georgia planters made claims on any black person including those who they knew were born free in Florida. Whites claimed because no blacks had immigrated from Africa as free people, any offspring of a fugitive was also their property. The United States launched several attacks on the Seminoles, including one led by General Andrew Jackson. As armed resistors to the established social orders of both United States and Creek nations, Black and Red closed ranks.

Following years of war, in 1832, the United States called for treating at Payne's Landing with the Red Seminoles alone. No amount of protest could get the federal government to include the Indians' black allies as council members at the meeting. If they recognized even born free Black Seminoles carrying free papers signed by the Chief Justice of the Supreme Court, it might set an unwanted precedent. With the Haitians eager to become a part of the world community, no black man, domestic or foreign, could be seen as an equal negotiator. The whites inserted a deliberately misleading clause which cost the Red Seminoles hundreds of thousands of square miles. They were also forbidden from having blacks in their community. The coalition of Seminoles developed a good faith strategy of allowing intermarriage, fighting as one, but keeping separate but equal nearby villages under the rule of locally selected leaders. They added an ingenious strategy whereby the blacks would pretend to be slaves of their red neighbors, being accepted as humans, free from rapes and lashes, paying them a small portion of their crops as "tribute."

The letter of Payne's Landing was honored although the treaty's spirit was as dishonored as the white authors had been dishonorable. Payne's Landing confirmed what all sides knew: the American goal was, by any means necessary, removal of the Red Seminoles from every acre of Florida and enslavement of all Black Seminoles.

* * *

In February of 1835, my 17 year-old brother, Luther, avoided poor whites who were the patrollers pretending to guard the porous border between the slaveocracy and Seminole freedom. The first border guards he came upon rode the northern banks of the Savannah River separating South Carolina, where he had been enslaved, from Georgia. He had been told the approximate place where the South Carolina and Georgia patrollers crossed as they traveled opposite directions. Unfortunately, the first night the Georgia patrol was delayed as they attempted to catch a runaway family who, like Luther, headed south to join the Seminoles. Luther heard later from slaves who gave him food on a plantation two days southwest walk from Savannah that the grapevine believed the runaways had successfully dodged the first patrol. There were certainly more policing other roads before they arrived in the freedom of Seminole-land.

On the third day the patrols crossed where predicted. Luther waited a while then thanked the Lord he had allowed me to teach him how to swim.

Much of Seminole territory already had been appropriated by white invaders but there were fewer settled areas which made dodging easier than in South Carolina and Georgia. All Luther had to his name were the clothes on his back, a good knife, and a few water-soaked books that he had stolen from his master. He had been living off the land for a week. Fish, wild greens and an occasional rock-killed bird had long lost their welcomed taste. There were times when the sound of his stomach reminded him of Mother reminiscing about African drums.

He came to the Okefenokee Swamp and recalled that he had been told it was shallow but dangerous. He saw two huge alligators sunning. He would have turned back but to where? He sat down to contemplate what came next and spied three others. All were too close to inspire confidence in his next move. Within an hour, a man wearing nothing more than a slouch hat, moccasins, a breach cloth, and a tattered European made vest, approached him in a canoe.

"Runaway are you?" Although no firearm was visible, the man could be a different kind of patroller. Luther stood and was ready to flee. "You don't have to fear me, son. Alligators and Crackers is your enemies, not Johnny Horn. My mother is Timucua and my father, wherever the bastard is, was a English trader. Come, I'll take you through. I know where you're heading." True to his word, Johnny guided him through the swamp and fed him well on maize, fish and alligator meat. "Where'd you get the corn?" Luther asked. "It can't grow here in the swamp can it?"

"For the most part, the swamp is best growing water moccasins and alligators. People have traded since before my time," said Johnny. Luther turned his eyes to look for the snakes and alligators, ending what might have been an enlightening conversation.

The next day they came to a place where Johnny guided the canoe to shore and said, "This is where you get off."

"How much do I owe you?" said Luther fully aware that he had but two coins in the pouch that carried his three books.

"I always ask the same fee," said Johnny with a smile. "If you see a white man on the road, kill him."

With that he pushed back into the swamp.

Luther had exhausted the traveling instructions he had been given before leaving South Carolina. He said to himself, 'Seminole-land appears to be like heaven. Everybody says it exists but nobody I know has come back to talk about it.'

He continued south until after three days walk on a small trail, eating wild fruits and a dead racoon, he came to Pilaklika-ha/Abraham's Old Town. Greeting him were the Black Seminoles' rich fields of cultivated beans, melons, pumpkins, corn, rice, and several types of field greens. To supplement hunting, they also owned domesticated chickens, geese and cattle. Luther saw black prosperity that reminded him of his mother's stories of Fante-land and his father's of heaven.

'Could it be, I am home,' he asked himself.

The first woman he saw invited him to help himself to a huge pot filled with chicken and beans. He ate the stew with a flat bread. Afterwards he enjoyed a melon he had never seen. It was the best meal he had eaten since his mother had fed him his last family supper eight years earlier. The next day, Luther, the young Virginia born slave had been sold and taken to Washington where he was sold to South Carolina. At each stop women he loved were sexually abused and both genders were beaten whenever the masters thought it might increase production.

'Not here,' Luther told himself. 'I am tired but no longer a slave and this woman seems to be unconcerned for her safety.'

In Luther's first taste of freedom, he had no idea what to expect next. Whatever happened, he expected his treatment would be far removed from the shackles he'd known in the Federal City and that there would be no vile names by villains pretending to be democratic. For a few days Luther ate well whenever he chose, received gifts of moccasins, a breechcloth and a colorful mantle for the cool evenings, clothes favored by the locals. He helped with labor and painted his face in what he thought were mere decorations.

A warrior about his age who he knew as Young Ensel came to him. "My daddy wants to see you?"

"I don't know him."

Pointing he said, "Go down that road about a quarter mile. On the right side there's only one man sitting under a live oak, just a stone's throw from the lake."

Luther followed the instructions, arrived at the appointed place and said to a grizzled and balding man, "Sir, unless I miss my guess, you're a Fante like my family. Mother taught me your name is a day of the week."

"My parents were both from Fante-land. I was born on the crossing but never knew my daddy. I expect he got killed trying to revolt on the big ship, least that's what Mama said. She saw to it I got my proper marking anyway." He pointed one at a time to horizontal scars on each side of his face. Luther said they mirrored our father's.

Luther failed to tell Ensel all he knew of the Fante language was how to count to ten and the names of the days of the week. Of course, that was more than I had learned from Mama. While I steadfastly resisted all things African, the youngest child in our family had been more malleable until he reached the age of seven and Mama let him choose to increase his knowledge of the old country or follow Daddy's dream of being an American.

"Most Black Seminoles is some kind of Akan or Ibo or Egba," said Ensel. "Back home our granddaddies mighta fought each other. Here, what's the point? We know the real enemy: the same devils that stole my younger kids and wife. Just call me a Seminole and all will be fine."

"Yes sir."

"I sent for you, young fellow, because I hear tell you can help me. Before we commence to talking for real, get somebody to teach you how to paint your face proper. Slapping some mess on it ain't what it's about. Paint tells a story that makes sense not nonsense. War's about to commence and men looking like fools don't get it with us."

Luther went away and worked up enough nerve to ask a friendly warrior, named Pete, to teach him the proper face painting. When he returned, Ensel said, "I'm not as big a interpreter as Abraham is for Micanopy or John Caesar for Emathla, but I suspect that sometimes the government agents read the treaties wrong to all three of us, setting us up to look bad. They say two or three times, Abraham got made out like he was the one lying. With folk looking sideways at him, if I can protect my reputation, I may be able to make the climb to replace Abraham. I need your help, son. I hear tell you can read and write better than anybody around here. How come? You a spy."

"I would rather die and go to Hell than spy against my own people. I can read and write because my daddy taught me how to read and write."

"You black as a moonless night in a cave. You trying to tell me your daddy is a white man?"

"No. A white man taught him."

"How's about you teaching me?"

"I'll be happy to teach you but I can't afford to risk being with you when you're around whites. I hear there are slave catchers looking for folk like me."

"Then you'll do it?"

"Yes, but in an even trade."

"You one of them uppity Nigras?"

"I believe free men practice reciprocity." Ensel frowned. "I mean fair exchange...give and take."

"I ain't rich."

"All I want is from you to teach me about this new world. All I know for sure is more than anyone should about slavery. It's freedom I need to learn about."

* * *

The two took turns as educators. Luther always began. Luther set a slow pace. He believed it was necessary to thoroughly know one section before moving on to the next he had in mind. When Ensel grew bored, he would say, "Hush up!" Then relate the shared Seminole history. Ensel explained that the Spanish had claimed Florida without paying or even defeating the Native Americans. Luther initially thought the Spanish was another Indian nation. "No fool!" said Ensel, impatiently. "They just a different kind of white man."

Recently the Spanish had sold the land to the United States without including the Seminoles in the negotiations.

"Seem like, no matter what happens, if you low man in the game, folk don't respect you enough to even ask your opinion. We might as well be babes at the tit."

"So will we be fighting both the Americans and the Spanish?" asked Luther.

"You is new to the fighting game. We ain't lost all our Spanish friends. Fishermen still come from Spanish Cuba and sell us guns and bullets."

"What's their government think about that?"

"I ain't asked. But my guess is they think about as much about their government as a buzzard thinks about ant turds. You ever heard of the Negro Fort?"

"What's a fort?"

"You about the dumbest smart man I ever seen," said Ensel laughing. "Let me take you back a ways. About 400 Negroes fought with the British in the Revolution. When the Americans won, the British deposited those of our people that helped 'em on the Apalachicola River. That's how one set of my granddaddies and grandmamas come to the area. They ran away from slavery. Granddaddy fought, Grandmama cooked, washed officers' clothes, patched up the wounded. The Brits took lots of folk with 'em but my kin was born in this country and didn't want to leave it. They run south to Florida and kept running til they got here."

He explained that a fort was a stockade, hewn trees stuck vertically into the ground, tied together to keep out attackers. The British had ordered blacks to build it for protection during the war of 1812 against Americans. At war's end, the fort was handed over to the Black Seminoles. Jackson's men, joined by Creek warriors, had crossed the border and massacred nearly 300 blacks and taken into slavery all but a few who managed to escape. That had begun a war that the Seminoles had lost. The Americans put them on a sizeable reservation in Central Florida, "No shore, so our Spanish friends would have a hard time getting weapons to us. That damn Jackson became President and said he wanted all Indians moved west and all blacks in slavery."

Rather than continue compromising their beliefs the Red Seminoles decided to resist being slave catchers for the whites and refuse to move west.

"Why were the Creeks helping the Americans? Aren't they cousins of the Seminoles?"

"Money rules the white man and his flunkies too. The Creeks want to be white so they keep sure enough slaves and sell 'em when the price is right. The Seminoles treat the black man like they want to be treated. Them two ways of looking at life clash. Can you wrap your mind around how dangerous this place is?"

"I have never lived in a safe place."

Ensel paused to silently consider Luther's words. "I wish you didn't, but you got a point. Anyway, when the new war start, them flying bullets will help you understand war can make slavery seem like every dawn is Christmas morning. One day I intend for me and my boy to be safe."

"Where will I be safest, sir?"

"Safest? The second safest place is in the swamps; without a Indjin or Nigra guide that done turned traitor, ain't no way for a white man to find Seminoles who don't wanna be found."

"I would have never made it here if a Indian named Johnny hadn't helped me through that big swamp on the Georgia border."

"John Horn still doing right up north?" asked Ensel rhetorically."That man is as good as grits on Sunday morning." He paused remembering something he did not disclose. "That brings me to the first safest place: stuck up under a white man, naturally. But if you afraid of being taken back into slavery by some cracker, you oughtta settle in Peliklakaha, Suwanee Old Town, King Heijah's Town, Bukra Woman's Town or Mulatto Girl's Town. All them places is chocked full of Black Seminoles living close by Red Seminoles. You get to go to the Red Seminole festivals with all the dancing and singing—Green Corn Dance coming up in a few weeks. You may even find you a good Red Seminole wife."

Luther said, "My mother was black."

"Get them kinda colors out your head. They about shades not living. Micanopy and Osceola both got Negro wives and Abraham got him a Red wife who was Micanopy's youngest stepmother. My grandmama didn't speak a lick of English or Spanish. A Seminole is a Seminole. Don't let nobody tell you different, son. We's joined like a fingers on the same hand."

He took a leaf from Luther's teaching style and paused before saying, "Red Seminoles tend not to expect more than ten bushels of corn a year from us; they'd rather hunt and let cattle stretch their food. Don't forget it's their land. What we give is only right for using it. Call it rent if it suits you. If we was back in Africa and they was on our land we'd do the same.

"Now let's get back to them As to Zs, I before E except after Cs," he gave a smile that revealed two missing teeth lost in battle and the lessons continued.

Day after day, Luther and Ensel alternated between training for war and studying. Bullets were hard to come by but Ensel preferred hatchets and hand to hand combat. To prevent himself from hurting his student he used weighted ax handles to compensate for the removal of the blades. In time Luther grew to love what he later described as an art form, claiming that each swing told a story. After working with the ax handles for nearly an hour, Luther feared the temptation to overdue pleasure. He overlooked the older man's prerogative signaled it was time to return to mind work.

"Already you know the alphabet, can spell your name as well as my name and spell to a hundred."

"Thank you very kindly for the compliments but I can do more than that. I bet I recognize near about 100 words in that book."

"More than that! I wish I had another book that was on your level?"

"What do you mean?"

"You're really just starting out and this little book must be boring."

"Boring is not knowing." Once more they repeatedly went over a recently raid-acquired McGuffy reader until, disgusted, Ensel suddenly said, "You cry over books. Unless we can get 'em from white peddlers—we stay short on guns, bullets, metal hatchets, knives and the like to keep them Lower Creeks from sneaking up on us. I believe we can handle the soldiers."

"How did we get from reading and writing to fighting."

"You must not like living. Books don't mean nothing to dead men or slaves. Them Creeks don't care a hoot about reading and writing."

"Are you saying other Indians are more dangerous than white soldiers?"

"Boy, once your own people are in the enemy's back pocket, they're more scary than taking a nap and waking up to a alligator about to bite your whatchamacallits."

Luther let his reflexes get the better of him, caught himself, and laughed falsely.

"Oh, the Creeks ain't the only Injins in the white man's back pocket. They mad at the Seminoles 'cause they think the Seminoles still belong to them. I guess it's sorta like the Brits feel about these white Americans. Folk don't wanna believe you can divorce 'em. You supposed to be married for life even if they sing outta tune every time they open their mouth and their breath smell like sick alligator stank." Ensel laughed at his own wit, gathered himself and said, "The just said, we'll be going to war before the year's out."

"How do you know this? Nobody else has said anything about war."

"You can read books but don't know nothing about drums. You hear how that music in the distance just changed?"

Luther listened closely, "Yes, yes I do."

"If you could read what it takes to save a life, you'd know war is upon us."

* * *

Luther told Pete about Ensel's words. Pete said, "I don't know if he was right. A war chief told me it will be a few days before we actually leave to join the others."

The two teenagers talked a while and then began practicing ax handle combat. Young Ensel joined them with a friend and played two on two for an hour, switching teams periodically. Young Ensel was on Luther's team when he said, "You had better watch my pa."

Luther said, "What do you mean?"

Distracted, Pete's partner caught Luther right behind the right leg and he found himself on the ground looking up."

"That's what I mean," said Young Ensel.

* * *

Osceola, who had risen to the most respected war chief, summoned a dozen of the principal interpreters. Ensel was honored to be among them. The old man asked Luther to accompany him. At a special council, Osceola had each interpreter read before several of his underchiefs. A warrior had stolen a book that turned out to be authored by John Locke. Ensel could only make out a few short words, placing him at the rear of the interpreters. In an attempt to recoup status, Ensel said to Osceola, "I have a new warrior with me. I bet he can do better."

Our father had loved words. He had drilled the necessity of reading clearly and with the proper shadings. Luther had the advantage of being the youngest reader in the family thus following me in age. I had made him practice to the point that, although I never told him, he could read better than I could when I was the age at which he had been when I had fled slavery. Before Osceola, Luther no doubt was a shining star reading Locke with alacrity. The high-minded English sprinkled with a few Latin words must have sounded impressive.

Unfortunately, Luther's knowledge of the Seminole language was far too weak to be elevated to treaty interpreter. Ensel had foreseen this before suggesting he audition. He suggested to Osecola that, should the need arise, Luther interpret and speak to him. He in turn would interpret in Seminole to the council. Osceola weighed the issue and decided that such a process would be too cumbersome. Instead, Ensel was told to expedite Luther's knowledge of Seminole while simultaneously learning to read English much better.

Osecola said, "Your reading sounds like a young red-bellied woodpecker who has no idea where food hides."

Everyone except Ensel laughed.

Alone Ensel said to Luther, "If I'd known that's what the council would say I would've left you behind. I'd rather be nothing but a warrior than see a upstart like you rise and me become the butt of jokes."

* * *

Luther said, "Ensel, Osecola said I need to hurry you along. No more applesauce. Here's the whole apple, rind and all. I know this is above your head, but just listen. It's special. In Carolina a white man can be lynched for having it, and a black man can be beaten half to death just for listening to it."

"How come your master had one and let you have it?"

"He didn't give it to me. I took it like he took my labor. As for why he had it, a black seaman smuggled it in and gave it to a slave sold first in Charleston and who later came to our plantation. The man could not even speak the language but when Master saw him with it he gave him 50 lashes. Why Master kept it I can't answer. When has a master explained any whys to a black man?"

Ensel conceded the point and prepared to be lifted higher.

"What you miss, I'll help you understand. I'll read slowly, just some small chunks that I think you can handle and we'll keep going back and forth until it sinks in."

"Damn it man! Is you going to read it or not?"

Luther was startled by the reaction and hurried his planned end to the introduction. "This great black man David Walker wrote, 'My dearly beloved Brethren and Fellow Citizens. ...we (coloured people of these United States,) are the most degraded, wretched, and abject set of beings that ever lived since the world began; and I pray God that none like us ever may live again until time shall be no more.... I am persuaded, that many of my brethren, particularly those who are ignorantly in league with slaveholders or tyrants...will rise up and call me cursed...I appeal...to awaken in the breasts of my afflicted, degraded and slumbering brethren, a spirit of inquiry and investigation respecting our miseries and wretchedness in this Republican Land of Liberty!...And yet they are calling for Peace!—Peace!! Will any peace be given unto them?"

Smiling, Luther looked up. Before he could read the section that he had saved for last, Ensel said, "First, how the Hell is it I'm smarter than you but you can read mess you think a man like me can't understand on first hearing?" Luther said nothing. "This smart talking brother sure ain't down here being shot at like I've been and you soon will be. Any fool knows the wrong in slavery. Them words you kept from me like you might be feeding a toothless baby ain't going shield nobody or free nobody. And some of the words you read must be showing off for white folk.

"Now you leave the book and get outta my face with your uppity ass. I'll teach my damned self how to read."

Luther opened his mouth to protest but Ensel made a gesture as though he might draw his knife. Had Luther been given the chance, he would have recited the portion he had memorized, "When I reflect that God is just, and that many of my wretched brethren would meet death with glory-yea, more plunge into the very mouths of cannons and be torn to pieces in preference to a mean submission to the lash of tyrants...Woe will be to you if we have to obtain our freedom by fighting."

. . .

Luther knew what I also realized upon reading Walker: the man may have been a scholar but he had the heart of a warrior.

* * *

"So the old man got sure enough mad at you," said Pete.

"For a minute I thought he might cut me."

Pete laughed. "That's the least of your worries, Luther. This is a place of love. Up in here, ain't no killing and cutting each other. Waiting to see if and when sure enough fighting starts is harder times than '29 but cutting each other... If you'd been up in Alabama you would have seen some boys who'd cut out your liver just to see if it reminded them of a chicken's."

"There's nothing funny about any of this."

"I guess you're right. I'll teach you what I got taught before the last time we raided across the Georgia line. First, Red or black, Osceola's is the best of the lot. He attracts blacks like good cooking brings hungry men."

"You know I met him and he thought I came up short."

"If he thought it, you did. Now listen to what I have to say. I doubt Osceola was scared of his own daddy and he won't never sell us out. A few years back they put the Treaty of Fort Gibson in front of the chiefs, I heard Osceola stuck a knife into it. The big general says, 'Let us keep this a secret,' and Osceola ignored him. He said, 'Do whatchou want with the knife but I ain't signing no man's treaty'. Wasn't that a mighty man? He don't want nobody 'round him but mighty warriors who won't blink at the sun, run from the hurricane."

"I have worked hard on my Seminole. I don't feel safe around here anymore. Let's go and do me a favor: talk mainly Seminole. My guess is Osceola will protect me more if it looks like I obeyed his orders."

* * *

Seminole religious practices had the deep spiritual connections to the natural world parallel to the ones Mother practiced. It appeared that many of those of African descent had brought vestiges of Christianity and its younger sibling, Islam into the mix. What united the threads with Seminole religion was neither had room for white hegemony and in a land of plenty, love for family and community were consistently practiced.

"I thought about praying my way up to Canady," said Pete.

"Praying?"

"Ain't no way for a nigger to find freedom unless he praying while he's running and my mama could be caught praying anytime she was awake."

"We're not running now," said Luther.

"Neither is we free when we fixing to go to war. Ain't no greater slave than a warrior. He knows he gotta be willing to die for the tribe."

Luther was shocked by the depth of Pete's ideas. "What besides distance stopped you from going to Canada?"

"The driver on my old plantation is the smartest nigger I ever knowed and he said it snows even in summer up there and white folk in Canady got one eye in the middle of their head and another on whichever elbow is on their good hand. That way, in a fight a smart man can know which hand to look for the knockout punch. I put that piece of news in a place where I could reach it. Whatchou think?"

"I think he was lying," said Luther. "If he knew you admired him and thought you might run, he probably wanted you to run to the closest place of safety. Besides, my daddy was the smartest man I ever knew, Pete. He never said anything about Canadian white folk being different, only that the best whites under God's heaven live in Philadelphia, 'The City of Brotherly Love'."

"No disrespect, Luther, but smart niggers I ain't never seen is to me like Jesus walking on top of water. The story sound good but—"

"Look Pete, let's not call each other niggers, but the point I'm trying to make is we're not in Canada, there's no snow here, and my daddy was like Osceola, 'a mighty man'."

The date of the beginning of hostilities was pushed back several times. The Seminole leaders appeared to be waiting for the Americans to initiate hostilities. Luther and Pete kept themselves apprised of the situation as they visited several Seminole towns, all the while working on Luther's fluency with Seminole. On the road, when they were not practicing Seminole, they exchanged Virginia, South Carolina and Alabama jokes or sang songs that took on new meaning with slavery behind them.

Usually the young men reveled in being able to proceed on their own pace and enjoy rather than curse the natural world.

Pete told Luther that Osecola was 22 when he married Morning Dew who was about seven years younger but the prettiest colored woman he had ever seen. "Hell, my master's wife was pale as fresh milk, smelled about the same, and face was so pretty she could make two roosters go cock-eyed. But next to Mornin Dew she looked like Old Man Henry's mule."

"Was Old Man Henry free?"

"He was white; that answers that question. Truth be told, he may've been as poor as a slave 'cause what chance he have to get ahead when master wasn't paying' nary one of us a penny for our labor?"

When they reached Micanopy, one of their first official greeters was John Caballo, a man whose mother was a black slave and whose father a full-blooded Red Seminole. Caballo, sometimes called Horse, was five years older than Luther, about 6' tall, well-built and a prominent war leader, considered fully free. Away from combat, he always dressed in colorful sashes, silver armbands and plumed head shawls. In war, he wore long sleeve cotton hunting shirts purchased from traders, buckskin leggings and single-piece moccasins. He was known to be a great marksman who never lost his cool and possessed uncommon ingenuity. Had his credentials been presented without mentioning his race, to the United States Senate he would have been called a genius and ranked a general. At a time when no black man was even ranked a sergeant among the Americans, among Seminoles he was revered as a commander of warriors.

Caballo's sister caught Luther's eye. Our older brothers Robin and Dan had taught Luther that a woman's brother might become offended by asking questions about his sister. Luther had learned many Seminole ways but not enough to risk

Caballo's wrath. In fact, Luther was daydreaming about Juana when John Caballo asked, "What's your last name?"

"Luther. Just plain Luther."

"A free man has to have a name even when he has stolen himself to freedom."

Luther thought a while. He despised each of his former masters and every American president he had learned about from Master Prescott through Daddy was a slaveholder. He liked the sound of a name of a Shakespearean character. "Here and now I'm going to be Luther Duncan."

"Why are you shading yourself? Either you are or you ain't Luther Duncan. Black man ain't got the right to be scratching his head about who he is. Take it or leave it alone."

"I am Luther Duncan."

"Well, Luther Duncan," said John Caballo. "Here's a new gun for you and your silent partner."

"Pete Love, sir," said Pete quickly.

"You don't have to 'sir' me. The whites have gone one hammock too far. Talking time is over. Next week we go to war. Since I was five years old, Jackson or his men have chased me from one place to the next. This time, whether it's Jackson or even Creeks by themselves, I intend to make a stand."

John Caballo left the boys and Pete said, "Thanks for doing the talking, Luther. I'm kinda shy and ain't quite learned how to speak to big men, especially when they think we came to be under them because we dallied getting to Osceola "

"God willing, we'll make it there sooner or later."

* * *

John Caballo had never been outside of Seminole-land. Even when others led raids in Georgia, he preferred to stay away from what was well-defined slave territory. Luther initially wondered if he feared capture and being enslaved himself but after spending time with him decided Caballo was a fearless warrior who recognized that any man his color was fair game for kidnapping anywhere in America. The war chief befriended Luther, building their relationship around stories of the fugitive's experiences in different parts of the country. Most nights Luther was invited to dinner and encouraged to tell stories of being enslaved in Virginia, the Federal City, while transported on the ocean, in South Carolina and in the journey to Seminole territory. Caballo had endless specific questions about working in the big house, picking tobacco and cotton, the streets and buildings of the Federal capital, sea storms, savage beatings, the way dandies dressed, where the most beautiful women or strongest men might be found, if free black men else-where walked or talked differently than their enslaved brethren... Sometimes he would catch himself shivering or cursing from rage. A man who believed in strict discipline, Caballo would sometimes close his eyes and relax before seeking more information. Because Caballo did not know Luther's most painful secrets and my brother did not even hint at the uncivilized way my mother, his sisters and other women were treated, such heinous behavior was not discussed. Surely Caballo had heard the stories. Perhaps because his wife and sister Juana were at the dinner table he never pursued informa-tion on such uncivilized behavior.

One evening Juana was helping her sister-in-law finish food preparation, which that evening included venison, fish, rice, squash and beans. Luther never allowed their eyes to meet. When Caballo had to leave quickly for an unscheduled council meeting and her sister-in-law, discreetly left the two younger people alone, Juana said, "Luther Duncan, why won't you look at me?"

"I have seen you."

"I know you have, but out of the corner of your eyes, not directly. Why?"

He hesitated. Remembering that he was supposed to be a fearless warrior, he pushed himself to look across the table into her dark eyes. "I never looked at you for fear that you are too beautiful and I might prove a fool for beauty."

"'Might prove'?" She considered his words. "You mean you've never kissed a woman?"

"I've never kissed anyone."

"I would ask you if you know what a good woman can do for a warrior, but by your confession you don't know what any woman can do for a warrior."

"That's an overstatement."

"Apparently not by much."

With her brother's tacit agreement, they began keeping company.

Luther's innocence was soon remedied. Juana took the willing student to places his past lives had not revealed existed. Sometimes he felt his head spinning. At other times, lights flashed in non-pastel colors and he did not know his right from his left.

* * *

Ensel, the elder, visited John Caballo. His goal was to arrange a marriage between the son who was named after him and Juana.

Addressing Caballo, he said, "You know my boy is one of the best warriors we got. Ain't afraid of nothing. Think of the kids they'd make!"

Caballo looked at Juana who sat silently. "My sister is spoken for. She's sweet on that new man from South Carolina, Luther Duncan. I'm just waiting for him to get up the gumption to propose."

"Is that true?" Ensel asked Juana.

"Now you ask me a question?" said Juana.

Ensel left in anger. When Juana told Luther what had happened she concluded, "You waited too late. Ensel doing what his son wasn't man enough to do and you were too slow doing what a real man would have done a week ago, made me think about this world. I will not marry any man in war time. The last thing I want is to be like my mama, a warrior's widow rearing one or two children alone, being preyed on by men who had pretended to be my husband's friends."

Luther had been thinking about proposing. He also had assumed their love was stronger than she made it sound. He turned silently away. "Aren't you willing to fight for me?" said Juana when he had barely taken two steps.

"I thought that was why I was in training."

"The more I try to teach you about our ways, the less you seem to understand. If I was to marry you and my children took after the father my children could be born dumber than a corn stalk."

* * *

War finally came. Through three skirmishes and one battle Luther and Pete were inseparable. Recognizing their strong relationship, Luther said, "I feel closer to you than I did with my older brothers."

"Since Master sold my three brothers away when I was a child, I've always wanted a brother."

Luther said, "My brothers were too old to be close to me but I think I understood them. What I don't understand is women."

"What's to figure? Is the gal pretty or ugly? Is she old or

young? Does she talk soft or scream? Is she loving or spiteful? Is she smart as a new water pump or dumb as a old stump?"

"It's more to a woman than that."

"Is it?"

"I'm talking about Juana. I know those things, but it's more to her than anybody I've ever known."

"The problem ain't women. The problem is you. Ask the question right if you want the right answer. Say, 'I can't figure Juana out'."

"Well?"

"I ain't studied up on that particular woman. You the one trying to work that field."

* * *

Luther and Pete were promoted to being scouts assigned to reconnoiter the white army. Many others stood far above them in combat importance but they were trusted and respected. They were instructed that if captured they were to pretend that they were escaping from wicked Seminole slavery. The two turned a bend in the road and thought they were accidentally running into Ensel.

"Well, you two young fellows are out here on a scout?"

"Yes, sir," said both young men together.

Luther added, "I haven't seen you in a while. I hope all is forgiven."

"What's to forgive?" said Ensel. "I'm on a scout too, for Osceola. He's disappointed in you. Thought you were going to come to his village and show off."

"We were but got waylaid."

"Is that what you call it?" said Ensel.

Luther noticed the weapons of the man who had trained him, "I see you have new weapons."

"The gun is new but these are the same battle hatchets I've carried for years. I keep what counts in good shape. You never saw them because your mind was stayed on playing with children's stuff."

"I said I was sorry."

Ensel ignored the apology. "One side of the white army is over there to the east," said Ensel pointing. "I saw smoke and reckon the other is just to the northwest. Why don't you go and check while I report back to the main body of Osceola's warriors?"

The young men followed his orders. Once removed from Ensel, Luther brought the discussion back to his favorite subject, finally asking what he had danced around, "Do you think Juana will wait?"

"Why shouldn't she?"

"There are things I don't know because I was born a slave."

"I was born a slave too," said Pete. "It ain't how you was born. It's how you living. The Good Book is clear about that and every woman I've ever known is more concerned with how you living than how your mama borned you."

Moments later, they were ambushed. Luther was fortunate enough to be missed by a poor shooter. Pete was killed instantly, his blood splashing all over Luther's body. Luther shot dead the man who had killed his friend. He could not load his single-shot rifle fast enough to shoot the fast fleeing poor marksman.

He was sobbing over his loss when Ensel's son appeared. "I knew you were in trouble," said Young Ensel.

"What do you mean?" said Luther.

"Daddy's sure the Seminoles can't win and the whites made him some promises. He took a lotta others with him too. I don't agree with betrayal, so I left on my own."

"You mean he sent us into a trap?"

"Yep. He hates you with a passion."

"Because Juana would not marry you?"

"I am too busy trying to get vengeance for what the whites did stealing Mama and my sisters to have my mind stayed on Juana or any other gal. Daddy was just trying to get some grandkids. All I know about him hating you is he said when you meet the Devil, you'd know why you was there: 'Hell is where all uppity niggers go'."

"Why are you helping me?"

"I'm one of those black men who can't be bought. I guess that makes me uppity too. Let's bury your friend quick. Daddy might circle back with some others."

They carried Pete into the woods. Young Ensel pointed toward a depression in the earth. They put Pete's corpse in it then piled leaves and broken branches on top. Both knew it was an insufficient resting place, but it was better than dying a slave in Alabama.

Young Ensel said, "I know you want to kill my father, but let me handle it. This was the last straw." Luther was shocked. "He's wearing my name, staining it like chicken poop on wet grass."

8

THE LITTLE CABIN

My middle sister, Fannie, was nearly Mother's physical twin. With Robin's death she was also the only one of us who knew our Fante history from the days before the Akan divided. From being a middle daughter who specialized in appeasing others, her personality was changed when she escaped by herself from a Kentucky breeding plantation. She ended up in Cincinnati where she was sorely abused by her first husband. For a second time she took control of her life. Clutching her free paper, she left in search of a better world with her best friend, a freed woman named Val. The two landed in St. Louis where they were wooed by twin trappers, Scipio and Marshall Lucky, who had returned temporarily to the states.

Scipio and Marshall took Fannie and Val to the Rocky Mountains where they joined two other trappers to form a multicultural partnership far from the eyes of American politicians and preachers who frowned on such blending of races.

. . .

As with my brother Luther, I was united with Fannie when she was an adult. Sadly, the occasion was our brother Dan's memorial service. Shaped by me, Sarah Ferguson, wife, mother, seamstress, this is Fannie's tale.

* * *

On a clear day replete with a medley of colors and great vistas of mountains, the Crow sisters, Her Mother's Voice and Wind Weaver, returned with their husbands, Pomp Charbonneau, son of a famous Shoshone who had been kidnapped and enslaved by Hidatsas and a French trapper, and Isaiah "Pock" Johnson, son of slaveholders. Her Mother's Voice and Wind Weaver had just taken their husbands for a short visit to the Crow village that was considered the women's true home. Along with their husbands were two male cousins, Six Coups and Bear in the Woods. Their labor was needed to help build a proper four-room cabin.

The site for their cabin had been chosen for its proximity to a salt spring that attracted elk and black tailed deer and other smaller animals. On the other side of the mountain wild sheep sometimes came down and were unfortunate enough to become succulent victims as well as to give up their skins for dresses.

The returning six travelers rode into the clearing. Before helping with the unpacking of tents and other gear Pomp asked Fannie and Val, "Where are your husbands?"

"Making sure we don't starve," said Val before Fannie could answer.

Fannie laughed. "There's good and bad to staying in one place. It can get hunted out and send them further and further afield. Never fear, we have plenty. We both shot rabbits and squirrels this morning and if they do not return with fresh meat for a few more days we will eat roots and jerky."

The four women hugged and the Crow cousins were introduced. Pomp had a note for Fannie from the well-known black trapper, Jim Beckwourth. With the note was a small package from the states.

"I thought Beckwourth lived in another village," said Fannie.

"He does. I had business with him," said Pomp. "I went to that village and he gave me these."

"Looks like he done gone off and done something half-way decent," said Val.

The four men respected Beckwourth, but Fannie and Val saw him as a lecherous blow hard. Since the trappers needed his connections, no one commented on Val's remark.

The sender of the correspondence was Patience Starbuck. Inside was a book of the Quaker author John Greenleaf Whittier's poems on the abolition of slavery, Charles Dickens' novel Oliver Twist, two pounds of slave-free trade sugar, and a bar of jasmine soap. The real prizes were letters from me and our brother Dan. I had written to my sister, niece Sally who was Dan's daughter, and Val, who had been my friend before meeting Fannie. Dan had been unable to find the proper words and had excluded his former lover Val from his letters.

"I'll read my brother's letter to you, Sally," said Fannie. Val left immediately. Afterwards Fannie said to Val, "Why'd you leave when I started reading Dan's letter?"

"I don't want to hear another word from that scoundrel."

If she had remained, she would have heard the words of a man struggling to show love to a never met child whose parentage he shared from his seduction of Val back in Ohio. Dan's guilt bogged him down in celebration of his personal successes as a businessman and Underground Railroad conductor. He had also skirted the fact that Sally had two half-brothers by Dan's wife Zephyrine as well as at least two others he knew of who were mothered by former lovers.

That evening Fannie visited Val's tent. "I so appreciate the books and letters. I knew Beckwourth had to be worth something."

"If you knowed it, you sure kept it secret from me," said Val. "But don't forget, when we met him the know-it-all claimed the Crow don't like the kinda work their cousins asked them to do. I know all men, 'cept for our husbands lie, but if Beck' was telling the truth for once, these Crow men may not stay to finish."

"Speaking of the Crows, they know less English than their cousins. We both speak Crow. Let's use it when they're around."

"I was thinking the same," said Val. "It was their country first."

"It still is their country."

Fannie's husband Marshall and his twin brother, Val's husband Scipio returned a day later. They had successfully hunted an elk and a mountain sheep. Two of the women removed the tongues, skinned them and boiled them immediately with Crow seasonings. Then they joined the others in skinning and cutting the game into roasts, steaks and stew chunks. Part way through the process, it was Fannie's and Her Mother's Voice's turn to begin the process of preparing the skins, something the other women would help with later.

"Why don't you let Sally help me," said Fannie to Val.

"She can watch the babies," said Val.

"The boys are both sleeping."

"She's only five years old!"

"You don't want to know all the things I was doing when I was five," said Fannie.

"You got that right! Or me either." Just when it appeared Val had given up she said, "I keep trying to remind myself that just because we ain't slaves don't mean we should be next to useless. Sallllllly!! Get on out that tent and make yourself useful."

Thankfully the babies were not awakened by a woman who had found her true voice when freed from slavery and allowed to be true self.

"You two Easterners are so funny," said Wind Weaver, "a Crow child can ride a horse at age three. A five year old is almost an old lady."

When the women finished laughing, Val said, "I will bet you that my boys will ride by that age."

Wind Weaver said, "That is no bet. With me as their aunt, those babies may be riding next week."

* * *

Beckwourth's knowledge proved limited. Laughing and flirting good-naturedly, the two Crow men worked as steadily as did the others. They were so competent as workers that one day Marshall and Scipio left them and went hunting for fresh meat. They returned only with a deer that appeared sickly.

"That's the best you can do?" asked Val.

"I aimed and shot but missed this huge elk," said Scipio.

"No, he didn't," said Marshall.

"What's your objection, your honor?" asked Scipio.

"He missed and aimed," said Marshall.

"Talk sense," said Val.

"I saw it from the ridge above. The shot was waiting to be made but my brother waited too long. The shot was missed before he took it."

Scipio laughed. "You got me that time."

"Well, Mr. Smarty," said Val, "you come back cold in hand and got the nerve to tease my man."

Marshall said, "Wait a bit." He went into the woods where he had stashed the elk his brother had missed. "That elk ran straight my way. I'm the one that got it."

"And you got me to," said Val laughing. "Hold tight, your time will come, you little weasel."

* * *

Because the builders were using muscles not often put to work, each night the ones with wives were given one of Val's boiled embrocations from witch hazel leaves. Her husband, Scipio, was resting on his stomach shirtless near the common fire around the five tents where the couples and visitors were spending the nights. Before he knew what she was about to do, Val had tossed the water out upon the fallen leaves and poured a bottle of his prized whisky on top of the leaves in a bowl.

Almost in shock, Scipio rose up. "I know you didn't just throw out that water and waste one of my last bottles of liquor!"

"'Less you blind that's what I just did," said Val.

"My mama would've used that water."

"Do I look like your mama?"

"Next time think like her and keep that boiled water," said Scipio.

The following night she followed his directions to the letter. "Y'owww!" he screamed.

Val laughed. "You the one tried to teach me how to do right by my own husband." He wondered if he had been scalded but she said, "Lay back down, honey. I was just funning. I got some cooler water to cut more of the whiskey. I saved most from last night. It wasn't as hot as you thought it was."

While the other were laughing, Scipio said, "Before y'all laugh at my back, it was the one felt the heat. That mess wasn't as cool as she claims it was.

Val kissed his back. "Does that make it better, honey?"

The third night, Six Coups, who knew some English, said, "Do us too."

"No sense in you and Bear getting jealous," said Val. "Get y'all's cousins to do right by you."

"That's not permitted," said Isaiah.

"Then they better do each other," said Val, "or get one of you boys to do 'em. My magic fingers don't work on nobody but Sip." While everyone except the guests laughed, Her Mother's Voice translated. The warriors saw nothing amusing about being left to apply the liniment to their own bodies.

After several days, a cabin stood carved into the wilderness. The cabin had a privacy room for each family and a great room for common meals, socializing, cooking and eating. The Lucky brothers rooms were slightly larger because Fannie and Marshall had one child while Val and Scipio had two children. Six Coups and Bear in the Woods celebrated with the others and left for home carrying one pony laden with beaver pelts as a gift for the time they had lost away from home. These they were expected either to trade with trappers near their village or to have made into robes.

"There it is," said Val, "solid as the brick house we built for Master back in Kentucky. I guess Beck' done lied again. The Crows flew True."

Using one of Val's favorite sayings, Her Mother's Voice said in English, "You got that right."

* * *

The women shed light within the cabin by putting holes in tin cans that held homemade candles. During dinner they ate elk, rabbit soup, a stew they called "rolling" because small game was added as it was come upon. Water from a nearby stream as a drink with the meal and coffee to top it off .

With the exception of using certain Crow or French words for what a speaker considered greater precision, most conversations were held in English. One evening, Pomp said, "We ran into Kit Carson on the trail from the Crow villages. He says the days of the Comanche Rendezvous appear over."

"I thought only white men held Rendezvous," said Val.

"Ours were the first," said Her Mother's Voice.

"In case you're wondering," said Wind Weaver, "the right word is ammatdiío."

"White men changed the name, hid the history and acted like they invented it," said Pock.

"What else are you hiding?" said Wind Weaver. When her white husband appeared befuddled, she answered for him. "I have seen all you own so at least one white man knows how to be naked with the truth."

When the laughter died down Marshall said, "We've been to the ones Comanches hold on the Upper Arkansas."

"There was a mess of strutting Comanche, Bannock, Shoshone, Kiowa, Cheyenne, and Arapaho, along with Americans and Mexican traders," said Scipio. "It was one of the onliest times in my life I was nervous. We was badly outnumbered, and if all Hell breaks out in Comanche territory, even if they fighting by theyself, you can cancel Christmas. Given a choice, I'd sooner die in bed 'long about in the evening like York."

"Then it'd better be with me instead of some 14 year-old child," said Val.

Others laughed but Val gave Scipio such a look that he thought better of joining in. Changing the subject, Scipio said, "Did you know Pomp's mother was a big woman?"

"I didn't know there was any big women out here," said Val, who was •at her lowest weight since childhood and still outweighed the other three women by several pounds.

"Not that kinda big," said Scipio.

"He meant big, like me," said Her Mother's Voice, who in her youth had spoken for her mother, a peace chief who had been captured in a battle and had her tongue ripped out and left for dead.

"Pomp's mama's name was Sackah-jah-way-wah," said Scipio.

"Can't the man speak for hisself?" said Val.

"He ain't a filled-up man like Beckwourth," said Pomp's sister-in-law, Wind Weaver. "It takes Pomp a while to get started."

"Not like some folk I know," said Isaiah.

"Husband, am I not a woe-man and not a man?" joked Wind Weaver.

Isaiah threw her a kiss. "She may get a couple pocks every night, but there's no woe in my woman."

Ignoring the sidebar reference to the residue from Isaiah's childhood illness, Fannie said, "Pomp, please tell us about this great mother of yours."

Reluctantly, the man who wore his hair long and full in the Crow tradition his wife favored, answered, "My mother was with William Clark and Meriwether Lewis."

"Who they?" said Val.

"The President of the United sent them to map and steal Indian land out here," said Pomp. "My mother is still alive."

"But that ain't why she's a big woman," said Scipio. "Plenty of folk is still alive."

"Even you," said Her Mother's Voice, laughing.

"My mother, Sacajawea, was born a Lemhi Shoshone, a cousin of the Bannocks, but when she met Clark and Lewis, she was a Hidatsa slave."

"I still can't wrap my mind 'round the number of Indian slaves out here," said Val, "and I ain't seen a black one yet."

"If you ever find your way to Comancheria, you'll see every shade of slave on God's good earth," said Marshall.

"Black, red, or white, slavery is wrong," said Fannie.

"Come on, Pomp," said Scipio, "tell them the good part."

"I was an enfant," said Pomp. "What do I know?"

"You know the story," said his wife. "That is enough."

"Ça suffit?" Pomp said in French, looking at his wife.

"Si! Ça suffit!" said Her Mother's Voice.

Pomp returned to English, "My first source in this story was William Clark; the next was York."

"The same York that spread babies from the Mississipp' to the ocean?" said Val.

"Yes," said Pomp, "but he was the only colored man on the trip."

"What's that supposed to mean?" said Val.

"Honey," said Scipio, "It means his trail was easy to follow."

Val turned on Scipio, "You musta liked that running off scoundrel?"

Scipio said, "It wasn't like what happened to you with Fannie's brother, honey."

"No," said Pomp, recapturing the floor that initially he had reluctantly accepted. "Clark and Lewis never kept the men anywhere long enough to see a pregnancy to an end. Most of the time they did not realize a woman was with child. They were traveling fast."

"Traveling fast, hummpf," said Val under her breath. "Ain't that just like a man? And five'll get you ten, they left a heap of half-white babies that ain't nobody claimed!"

Fannie put her finger on her lips and patted her friend's hand.

"If stories didn't match," said Pomp, "not only because she was the last to whom I spoke, she was Mother, the final arbiter."

"Does that last word mean what I think it should?" said Val.

"Mothers break all ties," said Fannie.

"Yes, of course," said Pomp, although he was reared away from his own, spending most of his youth with William Clark. "Later my mother confirmed that she was stolen as a child from the Lemhi Shoshone and raised with the Hidatsa who adopted her."

"You said that once," said Val, "and I forgot to ask, ain't the Hidatsa really Crows?"

"You got a good rememory," said Marshall.

"That ain't the only good I got," said Val.

"Like the old deacon said, 'Amen,'" said Scipio.

"Pomp's background helped him sneak into my heart," said Her Mother's Voice.

"If that's the case," said Val, "how'd Pock get in y'all's family?"

The laughter died down, and Isaiah said, "Ain't I one of the people?"

"In our house we come from many backgrounds," said Fannie. "But here we are The People."

"Pock, how does it feel to be outnumbered?" Val said to Isaiah.

"If I was worried about being in the majority, I wouldn't

have come west," he said. "Anyway, what the smallpox did to my face scares all but the best of people."

Isaiah's laughter had a slightly different shading to that of the others. His was a bittersweet joy: he was one of three members of his eight-person family to survive the disease.

"Come over here, you would-be Absa. I ain't scared of those pocks!"

Isaiah obeyed, placing his head in her open arms as though she were carrying the child they one day hoped to call their own. Pomp continued, "Mother was seventeen when she had me. Father named me Jean Baptiste Charbonneau."

"I like Pomp better," said Her Mother's Voice, laughing.

"According to Clark," continued Pomp, "Mother would have liked any name other than my father's Toussaint. My name means 'first born,' for I was Mother's first."

"They didn't like each other?" asked Val.

"My father liked her and many other women," said Pomp. "She did not like him. He bought her; she did not fall in love with him."

"We will keep him away from our home," said Wind Weaver. "This is a house of love."

"Even as a young woman, Mother was beautiful," continued Pomp. "Since my father was not an imposing man, she was sometimes insulted by the 30 other men on the expedition. I suppose he looked away."

"Thirty men and one woman!" exclaimed Fannie.

"Most men are dogs," said Val. "I'd rather clean cht'lins for a year and gut buffalo for two than be that outnumbered."

"Outnumbered or not," said Marshall. "If they'd insulted my wife, that'd be the last time."

Val looked at Scipio. It took a while before he got the hint that it was his turn to speak. "Marshall's my younger twin. If he was to come to the rescue, it would be after I done hurt somebody who insulted you, honey."

"Fortunately," said Pomp, "William Clark was more honorable than my father, who later made my mother abandon me. The men on the trip whined about everything and made their flirtatious remarks, but they did not touch her."

Each person in the room felt they had experienced insufficient time with their mother. Before reaching adulthood, both Fannie and Val had watched their mothers sold away. Scipio and Marshall had run away before reaching their teenage years, and Isaiah's mother had died while he was a mere child, leaving him essentially to be reared by his father's black slave. From a period of silence, Fannie said. "What a hateful thing for your father to do. He had no right to make her give you up."

"I will not talk about that," said Pomp. "I will summarize my mother's greatness. One day several journals fell overboard into the river, and the men panicked, staring helplessly. While keeping me safe in the canoe, Mother saved the only records of the assignment. Many times they might have starved if she hadn't taught them how to tell the good plants from the poisonous. When they needed horses, their luck held only because she met her old friends and relatives. On that fateful day, she declared to the Shoshone, 'Here is my Pomp. My son, look at these women. They are your grandmothers'."

"Like Esi, my mother, yours sounds like a strong woman," said Fannie.

"No one who meets my mother would describe her as weak," said Pomp. "Yet, when I found my mother, she told me that it nearly killed her when my father forced her to abandon me."

"Men are dogs," said Val.

"Pomp is a good man," said Her Mother's Voice.

* * *

The fierce Rocky Mountain winter arrived with first light snows in early November. The season advanced with frequent storms, some dropping fifteen inches or more of snow. Dried meat of every kind the four couples considered edible was the major source of food for the brutal season. By mid-December passing from one destination to the next was more dream than common. In their five-room log cabin, days removed from the nearest neighbors, the three couples wanted nothing more than to make the best of American life.

* * *

The men usually played three-card monte while the women worked on buckskins, darned clothing, nurtured babies, and laughed about life's little inconsistencies. Before Fannie and Val had entered their lives, the Ace of Spades was always the money card. Fannie insisted that the Queen of Hearts alternate. One January night, before the fourth game, Fannie said, "I want to play."

"A woman playing a man's game!" said Isaiah, yet again.

"Don't put unnecessary limits on me," said Fannie, reaching for the cards. "Let me deal."

"I like boss ladies," said Her Mother's Voice, laying down her sewing.

They were only playing for pebbles. Fannie, Marshall, and Scipio dropped out, and the other three women joined the game. Scipio introduced the subject of growing up in Mississippi.

"Did they lash y'all in Virginia?" Scipio asked Fannie.

"Yes, and in Kentucky too as well as on the walk in between the two places, but why talk of those days?" asked Fannie.

"What's the most lashes you ever seen a man take?" asked Scipio.

"Tell her if you mean take and live or just take," said Marshall.

"Marshall, you remember when Ebenezer took 66 and went dancing a week later?"

"Eb was a mighty man. Any fool could tell he was part of God's plan."

"Change the subject please," said Fannie.

"On a night like tonight, with the wind blowing through the trees, snow falling like it forgot how to quit, and a nice fire is going, something funny would probably be more to your liking." Scipio thought a long while and then said, "When we were li'l boys, we used to sit in swings that come down from the ceiling and shoo droves of flies away from Marse and Mrs. Hampton's plates."

"What did you use to brush away the flies?" asked Fannie.

"Long pheasant feathers," answered Marshall.

"One day after we'd helped in the fields, I was so tired," said Scipio, "I dropped off to sleep and fell down on the Mrs."

Everyone laughed. "Her fat head come back up covered with grits and red-eye gravy." The laughter grew louder until Scipio said, "The Hamptons said if we didn't 'straighten up and act right' they'd sell us apart. We whooped and holluhed, begged and pleaded."

"What'd they do then?" said Fannie.

"They didn't allow for no crying; Sip took 20 with the cat-o-nine tails." said Marshall. This was not the time for laughing. "They salted his stripes. Next day they got some new niggers to do the supper time shooing."

"You mean they was so rich they could just go to the auction at the drop of a hat?" asked Val.

"You mean at the drop of a nigger," said Marshall laughing.

"Didn't I ask you to stop using that word?" said Fannie.

"Sorry, darling," said Marshall.

"No, this was during hard times," said Scipio. "They was selling instead of buying. They just swapped us out for some other li'l boys already on the plantation. The night we got replaced and was in bed, we swore to each other if they mentioned selling us apart again, we'd run. Not long afterwards, the Hamptons commence to selling off good, strong slaves. Took our big brother Henry Junior. We couldn't wait round to see if and when our time be next—"

"So in the middle of the night we kissed Mama good-bye, runned away, and hid in the cotton bales on a steamboat," interrupted Marshall.

"Mama promised she'd pray for us 'til her dying day. We was ten or eleven when we runned away, but we made it to St. Louey," continued Scipio.

"That's how we become the Luckys," said Marshall.

"We sure wasn't going take Master Hampton's name and advertise where we done gone," said Scipio. "He didn't have a passel of bloodhounds just cause he liked feeding 'em table scraps."

"We met Beck when he was working in St. Louis as a blacksmith apprentice," said Marshall. "He wrote a note and sent us to his people living out in the country. His say-so was enough for them to take us in, and we worked for them for five years. Then, just like they promised, they gave us some free papers. Could be that without them Beckwourths we woulda starved or been took back into slavery." Marshall checked to make certain his words had registered with Fannie and Val. "We owe the Beckwourths...big time."

"St. Louey beats Mississip' by a long shot, but it don't exactly favor the colored man," said Scipio.

"Gangs of kidnappers be taking black folk back into slavery every time you turn around," said Marshall.

"I carried me a gun and a big knife in my dress," said Val. "I was praying some fool would try to snatch me."

"In '24, we high-tailed outta there for the mountains," said Scipio.

Marshall laid down his Ace and smiled. As he reached for the cards, Val said. "My Queen of Hearts says you be wrong Marshall!" She slammed the card down in the same fashion she had seen the men do. "Pow! I gotcha!"

The women applauded her play. "I told you a while back, Mr. Marshall Lucky, I was going to get you good. These 90-11 pebbles is mine."

While Val collected her "winnings" Fannie said to Marshall, "Let's call it a night, Marshall. I've got an early morning, and you men can stay up until the wee hours of the morning and still seem rested."

"If you take Marshall to bed who we supposed to play with?" asked Scipio.

"Playing with you is my job," said Val catching his hand and leading him to their quarters.

That night Fannie gave Marshall all of the passionate love that she could summon. At the point of his exhaustion she clung to him as though he had been the little boy who had been beaten as a child. Marshall responded so strongly that she imagined she were the luck that had arrived only because he had chosen a name worthy of all his mother's prayers.

9

THE WELL-TANNED GHOST

My brother Dan always dreamed of being both a lover and a hero. His widely scattered children speak for his ability to woo and procreate but, in all fairness, he was often a hero. He was a longtime Underground Railroad conductor. Prior to becoming one he had helped in an 1833 rescue of runaways who had been captured in Detroit. The tale of which we both are most proud is the one he repeated most often and I tell with certain tones down. He did love his self-congratulatory adjectives.

* * *

On an April day in 1842, Paddy Throughstone, Dan's Irish blacksmith entered The Lion and the Lamb Stagecoach head-quarters. Paddy was several inches shorter than Dan, but a well-built man whose eyes never blinked and whose brown hair always seemed in need of a comb. Unlike most men of the age, he rarely wore a hat. When he did, Cincinnati was already in a downpour when he left home. The Lion and the Lamb Stables

120

was not the grandest in town. The wood frame building had room for three coaches and stalls on either side usually held 8-10 horses. Most stables that I have seen had front and rear doors. To protect his backside, Dan had ordered carpenters to seal the rear door. He kept his fancy desk that he referred to as an escritoire, centered facing the front door with a stove on one side and an array of firearms on the other.

Dan was going over paperwork and Paddy was a few minutes late. Before Dan could ask why the tardiness, Paddy handed Dan a bottle and said, "For all you've done, a bottle of John Jameson's imported finest."

"Beware of Irishmen bearing gifts," said Dan, "especially when it's crossed the seas and is the wrong whiskey. I am a Bulleit's man."

"Trust me," said Paddy, smiling. "Jameson's is no imitation. It's the original." Dan was unmoved. "Not only have you donated money to help my people fight the famine, but when I was down and out you gave me a job. Many men have come and gone to work at the Lion and the Lamb Stagecoaches since then, but only one other white one. He left after a week. May I ask, sir, would you hire another white man, or in your mind, am I just the best of a bad lot?"

"I hire the best available," said Dan. "Right now, I have not a single opening."

"All due respect, Mr. Crispin, but the Brits taught us long ago that a man of means need not dress himself, leave alone manage his own day-to-day affairs. I believe your silent partner Miss Starbuck would agree. And every once in a while, Jerry Riley may be a good stand in, but he still has a wee bit to learn. I may have just the man to allow you to frolic more."

Dan looked in Paddy's eyes. His tone was respectful and only the year before he had risked his own life when the bully boys had attacked Cincinnati's black community with a

DWIGHT L. WILSON

cannon. On another occasion he had helped rescue fugitives. And yet Dan doubted that Paddy understood the full implications of denigrating Jerry Riley, his most trusted friend and employee. Perhaps something else was driving this conversation.

"Allow me the employer's privilege of speaking bluntly. How could I trust a white man with the management of my business? Whites are on the verge of stealing the whole continent; did steal my parents and millions of others from Africa; harass me at every turn...Need I go on?"

"Your points are well taken. For my part, I am not any more white than is a Jew. I am an Irishman, despised because I was raised a Catholic and my dear sainted wife is holier than the Pope. As for the man I have in mind, he too has a Irish mother and I think he has the skills to be your assistant. It wouldn't hurt to have a word with him, Mr. Crispin. He claims he's had years bossing others."

"Why this interest, Paddy?"

"You spoke blunt. My work is calling, I'll tell you the unpolished truth. I know you have interests beyond the Lion and the Lamb and business here is doing well." Paddy could see that Dan was not finding his argument compelling. He sighed. "I owe a few men money." Dan frowned. "It's not that you don't pay me well. I know what the other blacksmiths make, but I have a bit of a problem."

"Women? The cup? I've not seen you drunk since the day we met."

"I tried to explain once a while back, but something broke the chain of my thought. I no longer have problems with women or the cup. Like you, I try to walk a straight line. I learned the error of my ways in my wild youth, but you can only tame a man so much," said Paddy. "My good wife, Bess, won't have a drunk, but before she got me to say my vows, she overlooked the problem of the horses. I do love the horses, though I know gambling on them is not useful and try to hide it —I do love the horses. Plain and simple, sir, the man has no job and owes me enough to pay off my debts." He paused and pointed, "You see that stagecoach?"

"Of course."

"Broke, he can't make a down payment on a spoke."

* * *

Out of courtesy, Dan agreed to the interview, but had no intention of bypassing Jerry, a man whose loyalty was unquestioned. The next morning Dan was sitting at his well-polished escritoire when he looked up and saw before him John Hackley, the former overseer of Fruits of the Spirit Plantation. Among multiple injustices, Hackley's most egregious offense was lashing both Dan and our late brother Robin unmercifully for saving me from his attempted rape. Adding to his offenses, Hackley had lusted for our mother, beaten our gentle sister Fannie as well as raped several of our friends and made lewd remarks to black woman he saw.

It had been many years since they had seen each other. In those days Dan was beardless, weighed forty pounds less and lacked a surname. Hackley's hair had grayed and his wrinkles deepened. But the identity of this hated man was clear.

"Are you Mr. Crispin?"

Hackley held out his hand, but, seated, Dan ignored it. "You dare come to me for work? You who have stolen time, labor, virtue, dreams: an inveterate thief of the worst kind!"

The timbre of Dan's voice jolted Hackley more than the words. Our father's voice had been the pattern for Dan's.

Dan stood, towering over him, "Hackley, considering what

you did to me and my family, I wouldn't hire you if it took two to survive, and only you and I remained on earth."

"You? You're Dan, Kenneth and Esi's son!" said Hackley. "I would rather die and go to Hell than work for you, nigger."

"Rest assured both death and Hell are waiting for you, but as for working for me, nigger, I wouldn't work you as a slave."

Hackley left in a rage. Paddy had overheard much of the conversation. He hurried over and said, "Mr. Crispin, if I'd known—"

"Don't worry, Paddy. It was an honest mistake. I know you didn't summon the ghost, but unless I miss my guess, trouble's coming."

"Not to worry, sir. I won twice last night. My debts are retired. I'm free as a bird. I only brought him because I promised."

Dan paused, weighing matters. He refocused and said, "I may have brought the wrath of the law down on my own head."

"My dear mother often said, 'May the good saints protect you, and may troubles ignore you'."

"I often think of my own mother's comforting sayings, but unless the world has suddenly changed, ignoring what that snake Hackley might do would be inviting Satan into my home."

* * *

Hackley soon returned with the U.S. Marshal and two deputies, including the despised Bennett, a man known to have three brothers who were leaders among the most deprived bully boys.

"Alright boy," said the marshal, "let's see your free paper."

Dan produced the forged paper. This paper had been demanded so many times, including at least four times by the marshal, that he had concluded for the law officers harassing was a mean-spirited game. It only stayed in relatively good condition because periodically his wife spray starched and ironed it. Undetected, Paddy and the stable boy reached respectively for a rifle and a pitchfork.

"Certainly sir," said Dan as he handed over the document that Patience Starbuck had provided.

"That paper is false," sputtered Hackley.

Knowing that without proof of a job, Hackley would be jailed or run out of town, Paddy said, "And how would a vagrant like you have such knowledge?"

The marshal turned his gaze on Hackley. "Tell me how you have this knowledge. Be convincing so that I don't look foolish before a judge."

Hackley started stuttering, and Paddy said, "Marshal, look at this man's dark skin. He's the one whose papers you should check."

"Yeh, why are you so dark?" demanded Deputy Bennett.

"Overseers have to be the first up and the last in bed," said Hackley. "That much sun would turn Snow White dark."

"A likely story," said Paddy.

"Enough," said the marshal. "Niggers don't have blond hair and blue eyes, but do you have a job?"

"We're in a recession. I haven't been able to find a job yet."

"For wasting my time, yet ends at midnight," said the marshal. "After that, I'll personally tell the sheriff you're a vagrant. If dawn comes, and you're not working or out of town, my guess is you'll go to jail."

Bennett turned to Dan as the other officers were leaving. "Our eyes are watching you, boy."

Immediately after Bennett left, Dan turned to Paddy. "Why is that shotgun near the anvil?"

"Well, Danny boy—" Dan raised his eyebrow. "I mean, Mr.

Crispin, sir, the marshal's men would have had quite a time hustling you to jail or down south. The stable boy had his pitch fork, and I had already sent him for neighbors to reinforce our troops. Take a look at the street."

Dan walked just outside the door. Across the street, Dan's friend Eat-'em-Up waved a Bowie knife, and two stores removed three African-Americans and two white men were milling around to see if the law was going to double back. Each of them smiled and waved.

Dan reciprocated and said surprised, "Perhaps there is a God."

"Oh yes, sir," said Paddy, "you're loved more than you think, and many a friend in this town is indisposed toward slavery."

1 0

GRANDFATHER

My husband Charles came inside from working the farm. "My widowed grandfather has arrived early to visit Mother. We must be on our best behavior at tonight's dinner with him."

"Yes, thee must. It was thee who aggravated him the last time." Charles looked sheepish. "Thy mother told me that she was expecting him two days hence and has only started cooking for the planned family gathering with thy siblings. Will any of the others be there?"

"Only our family will be present tonight. As thee said, he was not yet expected. It is Grandfather's way to upset what has been laid. Mother reports that he has been eating less with the passage of time. Ready or not we must bring what we have."

"I fully understand that when it comes to hosting too much does not exist and too little is an abomination."

My husband was unusually nervous because he saw his grandfather as a rebellious hero. Both of my own grandfathers had been stolen from me before I had the chance to meet them. In Fante-land one had been murdered by kidnappers, the other captured and taken only the Holy One knows where. Cuba? Brazil? Puerto Rico? Mexico? Even in their absence I knew how to show deference to elders. Instead of reminding Charles he need not worry about me embarrassing him or that I must assist his nearly 60 year old mother, I set about putting away cloth and needles from my seamstress business, directing my 12 year old daughter as to which outfit she should dress two year old Eva. I personally cared for the infant twins, William and Henry. I also told Charles to hurry over what I had prepared for our weekday meal, a simple chicken hash and pickled cabbage.

* * *

When we entered Mary Crispin's and Charles Ferguson's darkening great room, her balding and wrinkled father, Jacob, was seated comfortably. He motioned for Charles to present his family. Silently the old man looked us over, finally declaring with a mischievous smile, "Thee seems to have been busy, grandson."

He had been father to ten himself. Even without his smile we knew he was teasing. He looked at me. "Well, Sarah, doth thee see me as too ancient to hold one of those fine twins?"

"Take this one, Grandfather." I handed him William, the only one who was awake.

He kissed William's tiny forehead then looked at my father-in-law. "Did thee hear that, Clark? She calls me Grandfather and thee, who hath been married to my daughter for nearly 40 years, yet wanders in a wilderness in such a fashion that ye have yet to call me by any name. I hope I live long enough for thee to make it to the Promised Land."

His eyes were laughing but not sufficiently to induce my

father-in-law to call any man other than his own deceased father by the honorific.

Charles still held the sleeping twin.

I said, "Please place Henry in the cradle in the next room." To Susan I said, "Thee may watch Eva as I help thy grandmother with the meal."

"Not quite yet, Granddaughter," said Jacob. "If all are assembled and Clark here can find a Bible I want to read aloud. By my count I am in my 28th cover to cover reading. The way my knees feel I doubt I'll see the 50th on this side."

Grandfather returned William to me. Clark handed him the big family Bible and sat down for what had long been a ritual beginning to an evening. The great room had no inner walls and each of the three facing the grounds had an uncovered window that occasionally showed a dear or even a fox. Mary Crispin had heard her father's words and came away from the stove. She knew what he referred to as a "public meeting" would only be the reading of a few instructive verses.

"Here is where I am today." He began with verse one of the 103rd Psalm, "Bless The Lord, oh my soul: and that is within me..." and ended with verse sixth "The Lord executeth righteousness and judgement for all that are oppressed."

Whether happenstance or craft, I knew both that I had been a slave and was far from free in the north. I also knew that once he had considered himself without liberty. Silently I approved of his selection.

* * *

Grandfather sat at one head of the table, opposite his son-in-law and led us in a silent grace by taking his daughter's hand on one side and mine on the other. We enjoyed a simple meal of chickens stewed with new corn, cornbread and beans that

Mary Crispin always referred to as "Quaker Beans," our Shawnee friend, Caesar, called "Rancocas Beans" after the Lenape who he said had introduced it to his mother and my own mother always called "Dunn-Colored Beans. Names fascinate me. I wish it were possible to ask Jehovah what is the proper name.

DURING THE MEAL MY DAUGHTER SUSAN SAID TO HER GREAT GRANDFATHER, "MY TEACHER SAID SOMETHING THAT I DOUBT IS CORRECT."

"Should thee not always trust thy teachers' knowledge?" asked Mary Crispin.

"Does thee always trust mine, daughter?" asked her father with a wink. "Ask and I will enlighten thee, child," said Grandfather.

"I thought that Philadelphia was the first Quaker settlement in America but Teacher said otherwise."

"The first of us in the new world came to New England." He paused and sipped a glass of buttermilk. "Even Burlington in New Jersey is older than Philadelphia. It is in Burlington, near the beautiful creek known as the Rancocas, that my family lived before I removed them to Ohio. In my mind that makes Burlington first in the heart of true Friends."

"My teacher is not a Quaker," said Susan. "They won't let me study there."

"What!" said Grandfather. "That oppression remains among us? What say thee to this abomination, grandson?"

Charles answered, "We have labored with the school committee for years. Thee knows it would take a sense of the meeting to reverse and the best we have done over the years is sixty affirmations. Always at least five have opposed letting in all children."

"The trend?" asked Grandfather.

"It has been steady," said Clark before my husband could admit that for fear he might physically attack one of those who blocked Susan and other colored children's entry into the meeting's school, I had begged him not to attend meetings where an integrated school was on the agenda.

Whatever the proper name of the beans, they were seasoned perfectly. The adults politely concentrated on finishing those on their personal plate in hopes of seeking a second helping before they vanished.

The conversation was moving more pleasantly than it had the other three times I had been present for one of Grandfather's visits. Peace was broken again when someone mentioned the word freedom. Although it was in an everyday context, Grandfather changed the course of the conversation and said, "I always distrusted our Stockton cousins. The Religious Society of Friends started out as the dregs of society but when the persecutions ended and our assumed honest ways brought increased money, our lot changed. Our people came to do good and the Stocktons did so well that they left Quakerism to become Episcopalians up in Mercer County. Give me time and I will condemn a slew of such apostates."

"Are Quakers the only righteous ones, Grandfather?" asked Susan.

"Two things. First, I am thy Great Grandfather," he smiled and she returned it. "Second, look around thee in Warren County, Ohio and America. Then answer thy question for thyself."

Ignoring Mary Crispin's signal not to feed her father's natural discontent, Charles asked , "Then, Grandfather, why did thee meet with thy cousin Richard who signed the Declaration of Independence?"

"My mother sent me. Honor thy father and thy mother says

the Bible. I hope such teaching still has currency among thy generation of near bone-idles." Charles could have told his grandfather that he had been in the fields before sunrise and had remaining chores to complete after this social hour. When he said nothing, his grandfather said, "I suppose respect for elders has been cast as far away as wigs on the frontier."

Charles laughed. "I respect both my parents and also each grandparent, including those who have gone on before me and those who tease."

"Respect the last of those beans this way, Grandson."

"I thought thee had little appetite," asked Mary Crispin.

"And when was it declared that the generation between Charles and me has the right to dictate what I eat? Which commandment in the Good Book or article in the Constitution?"

Grandfather led the laughter. Mary Crispin stood and kissed her father's forehead. "That is for being the same feisty man thee was when we crossed the Appalachians."

"Thee was but five years old when we came to the frontier."

"Thee grows addled," said Mary Crispin. "I was almost 15 and I can tell stories on thee that happened when I was but three."

"Peace, be still," said Grandfather. "The one we all love said, 'Peace be still'."

Grandfather finished his beans and Mary Crispin said, "By arriving early we have no pie or cake but I did save another bowl of beans."

"Puck is thee?" asked Grandfather. "I do believe the frontier made thee puckish. Thee was such a model child back in 'the old country'."

I have long been intrigued by this word "frontier." From the way both Quakers and other whites use it, I have determined that the frontier is the place most recently stolen from the tribes and where white hegemony is expected to reign imminently in its fullness. My husband had already requested I not put him in hot water with his mother and Susan had already demonstrated that she was in one of her minds to seek knowledge that might bring Grandfather to a place we would prefer to remain hidden. I said nothing about my frontier theory.

Grandfather needed no prompting from Susan or anyone besides his own still lithe mind. "My daughter has said that thee is most like me, Charles." We braced ourselves. "When I met with my cousin Richard Stockton he said pompously, 'I wrote a letter to the King trying to convince him Almighty God believes that it would be best to let the colonies self-govern as a commonwealth. Young cousin, he refused. Now I have signed the Declaration of Independence'."

"Did he mistake himself for the Light?" asked Charles.

All but the narrator and Mary Crispin laughed. We could see by Grandfather's demeanor that even almost 70 years after the conversation, and the fact that his kinsman had suffered mightily for his patriotism, he still nursed a grudge.

"I never bothered to ask," said Grandfather.

My self-discipline failed. "If thee harbored such distrust of thy recruiter, why did thee fight?"

"I was forced to choose my path," said Grandfather. "Not by men. Since my father's death, no man has ever forced Jacob Crispin to do anything. Not by circumstances. What are circumstances but an unswept barn floor? Choose right or left, front or back or middle, if thee pleases, but do clean them up!

"I was forced by the Holy One asking in my spirit, 'Whom shall ye serve?' Between the Religious Society's elders and justice, I chose justice. I supposed if the colonies won, all men would be free."

He paused before saying, "The same was true with some

slaves in north Jersey and others in Bucks County, just outside of Philadelphia. While the colonists were rebelling against the British, those slaves were trying to rebel against slavery. The Colonists sinned. They made the mistake of calling their own rebellion, the 'War for Independence' and the ones involving the slaves an insurrection."

"Whose independence did the colonists desire?" asked Susan innocently.

Grandfather looked around the table. When his eyes struck my father-in-law's, Clark said, "Don't look at me! That is the Crispin blood talking through a child."

Knowing that before he had won me, I had called myself Sarah Freedom, my husband said, "It could be Freedom blood."

I do not know if Grandfather caught the allusion. Emboldened by not being immediately corrected for entering into adult conversation, Susan said, "Great Grandfather thee mentioned New Jersey and Pennsylvania slaves. To hear people tell the story, slavery is only a southern thing."

"Phshaw!!" said Grandfather. "In those days there were slaves in both Pennsylvania and New Jersey. The last Pennsylvania slave died in 1831, around the time my dear wife Ann Chubb passed on and there are still slaves in New Jersey."

"Must thee speak of such painful things?" asked Mary Crispin.

"I will not be the GREAT Grandfather who kept his progeny in darkness. Living in darkness would make me a PUNY Grandfather."

"Why did the north hold onto slavery so long?" asked Susan still reeling over this news that her teacher had kept hidden. "And why did the elders try to keep thee from fighting for black freedom."

"They said we were breaking the law, so we were breaking the integrity testimony."

Giving up the struggle to control her father or stem her granddaughter's questions, Mary Crispin said, "Our Quaker testimony for justice is just after the love testimony."

"In fact," said Clark, "like our grandsons William and Henry, those two are twins."

"Hast thee told the child, son-in-law," said Grandfather to Clark, "How thee and my son John were nearly read out of Lee's Creek for supporting Elias Hicks at the split back in 1828."

"Only transferring membership," said Mary Crispin, "saved that abomination."

"I repeat," said Jacob, "hast thee told them the story?"

"Thee just did," said Clark with a smile. "Lee's Creek discontent was more with Hick's belief that all people have an equal right to freedom and less about how we put flesh to doctrine."

"This was one time thee did not overvalue words," said Grandfather with a twinkle. My father-in-law returned to silence. "Like most Quakers they were for freedom but not for equality."

I could not help myself. "There can be no freedom without equality," I said almost itching for someone to oppose me. "That is like asking for rain but no moisture."

Grandfather dropped his head. All entered a prayerful silence. Charles heard one of the twins cry out and quickly rose, fearing the other might be awakened in tandem. He had returned with William wanting to be fed. I covered my breast, began the feeding and broke the silence. "Grandfather, how did thee come to be so enlightened as to oppose the behavior of the majority?"

Before he could answer, Mary Crispin rose with Susan shadowing her. The two began clearing the table.

"I grew up with a neighbor named John Woolman who

convinced all Quakers to leave behind slavery but, as a youth, I was not fully enlightened," said Grandfather. "And like most 'Free' or 'Fighting' Quakers who fought in the War for Independence, I was less prophet and more fool."

"Father!" said Mary Crispin. "There are young ones present."

"If the word 'fool' is forbidden an old man looking back on mistakes, what value has it? We all know I am the wisest of all Great Grandfathers now!" He led the laughter. Then choked it off by saying, "If only the price for purchasing my wisdom had not been so high."

* * *

I excused myself leaving them still at the dining room table although the meal had ended. I laid down my now sleeping William. Kissed his brother on his forehead and went next door to my own home. No one who has not been enslaved can fully appreciate those last four words: to my own home.

After a few minutes I returned with dessert. "Grandfather," I said, "it is clear that you are a man who has a healthy appetite. I was saving this for the feast with your other grandchildren and their families, but I made three why not allow thee to sample one tonight?"

He clapped his hands. "Thee recalled my sweet tooth for cherry pie! I used to tell my wife, 'Ann, Sarah's pie is almost as good as Mary's and hers is almost as good as thine."

"That's high praise!" said Mary Crispin, kissing his head before carving the first slice for her father.

"It is even higher than thee might think," I added. "My mother-in-law is my teacher."

"Mother taught me," said Mary Crispin.

"And Anne's mother-in-law taught her," said Grandfather.

"That is how the circle remains unbroken. Four women taking care of one sweet-toothed man: Jacob Crispin!"

We laughed together. He tasted it, licked his lips like a child. "Crispin blood is powerful stuff."

"Mother was a Chubb before she was a Crispin."

"Mother was an Owen," said Grandfather. "The only constant Crispin is he who is enjoying this pie."

PEACE IN THE VALLEY

O nce more I leaned on my brother Dan for the kernel of a tale. However, removed from his eyes, I proudly played a role. For my part, I need of nothing beyond my own eyewitness account.

* * *

Dan loved to frequent Gates Saloon, a small place whose outside he commissioned to be painted white every other year despite the fact that on either side the buildings appeared to have never seen a stroke of paint. The saloon had room for four or five tables, each of which normally seated no more than four people and a bar that allowed perhaps five men to crowd up to stand closer to the spirits. Haynes Gates was a gentleman, only in the business in hopes that a lost relative or friend might walk through the door. He had a hard three drink per night limit. His regulars were not deterred. Most nights they came by for a single drink and camaraderie. When they had money for more, there were others similar places willing to serve colored folk as long as they had money.

Dan's friends Eat-'em-Up, Sweetnin' Water and Toad were already nursing a midweek drink when he arrived. Eat-'em-Up was the elder. I suppose at the time he was near fifty, dressed simply in the clothes he wore keeping clean a local general store and slightly bent from the years spent on a tobacco plantation. Sweetnin' Water and Toad were both near 40. The most distinctive characteristic to the former was his bowed legs. As for Toad, he walked as erect as a soldier and had a prominent scar above his right eye where he had been struck by a planter when he was a slave. In fact, only Toad was born free. He had come to America after being kidnapped as a teenager, long after the importation of slaves had been outlawed. Sweetnin' Water and Toad worked in separate slaughterhouses but the scents they carried on their bodies were the same.

* * *

"My friend," said Dan to Eat'-em-Up, "life is too short to be bent out of shape by every Tom, Dick and Mary."

Gates laughed. "I can get gold dust from a peanut and a thoroughbred from a mutt, but I can't talk a lick of sense into Eat-em-Up's head."

"That damn Deputy Bennett acted like he don't know who I am," said Eat-'em-Up. "I can't believe he made me step out in the street in front of a drove of hogs."

"Did you look down at your shoes?" asked Sweetnin' Water. Eat-'em-Up was puzzled. "That should've told you it happened." When the laughter that masked pain at a friend's humiliation died down, Sweetnin' Water added, "Don't go blaming Bennett for not recognizing you. I'd bet a penny your mama don't even know who you is and she was there when you was born.

"Don't talk about my mama!"

"I will talk about your mama long as she keep her big house slippers under my bed."

Eat-'em-Up reached for his knife and Sweetnin' Water said, "Ain't nothing shaking but the leaves on the trees."

Eat-'em-Up lunged and Sweetnin' lightly jumped out of the way. "If you was serious you wouldn't fight like a preacher's baby boy."

Sweetnin' Water put the knife back in his overalls and took a boxer's stance. "Okay, Mr. Big Eyes, you feeling froggy? Leap!"

Gates came from behind the bar. "None of that." Turning to Sweetnin' Water, he said, "Let his mama alone."

Sweetnin' Water said, "Where was you when he called mine everything but a child of God last week?" To Eat-'em-Up he said defiantly, "Yo' mama so greasy, she think Master is easy."

Eat-'em-Up withdrew his knife so fast, my brother said he didn't see the movement. With fury Eat-'em-Up lunged and ripped Sweetnin's coat.

"Boy, you sure enough done lost yo' mind?" said Sweetnin' drawing his own knife.

Gates reached behind the bar and retrieved his loaded shotgun. "I ain't too black to shoot both ya'll in the crack." To Sweetnin' Water he said, "I told you to let the man alone. Fourth of July is the day his master sold his mama down the river."

"That's just one reason we hate this day," said Dan. "The white man doesn't celebrate anything about a black man's life on this or any other day. Instead of fighting among ourselves, why don't you gentlemen shake hands and make up."

"Gentlemen?" said Toad, "ain't but two gentlemen in here and I'm both of 'em."

The men laughed. When they settled down Eat-'em-Up added, "Bennett'll get his."

Gates said, "Vengeance is the Lord's."

"Then today I am The Lord."

Lillith, a lovely street walker entered the saloon and said from the doorway, "Two lies told back to back. That's a position that ain't never satisfied."

Eat-'em-Up knew her voice. He simply ignored her and said to his drinking friends, "I want some satisfaction in this here life, not by and by."

Lillith said, "Before the '41 riot, I heard a Irishman say, 'I'm going to burn this Mary Finney down'."

"There's a idea," said Eat-'em-Up. "Where Bennett live? I'll wait 'til he goes to sleep and toast him like ash cake."

"Just 'cause he made you step into the street? You just talking like a fool," said Toad.

"If getting' back at Bennett is what this commotion is all about, I know where he lives," said Lillith.

"Why are you so interested in getting this man in trouble?" asked Dan. "He burns a deputy's house, gets caught, lynched, and you tell the story all of your life."

"I ain't all talk like these fools. I'll go with him," said Lillith. "Bennett done shorted me twice and took my bankroll once."

Sweetnin' Water was also game. "Let's go men!"

"No!" said Dan with such force that the room grew quiet. "I have two families of fugitives in hiding. I can take one up through an Eaton safehouse but I need at least a couple of you to take the others on up to my sister's in Waynesville. That's why I'm here tonight, not simply here to listen to crazy talk."

"Why ain't you going to Waynesville?" asked Toad. "That's where your kinfolk live."

"Have either of you ever been to Eaton?" When no one replied Dan said, "Eat-'em-Up knows the way to Waynesville because a few years ago I sent him to pick up a suit my sister made for me."

"I'll go with him," said Sweetnin' Water.

"Can I trust you two not to kill each other let alone to keep the fugitives safe?" asked Dan.

Both men swore the fun and games were over. Now they were all business.

"I'll go with 'em," said Toad. "I'll work like a justice of the peace."

"Boy, the last time you worked," said Eat-'em-Up, "the President was shining shoes on Broadway."

When the Underground Railroad strategy was laid out, Lillith said, "Dan, I was hoping for you to plan how best to use my new feather bed."

"Feather beds make me sneeze."

"Tell me how you like your bedding done and I'll get me a newer one."

Dan smiled. "I would say 'some other time,' but that lie would undress me."

* * *

I had been forewarned by the northbound stagecoach driver of my brother's Lion and the Lamb Stagecoach Line that as soon as possible Dan would be sending a family of fugitives to stop at our home for a quick meal. The message also said that Dan suggested my husband or father-in-law should move them up the line to a safehouse either in Xenia or Dayton.

When I shared this with Charles he said, "I respect thy brother's opinion but when they arrive, I'll move them to a new conductor, the plasterer, Napoleon Johnson in Springboro."

I said, "I don't know that name."

"Neither does my brother-in-law. Napoleon has recently come to Springboro after being freed. He feels a need to join in our work. Why not now, before he is well known, thus is no suspect?"

"All black men are suspects." He seemed hurt by an observation that he knew to be true. I thought a moment about his unspoken observation. "Doth thee think we are being spied on?"

"More than black men are being spied upon."

No white man married to a black woman could escape close scrutiny. I prayed more for my husband's well-being than my own. He had surrendered safety. I had never known it.

* * *

At the door I greeted Dan's three friends and their charges. They entered my immaculate house and the fugitives immediately apologized because their homespun was tattered because Dan had counseled not to make themselves conspicuous and filthy from the road. Dan's wife's Gold Circle Club had also supplied the freedom seekers with brand new clothing to be carried in a knapsack until they reached safety. The Waynesville area was so well known for its series of Underground Railroad stations that we had become a passthrough.

I asked the runaways not to worry about appearances, escorted them to a room that we set aside for just such an occasion, poured them bathing water and gave each a new set of clothes that I, a professional seamstress, kept for just such an occasion. They explained they already had one new set each. I said, "Now you have two."

When I returned Eat-'em-Up said to me, "I'm so hungry I

almost bit my own arm. You got pork chops and some of that sparrow grass Dan is always talkin'about?"

"I suppose you mean asparagus?"

"If it's green it's mean," said Sweetnin' Water.

"Pardon me?"

"Sweetnin' Water may be getting it confused with pepper grass," said Eat-'em-Up.

I said, "We are not reduced to eating weeds in my home."

"He didn't mean no offense," said Toad, "he ain't learned to like nothing but meat. "

"Any guest in my house will eat as fed. Tonight that does not happen to include pork chops. However, I do have both 'sparrow grass' and soup with cornbread." Toad fidgeted until I added, "There is much meat in the soup, both chicken and beef. That does meet with thy approval, sir?"

"Yes'm," said Sweetnin' Water. "I kept trying to tell my mind not to be dreaming of no chops or possum and sweet potatoes."

I wanted to laugh but why encourage them. I simply said, "If you men would find it pleasing, I can roast a few sweet potatoes. We have fresh churned butter to enhance them." I looked at Sweetnin' Water alone. "I am assuming thee realizes that neither sweet potatoes nor butter are green."

"If you would, Mrs. Sarah. I can make believe they possum dressing."

Before I could ask him to explain the leap in logic, Eat-'em-Up said, "Just eat that soup and shut up. And don't be trying to fish out all the chunks of meat like that other time."

"What other time?"

"Gentlemen, I prefer peace in my home and my surname is Ferguson but you may call me Sarah."

"Yes, ma'am," said Eat-'em-Up. "I been thinking, you got a glass of something wet?"

I knew these rascals, but they had somehow put me in a playful mood. "Sweet or buttermilk. Or if you prefer, pure country water not the slaughterhouse kind you drink in Cincinnati. What is your pleasure?"

Toad spoke quickly, "He meant—"

I cut him off, "We do not share your habits."

"He ain't got no habits," said Toad. "It's a everyday type thing and me and Sweetnin' got it too."

"Water, sweet or buttermilk?"

I took their requests and left to prepare the table, and checked on my three young children who should have been asleep but I had heard them in their shared room whispering and giggling.

After tucking them in I overheard Eat-'em-Up say, "I run into Jesus and he told me—"

"You a lie and the truth ain't in you," said Sweetnin' Water.

"If I'm lying I'm flying," said Eat-'em-Up.

"You wouldn't know a wing if you was on a blue jay," said Sweetnin' Water.

"Let the man alone," said Toad. "I wanna hear how he ties this mess up."

"All right," said Sweetnin' Water. "What was Jesus doing?"

"Eating a pork chop and sopping up the grease with a biscuit," said Eat-'em-Up.

The other two men started laughing. "Jews don't eat no pork," said Sweetnin' Water.

"Jesus ain't no Jew," said Eat-'em-Up. "John the Baptist baptized him, Reverend Nickens said that make him a Baptist."

"That remind me of when we stayed at the boarding house in Dayton and the woman set down five pork chops for eight men," said Toad.

"I enjoyed the two I had," said Sweetnin' Water.

"That was low down," said Eat-'em-Up. "We still had our

eyes closed praying when you gobbled down them chops like a starved hound on a ham bone."

They were laughing and I was back at the stove when my husband came through the door. Each stood and Toad said, "Good evening, Mr. Charles."

"Charles will do," said my husband.

"I told you he ain't like them other white men," said Eat-'em-Up.

Charles pretended he had not heard them. He walked quickly over to me and gave me a brief kiss. "I presume my charges are in the next room."

The fugitive parents and small child came to the table smiling with joy. The father held up his knapsack, "Inside this sack is the best good duds we ever done had."

"I sew too, Otis!" said his wife Bette.

"Excuse me, baby," said Otis, "but I said 'good' and Master ain't never allowed you to have no cloth this quality."

Beth still was not happy with his explanation.

"I understand," I said. "I was reared a slave and our master was equally evil."

"You was a slave?" said Toad.

"As was Dan and all others in our family. We help not because of what we've read or heard but because of who we are. Until the last of us is free we remain in bondage."

"That includes me," said my husband.

Various shades of doubt were on the adult faces but no one challenged him.

Bette said to my Cincinnati guests, "By helping us steal away our lives y'all proving yourselves Christians."

"I know that verse," said Eat-'em-Up.

"If you do," said Sweentin' Water, "the window must've been open when you walked by the church on a Sunday."

"Least I know what a church look like," said Eat-'em-Up.

He turned to the female fugitive and said, "My mama used to call slavery 'death before death'. Me and these men is blessed to get to help y'all."

"Thank you, sirs," said the husband and wife together.

"Don't disremember us when you go on your way," said Sweetnin' Water. "We the ones resurrected y'all."

* * *

The fugitives were eight hours down the road with Charles, my three guests had rested, and we were all at breakfast. Without knocking, Deputy Bennett kicked open the door of our house with a posse, all with rifles cocked.

Eat-'em-Up immediately put up his hands while saying, "Don't even blink." Sweetnin' Water and Toad already knew the proper response but I refused to do so.

Bennett saw me first and then my guests. To them he said, "I have reason to believe you Nigras were moving slaves. Where are they hiding?"

"There are no slaves in this house," I said. "And what is the meaning of you entering my house uninvited?"

"Are you deaf, wench? We're looking for contraband."

"You mean the folk that stole this country from the Shawnee?" said Eat-'em-Up.

"When I want a piece of dog leavings like you to talk, I'll ask him a question," said Bennett.

Meanwhile, akin to the way patrollers periodically searched slave quarters, the other three members of the posse were searching the premises of my home. Spitefully, one of the men said to Bennett, "There ain't nothing here."

Another said, "I knew when you set up that ambush it was on the wrong road."

"If you knew," said Bennett, "why didn't you say so?"

"When the marshal puts you in charge nobody can tell you anything."

"Just shut up Georgy."

"Excuse me, gentlemen, but we must finish our meal and begin our day," I said.

The posse stormed out with Bennett trying to kick my foot stool in his anger. When he missed and went flying, my guests wanted to laugh but feared reprisals. With no such restrictions, my children did laugh so hard that after a few moments I was forced to silence them.

"Could I help you up, deputy?" said Eat-'em-Up who had secretly maneuvered the foot stool into Bennett's path.

"Don't put your black hands on me," said Bennett standing on his own and doing his best not to limp out the door.

When the posse had disappeared, I said, "What great good fortune that his ambush failed."

"That weren't no good fortune," said Sweetnin' Water. "That was Eat-'em-Up taking us up through Mason Village instead of the main way through Lebanon."

"But if I hadn't told you to listen to him there'd be no peace in the valley," said Toad.

"Just stick with me," said Eat-'em-Up, "and when you gents get older I'll teach you how to do it."

"Do what?" asked.

"I didn't burn the Mary Finney down but I brought that low life down a peg,"

"Little by little, my man, little by little."

The three laughed raucously. I dared not ask about what.

BETWEEN US

W hen she returned to Ohio in September of 1850 for our brother's memorial service, my sister Fannie told me countless stories of her adventures in the west. I encouraged her to write them herself. She said, "My journal is enough for me. Most whites will overlook what is most significant and many whites may think me pretentious."

Her words were spoken like a true middle daughter, something I am not. I am retelling my sister's tale as though I had been where it occurred.

When Fannie's husband Marshall, brother-in-law Scipio and her best friend Val were murdered, my sister and her daughter, niece and nephew were rescued by Swift Eagle, a Bannock Indian who made her his wife and changed her name to what translates to 'River Woman.' Years later, in the autumn of 1847, Chooses Calico, her mother-in-law, asked to be taken to Comancheria for the winter. Chooses Calico's sister, Rainbow's

Breath was married to Downwind Wolf, a Comanchero trader. He and his partner's business ranged from two hundred miles above the Snake River to just below the Rio Grande over to Austin. The merchants agreed to take the Bannocks, offering safe passage in exchange for assistance with their business. By the time of the trip, all three of the children in Fannie's care were treated as though each were the child of her own body. As such, her husband also accepted them.

In route, from a bluff, Fannie watched a storm cross the plains near the border of their destination. The darkening sky and advancing lightning brought memories of our mother. Esi had assessed how planters treated slaves upon whom they held papers and predicted to her children that one day we would be separated. She had also promised that her presence would be in every 99th raindrop of each storm. Fannie believed she knew of Mama's essence then did all of us except our murdered brother Robin. The two of them had listened closely to Esi's stories and could recite the family lineage back more generations than either had ever stopped to count.

Fannie said aloud in Fante, "Mama, is there a message in the thunder or is it just Anansi playing with our minds?"

Running Buffalo, her father-in-law, overheard her but was not fluent in English. He had spent his life attuned to intuition which led him to say, "I wish my brother Tall Water was here." Fannie turned and saw his empathetic smile. "He knows when it is time to fear what comes next. You'd think that an old warrior like me would be able to read the danger signs better. I'm just old, not a seer."

Running Buffalo and Fannie gazed at each other for a moment as though somehow he might look into her soul and share any part that might be hidden from her. He spied movement over her shoulder and said, "Look, my daughter. There I see a faraway funnel!"

She turned. "By its direction it is no threat to us."

"Good eyes and good heart."

"Escaping the tornado does not free us from all other threats, Father. Are there others coming our way?"

"Whether in Bannock-Land, Comanche-Land or No-Soul's-Land, danger is a possibility."

◊◊◊◊◊◊

Before the storm caught up with them, the traders encamped high on a westward facing shelf overlooking a huge plain. A stone wall backed the lodges, a stand of trees offered wood for making fires for cooking and a nearby meadow supplied grazing for the animals. It appeared ideal. In last darkness, caws from the crows beat sunrise. The women rose to prepare breakfast. A hard rain hád passed and a fine mist was lifting. The air was fresh and clean.

With dawn's growing light, Sally, my sister's adopted daughter after her mother's and stepfather's death, said in English to Fannie, "Aunt Fante, look!"

Even Chooses Calico, who spoke no English, turned to where the startled child was pointing. A half-mile away, on the plain, was a poor white family still sheltering despite the lack of even the smallest cloud. The men came running. Chooses Calico asked her husband, "Running Buffalo, why might those strangers be on the muddy plain?"

"I will see," said Running Buffalo.

The men mounted their horses and followed a declivity onto the plain. Upon reaching the whites, Tongin', a man whose tongue had been removed during a torture, signed for Hosea, a black worker for the Comancheros, to be spokesman. The whites were powerless intruders. As such, even the Indians who knew English refused to speak a foreign tongue.

Hosea leaped down lithely. All but the designated interpreter remained on horseback. "What are ya'll doing here?"

"Ain't you going address me as, 'sir'," said the white man. Hosea received the words as unworthy of a response. The white man sized up the situation. "We's trying to get the Hell out, but don't know how."

"Then back track."

"Back to where? We had to sell our place to ransom my no-good wife and we is moving on west."

"Before we could leave some Injins took Mama again," piped in a fifteen year-old daughter.

The father added, "And all the metals from guns to tools, eight horses, both our slaves, all three cows, the grub, the blankets—"

"They treated you mighty kindly," said Hosea.

"Nigra, do you understand the word 'kindly'?" said the father.

"They left your scalps and life. More than that, ain't you got enough sense to know metal draws lightning? You could have been fried to a crisp out on this plain."

"I was thinking about how do I shoot a deer or a buffalo with my finger."

"Then you wasn't thinking good enough."

Perhaps the father concluded that he was in the wilderness and these armed men were not his friends. In a softer voice he said to the thirty-five year old man, "How we get outta here, boy?"

Hosea looked at Tongin' and Down Wind Wolf. The former gave him quick hand signals and he turned back to address the white man.

"Y'all ain't supposed to be out here. So just keep heading the way you going. If you don't dawdle and the Apaches ain't around, probably before nightfall day after tomorrow you'll strike the river. Follow it downstream and in a coupla days there's a li'l settlement. Least ways there was one when last we was over thata way."

"But we ain't got enough sustenance to travel that far."

"You got this wagon, your ox, and your lives. 'Cept for the last that's more'n my folks ever had."

"Are you serious, boy?"

With the patience of a gentle school teacher, Hosea said, "This ain't the season for joshing. If you can't find no water after that from last night's rain dries up, drink your own piss." The boy's eyes stretched in shock. "You still thirsty... drink the ox's piss. If you still is thirsty, kill the ox, suck her belly and intestines, use your hands to strip the colon. It's good eating locked up inside." The boy almost wretched. "Then tie up the colon to make a canteen in case you come across a pool of water. Eat the heart, kidneys, and livers raw. Cook up the ribs and haunches. Eat that on the trail until it spoils. That's enough food to keep a good man and his chillen going for weeks."

The white family was incredulous. "If you taibo ain't figured out this ain't New Orleans, heaven help you," said Hosea.

"How a farmer going to farm without livestock?" said the father.

"You didn't ask me about farming. You asked about staying alive."

"But--"

"You sure enough helpless," said Hosea. Then in his most compassionate voice, he said, "Try this: hold back on killing the ox long as you can. Meantime eat prickly pear, roots, careless weeds, and remember that anything that flies or creeps also dies and eats. Amongst the fliers and creepers is grasshoppers, frogs, lizards, 'squits and other bugs..."

Exasperated, Tongin' clapped his hands to get Hosea's

attention. He signaled, "Let's go. We are just wasting time on incompetents."

Hosea turned quickly and jumped on his horse. He fell to his place at the back of the line. Swift Eagle hung back and said to Hosea in English, "Those people are pitiful."

"Yes, sir, they are."

"It's a wonder they've lasted this long."

"Most don't," said Hosea. "Not out here in Comancheria. If they see two more sunrises it'll come as a surprise. And that village I'm sending 'em to ain't more than day and half's ride from where some Apaches live. Them fellows don't cotton to no visitors but Comancheros and then they gets tired of us some quick too."

◊◊◊◊◊◊

The men reported an edited version to the curious women. Fannie motioned with her eyes and she and Swift Eagle stepped away from the others. She said, "We must help those people."

"Why? They do not belong here."

"Please, let me give them some things. A gun, a kettle, a knife, bullets."

Down Wind Wolf was standing nearby pretending disinterest. His ears perked at the word "give." He entered the conversation to say, "This is my business. Do you know how much we can get in trade for that much product?"

Fannie quietly kept her eyes on Swift Eagle who said, "You may speak your mind, River Woman."

She spoke while looking at her husband only. "To turn our backs would be tantamount to killing them ourselves."

"But—" said Down Wind Wolf.

Swift Eagle interrupted, "Take what you want, River

Woman. Come with me and we ride back and do as you desire."

"You are listening to a woman who is giving away my goods?" said Down Wind Wolf.

"I am taking counsel from a friend. I am also giving counsel to a friend: when I am speaking to my wife, I am not speaking to you. As for your goods, is my assistance with your work that of a slave?"

Fannie put together a small package while Sally brought her mother's horse. The couple rode together to the plain. Easily they caught up with the encroachers. The daughter was the first to notice a woman was accompanying a warrior. "Pa, from here it looks like a black nigger squaw woman is with that Injin who I told you acted like he knows English."

"Mind your manners," said the father in a low voice. Swift Eagle silently offered the gifts but the father surmised that Fannie was responsible for the kindness. "Thank you kindly. You may be a Nigra slave, but you got a heart."

"I am not a slave," said Fannie. He did not acknowledge the correction. She overlooked his rudeness. "Who did this to you?"

"Mama knew some of 'em and said they was Nʉmʉnʉʉ--I guess they was sent by the chief of all them savages--but they looked Comanche to me," said the daughter.

Without explaining Comanche was a name given to them and no single person ruled any nation that she knew of, Fannie said, "Why didn't they take the rest of you captive?"

"Years ago when they came, we wasn't home," said the daughter. "This time, Mama acted ascared of us—her own kinfolk! Pa'd treated Mama so bad she didn't want to take none of us with her accepting her Injin baby."

"You wasn't no saint to her," said the father.

"None of us was too good to her," said the son. "I'm man

enough to admit she seemed happy to be rid of us, and I'm smart enough to know she saved our lives."

It was time to leave. "I hate to ask, ma'am," said the girl. "Y'all got any water? We's powerful thirsty and we can't drink what that mean Nigra told us to."

Although Fannie had not been told about their thirst, it never occurred to her that they might be out of water. "You sat in a rain storm wearing a bonnet and slouch hats and failed to catch any water?"

"We was so busy trying to shelter we wasn't thinking," said the girl. "Then the storm didn't leave nothing but muddy water. I been sick more than once drinking muddy water."

"My husband will send some clean water back from our camp. Never forget our kindness," said Fannie. "If you get the chance to do likewise—to your mother or any other person—act friendly."

The father had not spoken since Fannie had denied that she was a slave. Before leaving Swift Eagle said to him in English, "Were you simply born a fool or are too scared to say thank you?"

He was startled to hear an Indian speak fluent English.

"I told you, Pa," said the girl.

"Thanks. I mean thank you, sir. We is sure enough grateful."

* * *

The sun was shining unmercifully on a cloudless, sweltering day. The temperature might have been fifty degrees higher than the Bannocks' mountain sanctuary at this time of year. Below lay a huge valley.

"Mama, look at all those horses!" said Mourns His Losses to River Woman.

"That's more than I have seen in my lifetime," said Young-Man-Who-Chases-Antelope.

"Sons," said Swift Eagle, "here the horse is chief. No other animal comes close."

The valley was rimmed on one side with a herd of several thousand horses and on the other by a stream. Nearby the members of the caravan saw an estimated 400 buffalo skin lodges.

"My guess is there will be about 2500 people down there," said Swift Eagle to Fannie.

"That must be Old Owl's band," said Down Wind Wolf. "Theirs is the largest of about a dozen bands. They usually move every four or five days. I'm glad I guessed right and expected them to somewhere near here. They're always good customers."

The immensity of the sight temporarily disoriented River Woman. 'This is a new world,' thought River Woman. 'It is not my first. May it not be the last.'

◊◊◊◊◊◊

On the village outskirts the travelers were met by scores of snarling dogs. 'These guard dogs,' thought River Woman, 'want me to believe they are as vicious as wolves.' Emulating their parents, River Woman's and Swift Eagle's children pretended the animals were no more fearful than domesticated grasshoppers. Instead of kicking at those who nipped at their feet, they ignored them. In moments, several armed, but unpainted, warriors came out to welcome the special guests.

The morning before, the members of the caravan had been careful to set aside three of the most prized mounts per person to save for themselves and not to accept any bid for them that fell short of breathtaking. This was not the final destination. To move on riding inferior mounts would lead to open disrespect. Despite the fact that most Comanche warriors had a super-abundance of excellent horses, the warriors could not resist inspecting each . belonging to the newcomers. The Comancheros and Bannock men accepted a few bids of horses but no other products before the makeshift store was set up. They rejected purchase offers for the reserved horses even as they welcomed the opportunity to be judged well-bred judgers of horse flesh. Later they would purchase other horses from those who were now customers.

"The game is simple," reminded Down Wind Wolf.

"You are right," said Swift Eagle smiling. "We teach it to Bannock children when we teach them how to ride and you have repeated the lesson at least three times since we left home."

"I walked into that one," said Down Wind Wolf. "Just the same be cautious, here in Comancheria. But also be a warrior. Anything less is dangerous." He paused. "Oh yes, I have already taught that lesson as well."

Swift Eagle and Running Buffalo laughed.

As was the case with Bannock lodges, Comanche buffalo skin lodges were painted with scenes and figures indicating the sources of power claimed by the occupants. New to the Bannocks were stuck in the ground next to virtually each buffalo skin 16 or 18 pole lodge, a lance with waving scalp locks. The grisly flags were proof of the presence of an adult male who was loyal to his culture. Normally 8-10 people shared a lodge whose average size reflected Comanche wealth. A few Blackfoot lodges were larger and among the Bannock and Crows only the peace chief and most famous hunters could be expected to match the circumference of Comanche lodges. Inside each lodge was a stack or two of buffalo robes in various stages of treatment from fresh to being used for sleeping.

Everyone in the family shared the lodge: from warrior and wife, children and perhaps an elderly parent and a captive or two with no more rights than a slave and might be white, from another tribe, or even a black person.

Comanche prosperity was evident everywhere. At the vast majority of the lodges, women were hard at work preparing food, making clothing or robes, feeding watching children, supervising the work of older daughters or slaves. While passing several smoking lodges, the visitors saw 12-20 men relaxing, most of whom recognized Down Wind Wolf and Tongin'. These warriors smoked, laughed and teased while others concentrated on making weapons, practicing riding skills and deflecting both arrows and bullets with their well-stuffed shields. Mourns His Losses and Young-Man-Who-Chases-Antelope stared mouth agape at what appeared magic.

"It is a warrior culture, my grandsons," said Chooses Calico to the eleven-year old boys. She explained that as it was in Bannock-land, the primary responsibility of the warriors was to protect and hunt meat. However, in Comancheria, white encroachment into their empire was generations old. Only a few trappers had come into Bannock-land.

"That is because they are afraid of us," said Young-Man-Who-Chases-Antelope.

"My grandsons are too young to remember that your birth fathers were trappers encroaching, unafraid and far from respectful. Lack of respect is what caused them to surrender their lives." She paused. "I know what I have said. Tell me what you have learned from my teaching."

They conferred and agreed that respecting all strangers was the Bannock way.

Once upon a time, only a rare Apache or Ute raiding party in search of great honor dared make a suicidal attack on one of their villages. With the exception of the boldest traders, whites and Mexicans either did not know of their existence or religiously avoided all contact. Despite having some of the largest villages in the region, the secure life had disappeared with the arrival of the ones Mexicans called Tejanos.

They were still following the guide to where they would pitch their lodges Swift Eagle said to River Woman, "Did you notice the Comanches behind us before we came to the village outskirts."

"Yes."

"How many did you count?"

"Five."

"There were eight. The ones you counted wanted to be seen. River Woman, the next time you count, notice the hidden as well as the disclosed. When in doubt, look opposite."

"Yes."

"They weren't sentinels like the Bannock and Crow have," said Rainbow's Breath. "In their arrogance this village fears no attacks."

"Arrogance you say?" said River Woman.

"We trade not only with the Comanche but also with Blackfeet, Shoshone, Bannock, Crows, Utes, Apaches... even Mexicans and Whites. No one has the arrogance of the Comanches."

The traders headed for the village center where Old Owl, the peace chief's lodge sat prominently. His lodge was decorated with paintings of several running horses and an array of single riding warrior prancing eight scalps on a five-yard high lance. Following the previous peace chief's death, Old Owl had ascended to his position by matching ferocity, valor, generosity and no flagrant signs of ambition. Now he rarely fought, contenting himself with being surrounded by the lodges of his relatives and basking in the pampering of three wives. The second and third were each younger than his senior wife's last child.

Fannie noted that the village was the most multi-cultural she had ever seen. By quirks in their dress she recognized pure blood Comanches, Mexicans, blacks, Tejanos, Frenchmen, Apache, Bannock, Shoshone, Utes, and blends of all of the above. They lived integrated into Comanche life instead of in small segregated enclaves. Depending upon the acceptance within a given lodge, most were free. Others were slaves who had entered as captives. For now, all were Comanche and could be expected to help defend or attack if combat was required.

Fannie said to Swift Eagle, "How are free people who are darker than most Comanches discerned if free papers are not required? Do they brand them somewhere as some white slave owners do?"

"Branding others is as uncivilized as beating your own children. I only think of those foolish talking papers when you look at the one you carry in your puha bundle. Here your freedom is recognized because you speak Bannock and no Bannock is a Comanche slave."

"Like that of all people, my medicine bundle is to avoid as much trouble as possible. What if I, a black woman, did not speak Bannock?"

"By walking fearlessly among the Comanches you are presumed free."

In the 1840s for a colored woman to be presumed a citizen was an idea that had not even occurred to most abolitionists. Later her mother-in-law, Chooses Calico, explained to Fannie she should not be deceived: all people were not equal. Full-blooded Comanches, Bannocks and Shoshoni could expect more respect than others, "Protect yourself at all times, River

Woman." She smiled before adding, "People who can swim have been known to drown."

"Thank you, Mother."

On the trail Fannie had already learned that hers was a Northern Paiute accent. The knowledge made her begin mimicking Rainbow Breath's speech patterns. Once more she silently prayed in Fante to her biological mother, 'Mama, help me master this new culture. Help me to follow your example and never want what I do not need, keep what I should not have.'

She felt a light breeze on her neck and looked overhead. A wispy detached cirrus cloud continued east, following on the heels of others.

◊◊◊◊◊◊

It was tradition for the Comanche women to head the line of buyers. As they waited patiently, The Panther, one of the greatest war chiefs of his generation, swaggered up to the display. He was a few inches less than 6', wore his hair shoulder length with two feathers. He was strikingly handsome and never seemed to blink his eyes. He was wearing more jewelry than any warrior she had met: a gold disk around his neck, broad gold bands on his upper arms, a silver ring on his less dominant hand, and six small gold rings in each ear. His only clothing was leggings trimmed with the scalp locks of slain children—blond on one side and black on the other—a breech cloth that flapped in the winds while hanging beneath the knee, and newly made elaborately beaded moccasins. Most men only dressed so fine for ceremonies or war.

River Woman saw The Panther staring at her as though examining a fine horse. As a slave she should have looked down. As a free woman in the states she should have looked away. As a Bannock, River Woman, turned, flashed a sign of disdain with her eyes, then continued her work.

The Panther laughed aloud. After a cursory look at the trade wares The Panther motioned for his colleague, Broken Ear, to watch. In his booming voice he approached River Woman and demanded, "Whose woman are you?" She looked into his eyes but did not answer.

"Was the cost of your beauty being made speechless?" Broken Ear's laughed at the offensive joke. She remained straight faced. "Maybe I should confiscate a tender morsel like you or sell you to the Tejanos or the traders from New Orleans. I've heard they know what to do with beautiful, ripe, black-skinned women."

Chooses Calico, signaled to her son who was on the far side of the makeshift store of Comanchero goods. Swift Eagle pretended not to notice. All the while, he was measuring how well his wife handled herself. He could not always be at her side, and by being married to a rare beauty, he had known before leaving home that they both would be tested. Chooses Calico grew weary of The Panther's antics. She signaled again.

Broken Ear saw her signaling and sneered. She made a gesture that only a grandmother could have done safely. He laughed but said nothing.

Swift Eagle walked calmly over to The Panther and said, "She is mine."

"How many horses?"

"She is not for sale."

"You are a trader with a Bannock accent. All you north-erners have a price. How does ten horses sound? Twenty-five? Name your price before I take her right before you and your mother."

Instead of taking his words as an insult, Swift Eagle chuckled. "All Comanches have their stopping point. The price for my wife is the earth now; the sun and the moon at sundown, and the stars over your own head when you lay in the dark land wondering who ended your days."

The Panther snorted at the repartee, then laughed heartily. "One day I will use your words against my enemies."

"Not at any price will I be one of them," said Swift Eagle. "The Panther's fame makes his claws worthy of befriending not attacking."

The Panther smiled. Without introductions he was recognized.

Broken Ear said to no one in particular, "So this is the beautiful black Bannock woman who has lived back where the sun rises and the taibo originate."

When Swift Eagle did not deny the truth, The Panther said, "Pretend that this beauty is a scout. Debrief her about what she has learned of our common enemies and meet with me at the designated place at noon tomorrow."

The Panther left. River Woman said to Swift Eagle in Fante, "Why did he try to buy me?"

"They say he has the best eyesight on the plains," he said in Bannock. She did not laugh. "He would have accepted you as a gift if I had turned rabbit."

"Are these cousins without manners?"

"All people, even whites, have manners. It is positive manners you seek."

She thought, 'I expect a better answer than that,' but said nothing.

Swift Eagle turned serious and also used Fante, his wife's ancestral language. "If he had really wanted you, even if I had fought him and won, he had a Comanche village at his back. I would have died stopping him. We are guests. Comanche etiquette protected us. He was not displaying bad manners. He was testing me by seeing if I were weak enough to let him appropriate my wife and therefore unworthy of calling myself a warrior. I know you understand. You have read me a story in that Bible book where some chief was so weak as to deny his own wife. The Bible chief lied. I told the truth: try to take her, and one or more of us dies."

Fannie considered his words then smiled. "It is good to know that I am worth earth, sun, moon, and stars."

"Then forgive me. It should not have taken a great war chief playing as though he were a joking boy for you to realize that."

She let her eyes linger in a gaze with his before saying, "I knew."

Swift Eagle touched her face and changed back to Bannock. "Had he met my initial conditions I would have taken you back before he had taken a single step. I believe his scalp would fit nicely on my lance. He did have a beautiful shock of hair, didn't he?"

While speaking the last words, there was a rarely seen menacing, coldness in Swift Eagle's eyes. He turned and walked away to the far side of the display.

River Woman caught her mother-in-law's eyes. Chooses Calico was smiling and gave the hand signal. "That's my son."

◊◊◊◊◊◊

Fannie made the finishing touches to the display, straightening something here, adjusting elsewhere. Chooses Calico helped for a while then left to begin the next meal. Seeing Fannie alone, Rainbow's Breath stepped up to her and said, "Niece, you did not answer The Panther's question. Did you understand his Comanche accent?"

Thinking, 'There is a greater difference between the Virginia, Kentucky, and Mississippi English that colored people speak than Bannock, Shoshone and Comanche,' she simply said. "I understood him, my aunt. I do not like to speak to strange men, and my husband was nearby."

Rainbow's Breath said, "You were right then to stand your ground. It is well that I warned you of their arrogance. You will provide a great warrior with sons for whom he can be proud." After a pause she added, "The Panther showed us respect by visiting us early. My husband will set aside some of the best metals for The Panther's wives and sons to choose. He will expect no less."

"Are you two going to help?" called Swallowtail Butterfly, wife to Tongin'. "First Chooses Calico leaves our work and then you two Bannocks want to chat!"

They rejoined setting up their wares while the Comanche women who were clustered in a circle a few feet away had grown impatient and were repeatedly saying, "Now?" "Now?"

In the midst of the growing cacophony, The Panther's son arrived to speak with Swift Eagle who was with the male traders arranging guns, ammunition, Bowie knives and metal scraps.

"I am Wanders-the-Bravos, The Panther's son. They say your wife has great medicine. My father wants something made by her hand. What will you sell?"

Swift Eagle made eye contact with River Woman who was busy several yards away. She came to his side and he told her of the special request. She went back to their lodge. Upon returning she handed him a panther skin quiver and a metal knife with an antler handle. He smiled at her clever choices and held them out for the buyer's examination.

Wanders-the-Bravos said, "One horse for both."

"Six."

"You Bannock do not understand bartering. Three."

Swift Eagle removed the quiver and knife from the son's hands and gave them back to Fannie.

"Four and no more," said the son.

"Bring me a dozen horses worthy of a great Comanche war chief," the son almost swallowed hard at Swift Eagle's change in strategy, "and I will choose four."

The son went away disgusted with how the trade was progressing.

"My son is quite a trader," said Running Buffalo to Swift Eagle. "Maybe you were born to be a trader."

"I am what I was born to be: a warrior," said Swift Eagle, laughing at his father's joke. "Uncle Returning Cloud taught me 'even a rich man can be made poor if he is trying to please another.' This son overpaid me not from loving me, but from fearing his father."

"I don't understand," said River Woman.

"I had signaled my father and we had made a bet that. He said the son was only authorized to pay two horses," said Swift Eagle.

"And?"

"I said I would get him to pay at least three. We received three for your labor and another for the son's bad judgment," said Swift Eagle laughing.

"Then you may choose the first of the four for your personal use," said River Woman. "And, Father, you two may choose a horse after I choose the first."

Swift Eagle laughed again and turned toward Running Buffalo. "Father, would you like to bet that the son will have to make up the difference from his own herd?"

"I have learned my lesson," said Running Buffalo. "Today yours is the best medicine."

"Perhaps my wife's is even better."

"Generosity is not luck. It is heart.

13
THE OVERGROUND RAILROAD

M y brother Dan lived in Cincinnati where he owned a stagecoach business named The Lion and the Lamb, was an Underground Railroad conductor, lived with a family including wife and two sons and frequented a seedy saloon named after its owner Haynes Gates. When Gates entered our family through marriage, I learned much of this story. The rest comes from Dan's journal.

* * *

Shakespeare's Romeo and Juliet was being staged in Cincinnati. Ethan Jefferson, my sister Fannie's ex-husband, wanted his daughters to enjoy the best that western culture had to offer. Ethan often bragged that his daughters had only two African great grandparents among a sea of European ancestors. Those of us in the black community could see Africa in the daughters but, as often was the case, whites were oblivious to the obvious. Through white ignorance, their skin was light enough that one day they might pass for white, be accepted as sophisticated ladies and marry white gentlemen as had the blended daughters of former Vice President Richard Mentor Johnson of nearby Kentucky.

Ethan had a business relationship with a white man whose financial reversals following the Mexican War had pushed him almost to the point of suicide. Ethan pounced on his vulnerability and struck a deal with him to take his daughters to the theater.

The night of the performance the girls were resplendent in their new parallel-patterned pink or lavender gingham dresses and long brown hair, flowing out from their bonnets of opposite colors. Their rented "Uncle" met them at a remote place and accompanied them to 4th row, center seats. One of the ushers recognized them and pointed them out to the manager.

Immediately the girls were lifted out of their seats by the usher-guards who had as a primary assignment, to keep the audience pure. Kicking and shouting the girls were pulled across confused theater goers with the explanation, "These are niggers in white face." Meanwhile, the escort was pushed and kicked down the aisle by the manager. All three were summarily thrown into the street.

Quickly the story went through the grapevines. That night at Gates Saloon, Eat-'em-Up said, "I heard they called 'em everything but a child of God!"

Toad added, "That damned Jefferson always thought he was better than us. Trying to pass his daughters off as white! Who'd wanna see that Shakepeer anyway? That ain't no colored man's stuff. You seen them handbills? Men wearing tights and women uglier than your daddy. Church fairs and Negro Carnival Day outta be enough entertainment for any decent colored man."

"He shoulda hired a stranger," said Sweetnin' Water.

"Everybody knows that cracker they was with ain't got no kids that old."

"The grapevine say he's colored hisself, tryin'to pass," said Eat-'em-Up.

"He might as well just pass his ass on outta here," said Eat-'em-Up. "Them bullyboys will probably call him a 'nigger lover' and use him as a bulls-eye."

"No wonder he's got that 'Going Outta Business' sign in his window!" said a voice in the crowd.

"It makes you wonder," said Dan.

"What you think about it, Gates?" asked Eat-'em-Up.

"I know Ethan's not a likeable man. Some folk even say he's a spy for slave catchers. I doubt it," said Gates. "But it hurt me to my heart?"

"Why?" asked Dan.

"I've been trying to tell you men for years, to the white man there is no such thing as an individual colored man," said Gates. "They threw you and me in the street with those kids? Love them or hate them, those little girls took a asse-kicking for mama and your grandmama. Come to think of it, they also took a asse-kicking for you and for me."

The room grew quiet. Eat-'em-Up, Toad and Sweetnin' Water looked at Dan. Against his will he said, "That's how America works."

◊◊◊◊◊◊

A Quaker named Levi Coffin was friends with Dan. My brother both purchased slave-free goods from his store and was trusted in the Underground Railroad community in which Levi was Cincinnati's central figure. Levi knew Ethan Jefferson because his med delivered milk to the Coffins store. Coffin told those who warned him about that Ethan might be a spy. "Spies have existed since before Bible days. I know I am guilty of breaking the law, but in America, Ethan is innocent until proven guilty."

Two days following the rough handling of his daughters Ethan told his most trusted worker that he still felt much as he had the first time that his father had forced him to watch one of his older brothers being beaten with a whip. It was not his body, but tearfully he had shared in his brothers' shame. As did most of his employees, the man hated Ethan and spread the story around Cincinnati. The colored population was still buzzing over his comeuppance. Ethan's admission was received with glee.

Seeking comfort, Ethan made a milk delivery to the Coffins' general store. Ethan's business had grown to the point that rarely did he even mount a work wagon unless he was asked to help move runaways. Otherwise he had employees to do the grunt work. My nephew, Kenny Crispin summoned Levi to the door.

"Good morning, Ethan Jefferson," said Coffin, using Quaker formal.

"Mr. Coffin, sir, how are you?" Ethan held his hat in his hand despite the fact the proprietor followed Quaker practice and did not remove his own.

Coffin studied his face. "I am well, but it is a good morning, is it not?"

"Yes, sir, the sun is shining," said Ethan. "I need your help; I want to move some people." He had Coffin's attention.

"Come, would thee sit a spell?" Coffin led him to the privacy of a small room behind the shop.

Ethan carefully explained that he needed a trustworthy man to move his daughters to a gentleman in Indiana who was a friend of his father's. Coffin knew that Ethan's father was a white man and had heard rumors that he might be anyone from

The President to the Governor of Mississippi. Ethan carefully guarded specifics about his sire.

"I want my daughters to pass as white. After what happened in the theater that is unlikely in southern Ohio. Can you help me?"

"I have heard about that travesty and do not approve of what happened to thy daughters or what you see as a remedy. However, I know of one man and one man only whom you can trust for this mission."

"Who?" said Ethan, missing the shift from thee to you, Quaker-distant.

"Dan Crispin," said Coffin, "the owner of the Lion and the Lamb Stage Coach Lines."

"Patience Starbuck of Waynesville, the same woman who owns Nantucket Boat Builders, the Slave-Free Trade Warehouse, and Ohio Valley Iron Foundry, owns the Lion and the Lamb."

"Yes, her ownership of the stage line might be only one of the many rumors that circulate the area," said Levi. "Sham or real, for such as you desire, Dan Crispin is the only man I would trust."

"I need time to consider this," said Ethan.

"Take all the time you need," said Coffin, disgusted and by changing from thee to you, signaling there was a distance between them. "This is your desire not mine."

Dan's son Kenny was in the next room, putting stock on the shelves. He had been so quiet and Ethan so preoccupied that he did not realize this fact. Apparently, he also had no idea that Kenny was Dan's son.

"Kenny!" called Levi. "Perhaps thee heard something of this conversation."

Ethan's face was red. Unwilling to lie, Kenny said, "I will not tell a soul."

"That is not why I called thee," said Levi. "Even mice in straw are not quite so quiet as thee was stocking my shelves. I do expect thee to keep these matters hush, even as thee hast been ordered to do when fugitives are our guests. However, I called thee because if Ethan Jefferson here is willing and thy father consents, I would like both men to meet me here at 10:00am tomorrow morning. Will thee convey the message to Dan?"

"Yes, sir."

Kenny left and Ethan said, "If you knew he was nearby why did you not warn me?"

"That is the least of your worries." Coffin stood. "I will expect you back here at 10:00 am on the morrow."

◊◊◊◊◊◊

Levi and Kate Coffin were waiting for the meeting between the two colored men. Dan arrived at 9:56 a.m. and Ethan at 9:59 a.m. They sized each other up, silently recognizing that each appeared more dressed for a ball or a request for a bank loan than for a daytime conversation in a private home. Clean-shaven, Ethan wore an open gray waist coat with tails over black pants that were stretched by a band wrapping around each slipper, to keep the material smooth. Underneath the coat was a white cotton shirt and matching three-buttoned vest, set off by a burgundy necktie. A large black cravat purchased from a German importer accented the ensemble. Dan sported an open blue waist coat, with a matching seven-buttoned vest above tan pants. His white upturned collar shirt was accented with a red scarf and matching French cuff links. His boots were fine aged leather whose soles and heels had been replaced many times. Our brother Robin had made the originals more than twenty years earlier. Each boot bore a Fante symbol reminiscent of the stool that had been our family's insignia for centuries.

The colored men despised each other for being overdressed and inordinately ambitious. Furthermore, Dan had heard reports that Ethan had publicly referred to him as an ape with money and wondered, 'Does this wretch know Fannie's my sister?' Neither had criticized the other in the Coffins' presence, but Levi was the best-connected man in the Ohio Valley, and these men were among his partners in the work to abolish slavery. Despite their individual statures in the business world, all three men recognized that if peace was reached, Katie would be the key. The cultures of both colored people and Quakers demanded that she be respected.

"Dan Crispin and Ethan Jefferson," Katie said from her seat, "it is a pleasure to see men looking so healthy and prosperous."

"Thank you, ma'am," they said at the same time.

"I trust that neither of you distinguished men dresses so well for an ordinary work day," she said. Ethan blushed and Dan rubbed his beard and lowered his eyes. "Please, sit."

The three men obeyed. She lowered her head and took their hands as she led a silent grace. "Partake of a bit of this fresh cake with the hot coffee and then excuse us old folk. Levi and I have our morning chores to continue." Rising, with a butcher's knife in hand, she said in what they might have interpreted as a threat if she had not been a soft-spoken pacifist. "Treat our kitchen as tenderly as thee would thy own home, a locus of love built to last, free of hostility, dedicated to Truth."

They sat mute while she cut the cake. "My dear Aunt Hannah called this her Composition Cake. I doubt that either of you men bake but should you seek the recipe I will be happy to share. Along with the obvious flour, eggs, butter, milk and currants, there is a bit of nutmeg, mace and a few other spices."

She paused and they took the hint to take a small bit of the cake in her presence.

"Delectable," said Dan.

"Fine ma'am," said Ethan.

"May I have the recipe?" asked Dan. "My wife collects only the finest."

"I expected as much." She withdrew two sheets from an apron pocket and handed them to the men. Then she poured the first cups of coffee.

She stood to leave before her husband did the same. Dan and Ethan also stood, bowing as she disappeared. Levi shook hands with both men. "Indulging a good woman is a path to the stars." He bid them farewell, and left through a door on the other side of the room.

An awkward silence settled. Dan had promised himself not to be the first to speak or to disclose that Ethan's ex-wife was his sister. To himself he said, "I did not ask for this meeting and am only present out of curiosity. There is value in studying a cur. Should he try to bite later, I will know more of his moves and where to kick him."

In hope of ending the meeting as soon as possible, Ethan set aside most façades. "I need you to move my daughters to Indiana."

"Why me?" asked Dan.

"All you need to know is the address and to drive safely. In this letter are my detailed instructions to the party on the other end. I must be assured they will be delivered safely...and quietly. I have Coffin's oath," he said overstating his case, "that you can be trusted. None must know what I've done."

Dan listened to Ethan, thinking, 'You high yellow dog. I know you're lying about Coffin. Quakers do not take oaths or even make promises. Starting with your abuse of my sister, I hate everything about you, but I'll take your money.' He said, "How much are you offering?"

Ethan gave him the opening bid and Dan laughed. He thought he could read Ethan's eyes and that his adversary wanted to say, "Why you black bastard!" Instead Ethan swallowed. "I'll make it $50 more." Dan stopped laughing, but he still did not agree. "$100 more." Silence. "$125 more." Silence. "$150 more."

Dan said, "Name the date and I will work in such privacy their own mother won't know they have been removed."

Ethan flushed from the neck up. "I prefer you use the word 'moved'."

Dan's lone concession was to sit and wait for his adversary's next words. The deal was struck. Dan left feeling that Ethan's initial bid was more than fair. 'Unless I am mistaken, he is throwing away his daughters. But he could have given me the deed to the dairy farm, and it would not have been enough to repay me for driving my sister. out of town. We did not even have the chance to reunite as adults.'

◊◊◊◊◊◊

The next morning Dan came to the breakfast table and found his wife had prepared ham, bacon, pork sausage, eggs, and pancakes for him and their sons Abel and Kenny.

"Why so much?" Abel asked. "It's not even Sunday."

"Daddy's going away," said Zephyrine, "and he won't even tell me where. Maybe he's got hisself another woman."

Abel stared at his father.

"No, he doesn't," said Kenny.

"Say no more," said Dan sternly to his older son.

"Least ways, I know where to get my source when you leave," said Zephyrine.

"I'm sorry, Daddy," said Kenny, realizing it would be impossible to keep the information from Zephyrine.

"I know you are, son," said Dan. "Actually, so long as I don't let the cat out of the bag, I'm in the clear."

Dan had deliberately placed Kenny with the Coffins to obtain first-hand knowledge of the Underground Railroad world from the man who fancied himself the President. It was ironic, as distasteful as it was, now that the Overground Railroad was front and center in his life.

Early Sunday morning, Dan left home driving his personal long-distance coach instead of one with the company's Lion and Lamb insignia. This same coach had transported a few score fugitives from injustice. Janey Blakey, the girls' mother, had been Ethan's lover before and during his marriage to their father. Ethan had never formally married Janey, but he had moved her into his beautiful home on his dairy farm. There she had acted the role of wife as he had added a procession of mistresses to satisfy his desires.

Janey was disconsolate and wearing a rumpled dress with her hair in disarray when Ethan accompanied the seventeen year-old twins to the waiting coach. Dan noted how well outfitted they were in white bonnets, matching silk calico dresses, respectively with burgundy and royal blue bases. Dan stood by the coach awkwardly waiting to assist in any way he could, Janey choked. "Please, Ethan, don't do this to us. We are a family."

"Hush! Don't be selfish; this is what is best for the girls."

She reached out with both hands for one last touch. Ethan pushed her away before the girls could connect. Although it did not appear to Dan that it was a hard shove, Janey fell and crumpled to the ground. Overcome with grief, she could not rise. The girls both broke into tears. Dan helped Janey up and said to Ethan, "Where were you raised? In a pigsty?"

"One of us is being paid and I am not the one," said Ethan.

"Your best bet," said Dan, "is to remember I am neither a slave nor in need. I will hit you in the mouth, stomp on your worthless throat, and walk away this moment."

"No!!" said Janey. "I don't want to lose all three of you in one day."

"See what you've done, Janey?" asked Ethan. He snatched her away from Dan and motioned for two of his employees to hurry his daughters into the carriage. Once deposited the employees put huge trunks into the coach.

Still restraining Janey, Ethan said, "Daughters, tell not a soul of your true identity and your blessings will be uncountable."

Karen and Maria said as one, "I love you Daddy, don't do this."

"It may not appear so today but everything I do is for your betterment."

Before Dan could leave the grounds, he heard Ethan shouting at his employees, "Why did you not spring to my defense against that savage? You are fired."

* * *

The girls spoke openly around Dan as though the dark-skinned man were a slave, unworthy of notice. He overheard enough to verify his suspicions. 'Why am I doing this?' he said to himself. He concluded, 'I do not need the money, but knowing that Ethan will regret his actions for the rest of his life is worth the effort.'

He heard our mother's voice saying, "I done raised you

better." At the next rest stop he helped the girls out of the coach and waited under a lilac tree for their return from an outhouse off limits to him as a colored man. The girls were about to walk silently by him to wait beside the coach for him to help them climb the two steps.

He said, "Excuse me." They stopped a few yards from the coach. "I have figured out what's happening, and I'm sorry life has taken this turn. Please don't think less of yourself or colored people in general. If you were mine, I'd be proud to call you my daughters and keep you by my side."

The girls did not respond. Head pointed straight, they continued the short distance to the coach. He helped each in turn back into the cabin. Prior to Dan's talk there had been a small distance between them. Now they sat together tightly entwining their arms. Feeling as invisible as he had during the brief period in which he had been a house servant, Dan steadied himself by counting wild flower blossoms. Somewhere after 400 he wiped a tear and continued driving to an inn where each prayed the girls would be welcomed as white and he, for one, hoped it would not rain as he slept in the carriage.

14
THE FIELDS OF JOY

W hat follows is another tale told by my sister Fannie when she returned to the states for our brother Dan's memorial service. By the time of this story she had become River Woman, the wife of a Bannock Indian. Her new life in the Rocky Mountains seemed as different from Virginia slavery as the latter did from Fante freedom.

* * *

Annually the various Bannock villages joined with Shoshone villages at a wondrous place they called "The Fields of Joy." The journey taken by the one hundred souls led by Running Buffalo, my sister's father-in-law, led past the Soldier Mountains, through the Sawtooth Forest. Since the previous gathering of The People, the mountains had been ravaged by a huge fire begun by a lightning storm. Now the greening was wondrous and hunting the best in years. Elk and deer, sheep and bears all gave up their lives and were thanked for their part in the survival dance. When the travelers tired of meat, the fishing was plentiful. Roots and seeds were available for the taking. There was no hurrying, only anticipation.

Coming down to the valley, eagles and hawks seemed to grow more plentiful, sometimes gliding or deliberately changing directions, perhaps to dart after some small creature on the ground. Look at that one," said River Woman to her husband. "Was it he who gave you your name?"

Swift Eagle laughed and said, "Shall I fly up there and ask?"

"I have found my answer," she said.

"You are always about being who you are, River Woman," he said using her Bannock name, "keeping the flow of my life steady."

"Look!" said their daughter who was named Sally at birth. The Bannock had changed it to the Observer.

There before them was "The Fields of Joy" looking like a purple/blue velvet blanket interspersed here and there with thousands ˙of various colored wild flowers, dancing with sunlight, shaded with passing clouds. The band led by Running Buffalo was the first to arrive. Their approach led great flocks of geese and ducks rose to fill the air. However, hunters were able to shoot several partridge and sage grouse before the majority of them scurried to safety.

"We have known the starving times of winter," said River Woman. "Now we will feast."

* * *

The original reason for the trip was for the women to harvest camas, but "The People" as the various bands of Bannock and Shoshone called themselves, also enjoyed stationery games, races, courting and simply fraternizing.

On the second day in the gathering place Fannie was busily

using her pointed stick to harvest wild camas bulbs, a member of the asparagus family, when she heard ululating. She looked up. A special guest had arrived at the reunion. Coming toward her were three women, Fannie's best friend Paints-Her-Lodge, her mother Jumping Fish, and Sacajawea, one of the most famous women of the age. All of the women were dressed in buckskins but the designs on Sacajawea belied the fact that she had been among multiple cultures. River Woman identified symbols often found on the dresses of Shoshone, Bannock, Hidatsa and Comanche women but there were a few more that River Woman did not recognize.

Jumping Fish said, "The beauty who stands here is my daughter's good friend, River Woman. Here is my best friend Sacajawea."

The sun rays caught the great lady's medal given to her by George Rogers Clark. River Woman had heard stories about it but did not speak about the medal or say anything until her elder spoke first. "My first son has spoken of you," Sacajawea said to Fannie.

"Yes, Pomp and I once shared a lodge. It was a place where four couples and three children lived, loved, and danced. I hope all that he said was not bad."

"It's good to have a sense of humor when living among people with whom you were not reared."

"I am a Bannock now."

"I see. As slavery may also have taught you, wherever I flow, I have always been Sacajawea."

Fannie laughed with her. "Are you ever Janey?"

"Sacajawea. Never Janey. Never Pocahontas. Never Morning Dew."

"You have heard of Osceola's Negro wife?"

"She was born a Negro but she chose to be Seminole as you have chosen to be Bannock. I see that your skin's tone is more like York's than Beckwourth's. The one who lives as a Crow war chief has skin even lighter than mine," said Sacajawea.

Ignoring the reference to Beckwourth, a man she did not like, Fannie said, "I have heard much about York. Most came from men who never met him or knew very little. What can you tell me about the man?"

"I remember most that he was always respectful. He called me Mrs., never using 'Janey,' a name I despised and others used because they were too lazy to learn to pronounce 'Sacajawea'. York was tall and brave and missed his wife."

"I heard that like me he was born in Virginia."

"I have never been there, but yes, that was his country, a village called Ladysmith. Once he told me, 'You are a lady who smiths the way for all of us. I liked the way it sounded, but I'm not sure I understand it."

River Woman thought a while before saying, "I believe he meant that you work to make everything and everyone stronger...you have a vision that sees beyond the mountains."

"I knew his words were filled with kindness." Sacajawea paused before saying, "I would like to visit you in your lodge tomorrow morning."

My sister was still a middle child at heart. She was taken aback to think an important woman would seek her company. "I would be honored to host you."

◊◊◊◊◊◊

Soon after Fannie's husband Swift Eagle left to go hunting fresh meat with other warriors, there was a scratch on the lodge flap.

"Enter!" she said.

Sacajawea found Fannie working on a counsel robe. "I had hoped to find your baby awake."

"High Cloud had a late night and has yet to have his morning meal."

"That means you too had a 'late night'."

Fannie smiled. "I can awaken him if you like."

"We have enough to keep us occupied without waking a tired child," said Sacajawea. "May I help with your robe?" Without waiting for an answer, she got on her knees and picked up a spare needle kept for the possibility of a guest.

The women worked together silently, Sacajawea following Fannie's lead with the pattern. "I do not know this one."

"My ancestresses were Queen Mother of the Fantes in Africa. What you hold is a stool that symbolizes their positions as protectors of their people."

After several minutes of work had passed, Sacajawea said, "You know my name means 'Bird Woman' even as yours means 'River Woman'."

"I do, but the bird opposite the royal stool in this design is a male."

Sacajawea laughed. "I know that Swift Eagle is your husband. You are spoken of among many nations."

"I am?"

"Would you like to hear some of what they say?"

"No."

"That is a good answer, because surely much of it is false." Fannie still did not ask to hear the stories. "They also spread stories about me. People who were not there would have me believe that I really am someone who can fly." Sacajawea laughed and Fannie joined her. "I came to the Fields of Joy as much to meet you as I did to visit my old friend Jumping Fish."

"Why?"

"We have much in common that is not made up by gossipers. I was kidnapped and made a slave, and Pomp said that too happened with your mother."

"Yes."

"Many women have been enslaved. Few would want their child to also be a slave. From being an Hidatsa slave, I went to being Toussaint Charbonneau's slave. That is why I gave my son to William Clark. I could see that Clark was a powerful man who I believed could protect my son and make him a man of power. You understand this don't you?"

"I do, but not why you're telling me, a stranger."

"You are no stranger to me. As I suggested, our stories are not dissimilar. Pomp said that because of your parents' condition, you too spent your early years as a slave."

"I did."

"There are not many women in these mountains who understand what we experienced and live to talk freely about such a past."

"That is true."

"In the same village as Jumping Fish, I was born a Lemhi Shoshone. I live as a Lemhi Shoshone now. When the Hidatsa kidnapped me I became their slave, practicing their culture, eating their food, speaking their language, celebrating their festivals, wearing their styles. People thought I was Hidatsa. A sad one, but still Hidatsa. I did not. I was Sacajawea. I am who I believe am and I never understand myself to be a slave."

"Who were you when you traveled with Clark and Lewis?"

"They did not accept me as one of them. I was a 'squaw', such a hateful word. I knew that our hearts were not joined. Joined hearts make a people. How do you define yourself?

"A baby named Fante was called Fannie by her father, a man who wanted to be an American. In the course of time she married Swift Eagle who named her River Woman. The names have changed. I remain who I am. Only Nyame has the right to change me."

Sacajawea lifted up the side of the buffalo robe where she had been permitted to complete the stool. "How is my work?"

"No one could do it better."

High Cloud whimpered. Without waiting for a signal, Sacajawea stood, picked him up and handed him to his mother. Sacajawea moved on to another part of the robe while River Woman nursed the baby to the point of where he required burping. She handed him to her guest who spent the balance of the visit cuddling.

Over the course of an hour, Sacajawea talked about her French husband Charbonneau beating her and the necessity to run away from him many times. Finally, her brother Cameah-wait threatened him. "Do you have brothers whom you also loved?"

"I have not seen a brother in more than twenty years, but I have one who writes me, Dan. Yes, I love him. I have another whose whereabouts I do not know, and one who was killed by slave catchers."

"Cameahwait was killed by Blackfeet," said Sacajawea. "Without being able to live under his protection and wanting no new husband, I joined the Comanches. They are a fierce people, but not so fierce that they could make me marry against my will. Perhaps along with the Dakota and Cheyenne they are the only ones who can preserve us from being overrun by the whites."

"You do not count the Crow or the Apache as strong nations?"

"The Crow will help the whites against the Dakota and Cheyenne, and the Apache will do the same against the Comanche. Most of our people do not understand the ways of the whites. One day the whites will turn on even those who blindly help them today."

River Woman had listened when our mother had told her

how the decimation of Fante culture was aided by our cousins. She agreed that without unity there was little possibility of the survival of any Indian nation's way of life. She had no choice but to hope she was wrong.

"I have been such a traveler," said Sacajawea, "that many times those who did not know my whereabouts thought I had died. If death had become my second husband, you would think that I would be the first to know." The women laughed at her joke. "I know that you do not like the man that Pomp has become."

"He said that to you?" asked Fannie.

"He did not need to. People who have lived in slavery learn better than most how to study others. Pomp was corrupted by the white man's ideas. I know it and you know it. Do not blame him. It was I who placed him under their direct influence."

"I cannot presume to judge you. All I can do is love and admire you for how you have survived and helped others to do the same."

Sacajawea smiled, got off her knees and placed the sleeping baby back in his cradle. "I must be off to spend time with Jumping Fish. Before the kidnapping, she was like a sister. Now, you can think of me as an older sister. If for some reason you believe I can help you, send for me. When I love, my love is unstinting."

River Woman felt chill bumps. She had just been taken seriously by one of her idols. For days she queried Nyame, asking why Sacajawea had made the visit. Finally, she heard inside, "Be grateful and do not ask why I brought you two together. Many of my plans are foiled by those who refuse my gifts. I am grateful that, this time, you both accepted the joy I intended."

15

WORDS

I n the midst of yet another cholera epidemic, and six
months after my brother Dan's death, his widow had delivered a child. Upon receiving the news, I left my own children
under the care of my mother-in-law and had my husband drive
me down to Cincinnati. When he protested that I was putting
myself and "his" family at risk I reminded him that in view of a
neighbor dying in childbirth only a week earlier I had taken
greater risks initiated by his actions, he was not my master, and
if the children are not also the mother's, by whose authority has
she lost them? Perhaps my response would have been gentler
had I not been born in slavery and near the end of the line of
several children.

* * *

Zephyrine and child seemed well but there were bags under
her eyes I had never seen before and her hair needed tending.
She obviously required more rest than I. Although she had no

plans to leave the house or receive visitors, she allowed me to comb her long black hair and change Dan, Jr.'s wetness.

"I hired that nurse to take care of him," said Zephyrine.

"Thy mother was nurse on Fruits of the Spirit," I reminded her. "I heard her say many times, 'It ain't but one Eula!'"

Had she been well she would have laughed at the reminder. Instead she closed her eyes trying to fight back her nausea. I rang for the nurse, who came running from the kitchen where she was helping a second servant prepare a quick meal for my husband and me before he left to visit cousins.

Zephyrine fell asleep even before the nurse and I had finished cleaning up the latest mess . Fried chicken, corn on the cob and a simple green salad were already on the table and the biscuits were in the oven. The cook led us in an extended grace that only ended when it was time to remove the biscuits.

Charles kissed me and left the room. "He your man?" asked the nurse who had only been hired to help during Zephyrine's sickness, in hope that she could help protect the child from becoming ill.

Annie, the cook and usually own regular servant said, "Yes and he's her husband. Kaye, I done told you, don't be so nosy, if you wanna keep this job."

There was no need for me to say more so I excused myself and went to my brother's library. Before the illness, Zephyrine had given me permission to read my brother's journals, "And no more," she had said leaving no room for discussion. I perused my brother's papers that were not legal documents.

I came across a file marked "Incendiary." Having no reason to believe these were among the off-limit papers, I came upon abolitionist articles, statements by enraged blacks, Indians and Mexicans. The latter were in translation. By whom I wondered? I knew Dan read Latin and had spoken some French in the years that he had resided in Detroit. I was trying to solve the riddle of the Spanish translations when I came upon David Walker's famed appeal. I had heard its contents touched upon, but no more. It took away my breath. Had Dan thought me too meringue-like, or a sable version of a slave master's fairy princess? Surely, he knew me better than that. When I finished reading, I closed the pamphlet and thought to myself, 'Walker's words speak to my condition more than does the Quaker Book of Discipline. Is this truth more the reason I cannot make myself apply for membership than the lack of anyone save my mother-in-law and Patience Starbuck inviting me to join?'

The second morning, when I arose, I looked in on Zephyrine. With Kaye, her nurse beside her, she was resting well. I went to the next room and found the cook cradling the baby. I exchanged whispered greetings with Annie and kissed Dan, Jr.'s tiny head and turned to leave. There was a knock at the door. Rather than risk the cook carrying the baby to answer, perhaps awaking him in the process, I answered it myself.

Before me was a striking woman wearing a well-tailored cyan based dress with touches of what appeared to be a crisp burnt orange color that I, a seamstress, had never seen. I recognized the woman for I had seen, but not been introduced to her, at Dan's funeral. I had heard whispers from uncouth men, but she who placed faith in men's words concerning lovely women will believe virtually anything.

"May I help you, sister?"

"I know whose sister you are. I'm afraid it ain't mine. My name is Lillith Whitfield. I come for to see Zee."

"I'm afraid I must ask, do you have or have you been exposed to cholera."

She turned slowly around clockwise and then reversed herself. "Do I look like I have the cholera?"

It was so embarrassing. We were clearly of the same race and gender but the featured comparisons ceased there. She struck me as verging on being shameless.

"Zephyrine is sleeping."

"I'll wait. This ain't my busy time and even if it was, she takes first place."

I had not fully opened the door. Noting my rudeness, I suggested we sit together in the larger parlor.

Lillith said, "I seen enough of clothes you made for Zee and Dan to know you're a businesswoman too."

"What line of work are you in?"

"You don't know?"

"We have never met."

"I don't make no clothes and sure don't do laundry or clean no white fools' houses. Ain't much left is it?"

Embarrassed I said, "I am a seamstress."

"Didn't I say I knowed that?" For once, the whispering men had been correct. Before I could ask how she knew Zephyrine, she said, "Can I get you to make me a dress? Why do you think I showed you my fine brown frame?"

"Every day, Sunday-go-to-meeting—"

"At the door I showed you what I got. Make it look inviting and call it a man-come-to-Mama dress," she said laughing. There was no mirror but surely I blushed. "How soon will you have it ready?"

"My mother-in-law may have so good an eye as to make a dress without taking measurements. I do not."

"36-22-36 is all you need to know. My body ain't been

touched by a woman since I left my mama's place. I aim to keep my streak."

"I'm afraid I need a tape for more than you suggest."

"That wasn't no suggestion. That was a real as a orange peel keeping in the juice."

I needed to reassert myself. "When Zephyrine wakes up I'll borrow her tape measure. I leave in the morning two days from now. When I return you will be third in line."

"I know you ain't going to tell me some white wenches is up ahead of me."

I did not bother to explain that she who arrives first is served first. We both were aware that white business people did not abide such courtesy to colored customers, but, as I tell my children, if we want a better world, we must lead the way.

"This is how I do business. First the tape measure, then third in line."

She laughed. "Yeh, you may be high yellow on the outside but you are sure enough Dan's sister. Stubborn as that boulder in Farmer Jones' wheat field. He gave up trying to move it; I will too."

I had measured Lillith and she was visiting with Zephyrine when I heard another knock. This time Kaye led Patience Starbuck into Dan's library where I was reading Dickens.

She appeared frazzled but I was still basking in the glow of having held my ground with another strong woman. Ignoring her anxiety, I said, "What brings thee this way? Had I known thy plans I could have traveled here with thee."

"We must go, hurry!"

"Ordering does not become thee. My question."

"Harriet Stowe has lost her beloved son and she is beyond distraught. My driver awaits."

On the way to Harriet's I reminded Patience that I had only met the woman once. That was before she had married. Even then we had not held a proper conversation. Patience explained while it was true that she and Harriet had been friends for years, she herself was out of her element. She had lost her mother, father, brothers, sister as well as my brothers Robin and Dan. "But I have never been a grieving mother. I do not know how to touch the subject, let alone shape it into something bearable."

Patience led me into the room where, in a black mourner's dress, Harriet sat crying and surrounded by her remaining five children, some of whom had cried themselves out, others sat in shock. The room was so aphotic that I too almost wept. The last time I had been in a living space so dark, was in our windowless hut on Fruits of the Spirit plantation and the master had just raped my mother.

"Harriet," said Patience. There was no response, "Harriet, I am here with the woman of whom I spoke, the Underground Railroad conductor, Dan Crispin's younger sister, Sarah."

Harriet looked up and said weakly, "Will you have a seat, Sarah?"

The children moved closer to her, leaving me a seat more appropriate for a small child. I am only 5' tall and my body was quite thin at the time. However, squeezing myself into the remaining chair would have required more dexterity than I believed I possessed.

"Please, darling children," said Harriet, "would you be so good as to go with Miss Starbuck?"

At any other time, Patience would have insisted they call her either by her first name or use Quaker formal which is both names. Perhaps the childless woman was so stunned by being directed—not asked—to care for a passel of children that she did not correct Harriet.

I surprised Harriet by taking her hand, she flinched a little then relaxed. "I am here to help thee if I may."

The subsequent conversation was a difficult one to enter. More than once one of us tried unsuccessfully to begin a sentence that would allow the other to meet in common space. After a few moments, I succumbed to a Quaker silence. We sat together for some time before Harriet said, "Sarah, people brighter than I speak of bittersweet tears. I have no more tears of any flavor to shed. Inside my heart is crying drops of blood."

She was the mistress of words that I hoped one day to be. I waited for more. "This is a painful dark time for me, Sarah. Have you ever lost a child?"

"Oh yes. In between my first and second live birth I lost three."

"My Charley was 18 months old when he died."

"Your loss is much different from my own."

"All losses differ in quality." I had no follow up statement. "We women are the ones who build the bearable structure in this society. Tell me of your losses and how it has constructed your present composure."

Knowing they were not the same magnitude as losing a child who could walk and was forming words, I told her that between the 1832 birth of Susan, my first child and my now eight year-old Eva, I had suffered three miscarriages. I knew each birth/ death day, how the little one appeared when the midwife showed me a small bundle of lifelessness, the face of my grief-stricken husband. I even recalled the names for each, names that heretofore, I had never disclosed to anyone: Kenneth, Marybeth and Hannah.

I had known before touching the cloth that no scissors have the power to precisely cut another's pain. When she predictably appeared unaffected, I took a great chance. Instead of seeking empathy from a drowning woman, I channeled my dear mother. Matriarchs hold keys that mere mortals do not. Silently seizing on an idea Harriet had introduced, I allowed myself to feel the bitter sweetness that I imagine was Mother's. I told Harriet that my mother had lost three teenage children when they had escaped seeking freedom. Before we left, Mother had acted as though she had a premonition that this would be our last time together before Heaven's Gate. Harriet let a tear fall. I went even further. I told her my mother was forced to watch her remaining children and her husband sold one by one to slave dealers. Harriet wept. I joined her, touching on-going hurts that I had never permitted myself to fully appreciate. Once inside the cave, I spoke of my dreams for each, one dashed after another and the fear no living soul would come to help my life feel more complete. It was not my intention but somewhere in the midst of my tale I too was crying. Before I lost total control I said, "She was carrying a new baby when she was sold away from us. I imagine she told herself for the unborn's sake she must find a way to let her spirit rise again."

She was not yet ready to say farewell to Charley--in my mind she could sustain his spirit until the day after eternity's end and Jehovah would find no fault. She spoke of Charley's budding personality and the man she had envisioned he would be. I believe the author's words landed on living Truth. She stood, opened the curtains and we both wiped our eyes, more from the vanishing darkness inside than the setting sun.

"We never learn love's definition until we try to stop loving those we have held and nurtured," said Harriet. I had nearly exhausted whatever bits of consolation I could easily reach so I held my silence. "I am so very sorry for your losses and those of you mother. Under the circumstances, I feel as though I have your dear mother's pain is a part of my own. What was her name?'

"Esi."

"'She cares' yet a man who could only see his own 'I' abused her?"

I heard her words as that of a writer not as a true guess.

I stood to leave. She was still standing unsteadily. "Is it not a great irony that I have spent so much of life trying to find ways to help you people and it is you who has helped me move forward?"

"If thy efforts is not to help with us instead of help for us is not something missing in the garment?"

When I began my pivot for the door, she touched my sleeve. I turned to fully face her and she opened her arms. We embraced as equals.

* * *

In the carriage, Patience asked what had unfolded with Harriett. I was still coming to terms with many things in our exchange. I took advantage of the Quakers love of silence and remained so for perhaps a mile or two of our five mile trip. Then I took her hand while usually looking off into the distance

"It is possible that nothing has more power to redeem than the death of a small child." I could feel by the change in her hand's pressure that she was surprised by my opening. I used my thumb to gently press her hand as signal that I had only just begun.

"Purity evaporating before a person's eyes, or an innocent

stillborn in whom you had hopes that must be denied, can bring out the best in anyone endowed with compassion."

"All mankind is endowed with compassion."

"Kind men do not support slavery and racial inequities. I was speaking primarily of mothers who have loved their baby for nine months before they have seen their babies. As for Harriett, I envy her having Charley for 18 months."

"It seems to be that such would make it harder to lose him."

"I am not denying thy observation. I am saying that to share a love, no matter the brevity, is a gift."

"Then thee thinks she is better?"

"I know that I am. Through her I allowed myself to feel the three miscarriages. When they happened, one by one, I put the love stored for each into Susan and occupied my mind with more focus on my seamstress work."

"And into thy husband?"

"There is no more than 100%. I am a Daddy's girl whose own father never shorted his mate. I consciously put increased love in my living child Susan and forced myself to work more focused with fabrics. Turning to face Patience, whose face was undefined in the near-darkness, "I filled space my babies deserved."

"Thee said forced."

"That was no slip of the tongue. I forced myself to forget. Through thy request that I help another I was led with Harriett to do what my mother would call, 're-remember' what never should have been overlooked or forgotten.

* * *

Kaye let me in, told me Zephyrine was feeling better. Indeed, she was at the dinner table eating dinner with her older sons. Kaye pointed toward Dan's office where a light was shining. I entered the room and was surprised to discover Lilith sitting at the desk. She had moved the papers I was perusing and was holding a pen. Seeing me she folded a paper on which she had sketched something for her eyes only.

"What may I ask is thee doing?"

"You can ask but that don't mean I'm going tell you."

I was exhausted and hungry. Although I had advanced toward her, abruptly I turned to leave her to her own business.

"Come back, child!"

I was nobody's child. For all I know we were about the same age. I kept walking.

"Don't be so high and mighty," she said in a conciliatory voice that I was surprised she possessed. She unfolded and held up her sketching. "This is for my gratitude journal. I been keeping one since I was breast high to a cricket."

Intrigued, I came nearer. I had seen hundreds of drawings in magazines and Patience had several paintings on her second floor, away from prying and disapproving Quaker eyes-- the Religious Society of Friends considers art frivolity. Lillith's lines were drawn with bold precision. Even when they undulated, or moved in circles, they did so with God's grace. Her spaces were filled with power instead of love. I could not imagine that such a woman had been inside a museum. Her influences must have been her own experiences. Who might she have been in another world?

I told myself it was magnificent. As I searched for a word that she might understand, she said, "I'm just grateful that Zee and her baby is fine. What do you think about what I drawed?"

"I am speechless. I don't know if it calls for thinking. Perhaps I should just feel."

"That's just why I won't let nobody teach me writing. What I want to say, words can't touch."

16

TIME

My youngest brother Babatunde is the source of this story. The preamble he learned from a friend of our mother who I never met and thus cannot vouchsafe for its contents. In fact, I did not even know of Babatunde, who others called Tune, until he hunted me down 26 years after Mother's death coincided with his own birth.

At the time of Mother's sale in 1827, slavery was more ubiquitous than the popular narrative describes it. As late as 1830, only Vermont was totally free of slaves. It was common-place for slaves in Virginia, Maryland, Delaware, Kentucky, and other upper south states to be sold to the faster growing states Louisiana, Mississippi, Alabama, and Georgia. Later Texas and Arkansas became destinations for torn asunder slave families and communities. Yes, as did the Shawnee and Wyandotte and later the Cherokee and Creek, we had our own Black Trail of Tears. It was larger than all of the Indian removals combined. Yes, it was an extension of the Middle Passage, but it was out in the open, beginning north of the Federal City, where thousands were gathered and flowing south and west. Yet its details were seldom discussed in the north and virtually ignored by Christian churches.

Colored folk in the long coffle marching south with Mama were chained or tied around the necks with ropes. The men had padlocks attached to their neck chains. Mama began on foot rope-tied with the other women. Both males and females had iron chains with staples and bolts on their wrists, alternately right and left to the people next to them. Mama's pregnancy increased her despondency and after several days she began to stumble involuntarily. Initially she was given a few lashes to encourage her but the foreman feared losing her and having his pay docked. He ordered the guards to place her in one of the caravan's wagons beside barrels of Sunday morning salt pork; whiskey for the guards; the bags of peppers, potatoes, yams, rice, beans, grits dried and corn on the cob. The slavers fed some of the same food to horses, mules and people.

Even in the wagon, her wrist was chained to a rusty clench in the wagon. When Mama's dear friend Yejide spoke of the long journey to my brother, she always explained that pregnant women were considered not only "2 for the price of one" bargains, but also proof that "more product was almost guaranteed."

Along the way, the slaves slept chained in jails or in fields while the guards took turns sleeping in taverns located near stores that sold additional foodstuffs and supplies. The slaves drank water on their knees beside the horses and mules drawing the wagons. Much of the way someone had a sorrow song going. After a sale in the Carolinas two fiddlers were purchased. After each of two daily meals they had to play until the foreman told them to stop. When they chose to do so, sometimes they would play at other times. Yejide said the music on their own time tended to be sadder and remind her of home. Some of the songs sung were old. Others were improvised as they walked along, mourning for those left behind or the expectation that they would be sold apart once the next sale began.

Mama died in childbirth. Some have said her real ailment was a broken heart caused by the times in which she lived.

Yejide, had recently been purchased right off the boat in Richmond and joined the coffle a few days after Mama did. Because they were both Fante, they had gravitated to each other. Yejide's kidnapping and purchase came almost twenty years after Federal law forbade the importation of slaves. I am writing in 1860 and those infernal slave ships are still arriving in American ports.

Mama died soon after childbirth. Yejide said when she saw her baby, she kissed his forehead and uttered what were to be her last words, "Thank Nyame." Yejide spent the rest of her life puzzling over Mother's words, but each of her older children understood them perfectly.

Yejide was sold as Judy. Along with her own small sons, she had claimed Esi's final child as hers. The slave dealer was happy to participate in the deception, for a baby with a mother brought more money than an orphan and Carwell Mustin believed purchasing whole families proved his Christianity. If he ever asked about the missing father, Yejide never mentioned it to Tune.

By Esi's final request her baby was named Babatunde. Mustin renamed him Tune and never asked Yejide if Judy was her real name. Yejide was the lone person on the plantation who called him by his mother-given name. Our sister Fannie, the keeper of the flame, told us Babatunde means "Father comes again."

* * *

Carolina Halam, Tune's teacher, had learned his banjo playing in the Piedmont and spent the prime of his life in southwestern Tennessee, before being sold across the river to Texas. Tune was his protégé and learned the craft so well that his playing had made his teacher expendable in the sight of Master Carwell. One of my brother's favorite compositions was the following:

ESI WAS MY MOTHER

Esi was my mama
'though I never felt her love
Esi was my mama
'though I never felt her love.
Died wearing chains.
Roof was sky above.

Mama, Mama
what they done did?
'lone ain't no way
for a li'l kid.

Esi was my mama
'though I never felt her love
Esi was my mama
'though I never felt her love.
One day by and by
meet again up in the sky.
You and me riding side by side
nobody know, how Tune done cried."

* * *

Carwell Mustin's plantation lay less than fifteen miles south of Memphis and equidistant east of the Mississippi River in Shelby County, Tennessee. Perhaps a quarter of his land was in DeSoto County, Mississippi. It had been stolen from the Chickasaw Indians and populated primarily with slaves imported from the Upper South. The big house was a Greek Revival Mansion supported by a slave quarters made up of a few dozen drafty log cabins, a carriage house. smoke house, shed, overseer's cabin and a huge sturdy horse stable capable of housing up to fifty horses.

Mustin stood before the assembly of five members of the household staff. "I and you are living in the time of America's Golden Age. As I remind you each time I have a birthday, I will make the gold. Together I and you will make it our business to be better Christians. Is that understood?"

"Yes sir, Cap'n Mustin, sir," was the universal reply.

When all but Eliza Bailey, the most trusted house slave, were dismissed, Mindy, his wife, said, "Why when their language is already so abomible do you deliberately teach them bad grammar?"

"When I speak to slaves, I am always teaching them reality. Only white trash would put them before himself in sentence or deed. To the refined, at all times, it is quality and then the quantity."

"I still believe they need to speak much more better."

"All they need to know is who rules, to keep clean, the time to go to work, and not to stop working too soon."

Mustin left the house to check on his race horses. As usual he saw one of his teenage slaves with Cocoa Dust, the prize horse of the area. From a young age my multi-talented brother had been drawn to horses. The first time he mounted one was because Zeb Campbell, son of the former overseer, had let him ride. Tune and Zeb had become friends as youngsters. In those days they had played games with the Mustins' two sons. At about age eight the fun and games ended. From then on the master forbade his sons from playing with "niggers and white trash." The abrupt ending had been difficult for all four boys, but in less than a year's time, the Mustin boys never spoke to Zeb or Tune unless they were giving one or the other an order or deriding the outcast's poverty.

When a mere sprite, Tune began sneaking out on moonless nights and taking horses on short rides around the area. More than once patrollers heard him and failed in their attempt to run him down to make certain the rider was not a slave. By the time Tune was in his early teens the master himself marveled at Tune's Sunday afternoon horse performances on the plantation. Tune could do more than race like a tornado. He had an uncanny ability to sit silently, barely moving the rope as he guided a horse left, right, clockwise, counterclockwise, forward, backward, horizontally, and diagonally. Some of his neighbors swore he was practicing "the black arts."

One afternoon, Mustin walked his wife down to the race track. She was so enthralled by his abilities that she called him, "A black unicorn."

"I dislike the nickname but Mendacity—"

"You know very well that I dislike that despised name my brother Albert gave to me."

"Forgive me yet again, Mindy, dear, but you have just given me a great idea on how best to capitalize on Tune's skills."

He called Tune over. "I've seen you racing around my track and riding around my plantation. You're a horse boy, sure as I was born. I'm going to give you a chance to be a man. I pronounce you a jockey. Every time you win, I'll give you a dollar a day until the next race. Lose and you get nothing. It's kind of like, what the Good Book says, 'for whosoever hath, to him shall be given; and whosoever hath not, from him shall be taken even that which he seemeth to have.' I and you will make the best of this situation."

Tune loved horses for reasons other than racing, but the possibility of earning a dollar a day was intriguing, especially when it was clear he was not being given an option.

From Nashville to New Orleans and a score of lesser towns, Tune became so successful that Mustin increased his generosity. He surprised everyone on the plantation by having other slaves build a small cabin for his favorite jockey. Furthermore, regardless of the workload in the fields, Mustin allowed Tune to sit with his banjo for hours at a time. Instead of begrudging Tune's release from the fields, the residents of the slave quarters felt blessed that Tune played wonderful music into the wee hours of the morning. Until proven otherwise, the one they called Tune was the greatest musician in the known world.

Tune's preferred audience lived on the next plantation, just across the Mississippi line. When he was in town, from Saturday night to Monday field call, his beloved Irene could spend the night being serenaded by her banjo playing lover.

One Sunday after church services, the heat was unbearable in his windowless cabin. Irene said, "Honey, couldn't your master've put at least one window in the cabin?"

"Sweets, he didn't build it. The fellows did."

"They just do what he tells them to."

"'Let's just be grateful for what we got and not worry what's not,' that's what Mama Yejide used to say.

The lovers left the cabin in search of a breeze. They found a westward leaning umbrageousness formed by a triangle of disparate trees standing in small clusters: maple, willow, and red oak. Their rendezvous was both canopied and close enough to a brook that in the background they could hear nature's music.

After kissing and hugging Tune plucked a medley of slow songs. He kissed Irene's thick braids at intervals and played with lyrics as they came to him. The lovers acted as though Sunday's sun would never set. Time is not as kind as soft words and tender strokes from hands made rough by slave drivers and clutching raw hide.

"What I wouldn't give for the free life," Tune said.

"You the freest nigger I know."

"I seen men that got their own free papers in their pocket and strut like a li'l red rooster too sorry to crow for day."

"You mean free like white folk be free, bossing us 'round, sipping toddies and such, wearing fine clothes and eating' like everyday is Christmas?"

"There's more to free than that, honey. When that sun go down tonight we soon be going our separate ways. Master Mustin and Master Warren will be laying back in the cut with their wives. They got in their hands all the time in the world."

"I can't deny what you say but them four don't have the kinda love we got."

"Nobody got our kinda love. The point is, we could have more love if we had more time."

"I know me some Tune, but I'm yet to figure out time. I can be in them cotton fields and time will last for what seems like now on. Then we can have our time together and time seem like the space between breaths."

"Hold your breath." He kissed her. "You can breathe now."

She opened her eyes. "Can I?"

* * *

A few weeks later, slaves from five plantations gathered for a rare Saturday night dance timed to lift spirits and insure a bountiful harvest. In the trees were scores of gourds brought from the fields and filled with fresh water to cool the sweaty and tone down the fire from the homemade brews allowed by the masters as a special treat.

Tune was the featured musician. While waiting for the slaves from the last plantation to arrive, a trio of elders sat together. They were the last three men left from those who had cleared virgin forest and built the Mustin's first log cabin--which was now used by the overseer--plowed and planted the first fields, and made the first roads in the area. Although still in the fields, they were too old to dance. Aging did not prevent them from enjoying good company and music. While holding a wide-ranging conversation, they chewed tobacco and listened to Tune strum his latest slow song.

Talk turned to Tune's playing. They knew he was eaves-dropping or "signifying," as they referred to listening to the conversations of others. However, as he prepared for the evening's festivities, he was unlikely to be critical of their banter.

"You should've run like your brother did when the flood almost took y'all's field back to Noah's days," said the first man.

Before the man addressed could speak, the second man said, "I wonder where that nigger run to. It was more moccasins in the water than mosquitoes on old grandad at sundown in mid-August."

"In case you missed it, he was talking to me," said the third man. Turning to the first man he said, "How the Hell I'm supposed to know where he ran? My brother always tried to act like he was gooder than Jesus. Maybe he walked on water all the way to Canada."

"I bet he drowned," said the first man.

"Then why'd you ask me?"

Tune played a part of a composition he'd been working on for days. Unsatisfied he quit and thought a while, still playing a few notes on his banjo every few seconds. When the composition seemed to come to him whole cloth, Tune continued strumming slowly and listening so deeply to the beauty of his own playing that his mind appeared closed to all else in the world.

First man took a sip from the moonshine jug, pointed to Tune and said, "I knew the boy before he knew what a banjo was."

"Yeh, well, I knowed him when he was named Baby or Baba or something else off the barn wall."

Third man said, "Pass that bottle while you resting. First man obliged. "Y'all niggers don't know nothing. I knowed his granddaddy. He was as tall as Tune is short."

"You just a lie and the truth ain't in you," said the first man. "He come here a orphan. How you know a granddaddy when the boy don't know the daddy?"

"I know who your daddy is and he a fine looking nigger if I have to say so about myself!"

"Why don't y'all shut up and let the man warm up?" asked Eliza Bailey. "Y'all so drunk on Campbell's whiskey you don't even know yourselves. If you did you could keep good time instead of being all off the beat with your feet and talking dumb with your toothless gums."

Tune was ready for his opening song.

SUGAR CANE

"Mr. Charley took my sugar cane.
Mr. Charley took my sugar cane.
Now even when it's sunny

feel like all day Sunday rain.

"Come home for my wife,
done drove me like a dog.
My bed been swept clean.
Is this the fire?
Am I the log?

"Mr. Charley how this be right?
You got yours and mine,
both wrapped up tight.

"Mr. Charley took my sugar cane.
Now even when it's sunny
feel like all day Sunday rain.

"Darling, give me your hand
tell me I'm your man
I ain't mad at you.
Just can't live life
with my tan turning blue."

The music was well played but Tune noted the quiet reaction to the lyrics. Perhaps he had exposed other folks' nightmares. The people did not come to sulk, and Tune was one of the people.

"Now here come Slim Jake and his jumping fiddle, and Apeony the great Chickasaw cane flute man. Slim Jake can keep time like raindrops on a hot day and Apeony can make a sweet singing bird weep. Listen to this li'l shuffle some Cherokees taught me the last time I was in East Alabama. We going do like Grandpa told Grandma. We going take it north of your toes."

The musicians started at a tempo just a little faster than that of the opening song. By the fourth verse of the word-free song they were speeding and the crowd was whirling with abandon.

Midway through the dance, one of the three elders pointed at the Mustins. The master and his wife were up and moving.

"Is that supposed to be dancing?" asked the first man.

"Master's big feet couldn't keep time if he was Judge Warren's clock," said the second.

"Quit talking so loud," said the third. "If he hear us we could take 40 lashes."

The first said, "Hear us? Hell fire, judging from the way they stumbling about, they can't even hear the music."

The musicians closed with:

THREE IN THE MORNING

"Irene it's three in the morning
and you just keep' dancing.
Irene it's three in the morning
and you just keep' dancing.
Your big feet is all dirty
and you still dancing
"Dance, baby, dance.
You all I need.
You my only cotton.
I'm your only seed.
"Irene, it's sure enough three.
Them fields is waiting
for you and for me.
One more dance, baby.
That's all I got in me.
Baby, slow down,

My lungs about to pin me.
"Irene it's three in the morning
and you just keep' dancing."

As people applauded and begged for more, Eliza Bailey came up to Irene and whispered in her ear, "That boy sure does love you."

"You can say it out loud," said Irene. "He declares the truth just like this, 'I love me some Irene!'"

The people laughed and Tune called Irene over. She said, "You the best banjo stroker I ever heard, Tune."

"You just trying to make me feel good. Old Man Halam could pick circles around me."

"Not so and you know it!" said Irene. "Everybody say Mister Halam picked old timey music. He ain't been places you done seen. You know what young folk want."

He pulled her close. "I know what Tune want. 'Cause of all them races I won, I been too long on the road and that new cabin ain't quite broke in yet. It's high time we made up for the strokes that's been lost."

During the dance, some of Campbell family members sneaked over from Scotch Hollow and stole eight chickens and several dozen eggs. In the morning Eliza went to feed the chickens and collect eggs. She immediately reported the thefts.

Captain Mustin had the slaves assembled. They stood in little groups waiting for whatever bad news came next. Mustin ranted for what felt like an hour blaming the slaves for the lost chickens, last spring's hard rains, the present heat, wasting his time. He circled back to the chickens and declared, "Ya'll's guilty as sin!"

Although they were not above taking what they believed they had earned but were denied, in this incident they were innocent. Several had seen the Campbells making the thefts. Still they refused to inform the Mustins.

"I know you niggers," said Mustin. "Y'all love chicken like Jesus loved wine. Let's see if you can change water to chicken because water's all you get today, and then they'll be vegetables only and no chicken until I say when."

"I may be good at more than one thing," said Tune, "but how could I steal chickens and play banjo at the same time?"

The others thought Mustin would be outraged by being publicly questioned by a slave. Instead Mustin stopped the overseer from cocking his whip and said, "I wasn't talking about you, Tune. You can still eat chicken. I might even send you a pork chop."

"No, thank you master," said Tune recognizing such treatment might make his neighbors envious. "I won't eat what they can't eat."

Mustin talked a better punishment than he could control. The delay in rations did not relegate his slaves to water that Sunday. They kept their own small vegetable plots, were plentiful and possums careless. Sunday's squirrel stew did not compare with chicken stewed or fried. Two weeks without domesticated meat and only potatoes and beans from the Big House garden, galled. It did not make them vegetarians.

Eliza Bailey finished her chores in the big house, took off her full- length apron, straightened her head rag and ran over to Tune's shanty. "Guess what happened while you were away, Tune?"

"Master said, 'Eliza Mae Bailey, you is a free woman!'"

"I done told you ninety-eleven times, ain't no downhome Mae in this Maryland gal's name! Guess like you got some sense."

"I give up."

"You just a liar in love with lazy thinking." He laughed and she said, "I found a baby and I'm gonna keep it."

"I thought you said you was through with that kinda business."

"This baby got as much black blood as I got white blood."

"Blood ain't nothing but blood," said Tune. "If it's a folk it's a folk."

"I don't need yo' young ass to teach me sense, Tune. What I'm talking about is ain't no slave around here done had this baby. I asked those in the know."

Tune paused. "You reckon that wild Campbell gal done left it?"

"It ain't my job to reckon what white folk done did. I'm just taking this girl child for my own, and when she grow up, I ain't going play the game Aunt Judy did with you. All she going know is Eliza Bailey is her mama."

"Sounds good but what did Master Mustin say?"

"I ain't seen that rascal in two days but I asked Mistress Mindy and she said he won't mind so long as he got papers on the baby. Me and her get along like two peas in a pod. She went to see Judge Warren and..." She withdrew a paper from the top of her dress. Here's the paper. It's my time to be happy. I named him after my long lost favorite brother, Frederick Bailey, the second."

"What's that 'the second' for?"

"Master Mustin named his boy after hisself Carwell Mustin, II."

"Don't this beat all, a woman with grown kids done become a mama again."

* * *

While seated together in the church balcony, Tune and Irene and the other slaves watched the whites take the bread and wine. Few questioned the separation of faith and slaves but some whispered among themselves about the happenings on various plantations.

"Ain't it about time for us to have a baby like Eliza's?" asked Irene.

"A baby?" said Tune. "Who in their right mind would bring a baby into slavery. Eliza is about as crazy as a addled hound that's got into the moonshine." He chuckled at his own joke then in a panic said, "You still doing what Miss Sadie taught you about baby stopping?"

"If I ain't you won't know 'til it's too late to do anything but be happy."

All day long Tune thought about the unsatisfactory exchange in the balcony. When it came time to separate for the six-day work week he said, "Honey, when the time is right—I done saved every dollar I done made and bet on myself enough to make a lot more than Mustin gave me—"

"That cheat ain't gave you nothing. You the one making him money!"

"One way or the other, I'm going buy me and you out. But if it's a baby in your belly, Judge Warren going own that baby too."

"You mean we ain't got time for no baby?"

"Time for anything is the space after slavery."

17

LET THERE BE LIGHT

T his is my tale. However, I received priceless aid from my younger brother Luther.

* * *

We learned that Frederick Douglass was coming by train from Cincinnati to nearby Harveysburg. Douglass had made a tour as an associate with the publisher of The Liberator, William Lloyd Garrison in 1847 but I had not been able to hear them. Later they had argued because Douglass wanted the freedom to print his own newspaper, the North Star. Patience had long been friends with both men but seemed to prefer Douglass because he was one of the few male abolitionists to openly support the women's conference that was held in Seneca Falls in 1848. Removed from his mentor's shadow, Douglass often traveled as the featured speaker.

Luther Duncan settled down in the train seat next to his employer. Douglass said, "I assure you I was pained to hear our host so denigrate the Irish."

"If they were the leaders in the attacks on our people in '29 and '41, it would be incomprehensible for there to be a lack of enmity from a colored leader."

"Ah, that mystifying word 'they'. It is unwise to paint all people of any race with the same brush. There are good Irish just as there are black informers in the back pockets of those who oppress us. Did I ever tell you that when I was abroad, I heard Irish field workers sing songs with the same heartfelt tones as we hear in the south and that all over 'the Emerald Isle' I was treated like a hero? Moreover, it was two Irishmen who first gave me the idea to run away. Those good men were dock workers, not successful robbers like the slavers."

"I don't know these stories."

"As for those noble dock workers, one day when I was 12 or 13, I volunteered to help these men, Seamus and Brendan. While I was on my break for the noontime meal, the Irishmen were unloading ballast for my master. Through what a preacher such as yourself would call Divine Providence, I walked toward the ship grabbing stones with each step."

"Why would a master waste a slave's time ordering him to pick up stones?"

"We both know that all of slavery is a waste of time...something the oppressed will never regain. To your point, ballast are stones stored in the bottom of ships...the same ballast sacks that Seamus and Brendan were unloading. These men were one step up from me, Frederick Bailey, the bonded boy. They were these underpaid, despised men.

"Brendan asked me if I were a slave. I picked up another stone and, without looking at him, said, 'For life.' The affirmative answer I was forced to give shamed me. Baltimore had twenty times more slaves than there was ballast in the ship. I wished they would not shame me even as I was voluntarily helping them. To my surprise Seamus said, 'There is no justice to that' and Brendan added, 'If I was you, laddie, I'd run away up north'.

"They were not shaming. They were empowering. If I live to be 100 I will always credit those 'Sons of Erin' with much of my life's alacrity."

Luther paused before saying, "I needed no Irishmen to plant the idea of freedom in my mind. In time you would have concluded the same thing by yourself."

"Of that I am certain, but in the interim would have been many a wasted month or year or five. The finder's fee goes to Seamus and Brendan."

Douglass looked out the window at the passing countryside that included an occasional stream; gently undulating low hills in the distance; ash, oak and beech trees; corn and wheat fields. Everywhere he looked was greens in myriad shades broken up by the occasional browns of prairies, dirt road and scattered herds of cows, pigs and horses.

He turned his back to Luther who was studying a Latin book and said, "I suppose each man is guided by little happenings."

The aisle seat was Luther's. He laid down his book. "As for little things, once when I was but a small boy, I was walking with my mother. She tightened her hand when the master looked her way. 'Be a warrior, Luther,' said Mama. "All my life I've wondered if she were talking more to herself or to me. I would sooner die than have my wife or daughter placed in such a position of pain, by American, Englishman, Lunarian, Irishman. When the Seminoles called, I became a warrior."

"You certainly were that when I was attacked in Pendleton!" said Douglass.

Luther savored the memory of their meeting, his rescue from a mob of the man who would become his employer, was one of his life's highlights. They both watched the countryside whizz by. For an hour Douglass was more pensive than usual. Meanwhile Luther read. Finally, Douglass said, "Although she forbade you accompany me to England, it was so good of your wife to let you come with me this last time, 'for old time's sake'."

Instead of admitting the difficulty it had convincing Angelica that he was not shirking his responsibility to his family, he said, "Did it ever occur to you that it might have been more difficult getting my congregation to free me?"

"Angelica grows tired of your face?"

Luther showed his profile and said, "No sane woman could tire of this." They laughed.

"Perhaps Angelica, seeing how in all these years Anna has been the model of faithfulness, has chosen to do likewise."

"They have never met."

"That is a great misfortune, but the story of Anna's staking me the money to escape after the conversation with the Irishmen and her skill in rearing our children while I spent most of time on the road helping to free our people must be well known."

Luther paused before saying, "I am afraid that women like your wife and my mother are often lost to history."

"This is a lost world," Douglass sighed. A moment later he clapped his hands. "But men such as we two will save it."

"I must also credit Angelica more fully. Her father was one of the biggest colored preachers in Philadelphia. She was educated and comely. She could have chosen anyone. Through divine Providence, she chose me, a nobody to Philadelphia's black society."

"You are a modest man, Luther. From slave to runaway youth, to Seminole warrior, to minister of the gospel is an impressive journey. Your father-in-law did not give you that tiny congregation which you have built into a large voice in Philadelphia. You founded it. Respect yourself more." Douglass mused. "Yet, I still have a difficult time thinking of you as a preacher."

"I am not alone in my ministry, Fred. Some call you a preacher."

"I may preach but preacher with a single flock I could never be. There is something missing in your major pillar called prayer. Until I fled for freedom, I prayed with each breath. God was as silent as a slave's unmarked grave. Then I prayed with my legs. There was my answer."

"Have you not heard the old saying, 'The Lord helps those who help themselves'?"

Douglass smiled. "The first time I heard it, I said like the prophet, Isaiah, 'Here am I send me'."

"They are right. Frederick Douglass is a preacher!" The two laughed. "Do you know verse 14 from Obadiah 's only chapter?"

"So short a tale should be easily memorized, but no. It escapes me."

"Good word choice. It reads, "Neither shouldest thou have stood in the crossway, to cut off those of his that did escape; neither shouldest thou have delivered up those of his that did remain in the day of distress'."

"Had I known that the good prophet was an abolitionist, I would have enlisted his services long ago!" Both laughed. "Ah, Luther we have been away from each other far too long. No one is more loyal nor makes me laugh though these demonic days as you do."

"You have spent a lifetime traveling with sober sides."

"It's not their sobriety that bothers me. It is the fact that despite ample evidence to the contrary, they continue believing the immoral can suddenly become moral. They seek light when we need fire. They seek love in a mist when we need lightning in the storm. What say you, Reverend?"

"You grow formal?" they chuckled. "Looking back on my life, I remember myself as the Black Seminole who killed no less than six American soldiers who were invading the best sanctuary I have ever known; one where I was a full citizen. Now I travel with a passport in my own country and am almost without rights. I must admit I have to believe in the hope of white redemption."

"Does the story end there?"

"If I have my way it does. And peacefully. But before I was Seminole warrior, I was the descendant of Fante warriors. Furthermore, Jesus traced his line to David the warrior king. If cornered, I will pray with my fists, pikes, guns, bows and arrows, cannons... "

"Unlike with other abolitionists, I have no reason to doubt your heart. Let us change the subject to more down to earth things."

"As in the old days, before I was a preacher, I am traveling with you as secretary. Dictate."

Douglass laughed. "Don't take this down!" Both chuckled. "I think I'll miss Julia more than I anticipated."

"Miss Griffiths was a fine tutor and secretary," said Luther.

"I hear a but hidden from the wind."

"If so, it's your own."

"My task would be lighter, and my burden easier and more delightful, if not for the belief of most that friends from the opposite sex jeopardize relationships. What are your thoughts on the matter?"

"Don't worry about Garrison's charges. Even with your recent dispute, he's more friend and ally than prosecuting attorney and hostile judge."

"Garrison helped make me, but in the end, I had to be true to Douglass or risk despising myself." He sighed. "How many times have I said no struggle, no progress. Being absent one from the other is more than struggle. It is an added burden."

Luther wondered if Douglass were referring to Griffith or to Garrison.

The men rode in silence for a while before Douglass returned to the subject that bothered him most that day. "It is scorching irony that, to me, sometimes Julia was like a mermaid."

"A mermaid?"

"Yes, a woman of myth: half female and half..."

"Male?"

"No, no, my friend," said Douglass. "The secretary who puts words in an employer's mouth risks cutting off his feet. Half woman, half fish."

Luther considered the women he had loved. Neither the Black Seminole Adriana nor his wife Angelica reminded him anything of a fish and if anyone had been caught, he was the one. Douglass watched Luther's perplexed face, laughed. "My friend, there is a somber sense of disparity between us. You have an underdeveloped imagination and mine is as fertile as natural justice."

Embarrassed, Luther said, "I can imagine our people free. That's enough imagination for me."

"When we reach the National Black Convention in Rochester, I will speak on unifying our activism and opposing emigration to Africa, Canada or the West Indies. You, my friend, give the assembly a few stirring moments concentrating on rededication to ending this madness."

"I will be allowed to speak?" asked Luther in surprise.

"Why not? Haven't we been silenced enough in this country without me muzzling a preacher?"

The issue settled, Douglass said sadly, "The two of us traverse these metal rails everywhere meeting invisible fences stronger than steel that deny our worth. Only the belief that one day America will grant us respect, if not love, fuels my continuation. I would suppose I also speak for you?"

"The employer has every right to speak for the secretary."

"Do not even say so in jest. Men must have their own voices or there is no justice."

* * *

The train pulled into the Harveysburg station. Douglass rose from his seat, took a few steps toward the exit, paused, and returned to the subject of the Englishwoman. "There are those with diabolical intent who claim Julia wrote and I spoke."

'I wish it had stopped there,' thought Luther. 'I wish it would all stop. We have to prepare for these country bumpkins.'

"That is why I so often speak spontaneously," said Douglass. "Let them see that I am the author of my genius. It is her companionship that I will miss most, Luther. That and the faces of whites as they saw her constantly by my side. She was a symbol that we were defying society. What say you, my friend?"

Luther stood. "As my father would say, 'fiat lux'."

"I love your new rallying call, 'Let there be light'. You are a precious man, Luther. And you are right. Let's put aside the missing white friend and concentrate on the captives and these kind souls who are looking for entertainment if not truth. It is time to give our guests that for which they came. Now is the time; the important time."

Douglass sent out Luther first. The bodyguard turned protégé/secretary was well-dressed but too intelligent to have his suit outshine his employer's. Silently Luther bowed slightly and pointed toward the main attraction. Amidst cheers,

Douglass disembarked and moved toward a makeshift platform. Luther fell in behind him. A deafening welcome greeted the man who was more famous than the combined reputations of all other black men of his era.

None in the crowd were more excited than my visiting sister Fannie, Patience and most of their abolitionist friends and relatives. I was merely in attendance for the excitement. My mind had been made up on the subject the first day I recognized that I was able to think. At Patience's urging, as though we were an update version of the Black-Frenchman's Three Musketeers, I had made matching silk dresses and reticules for Fannie, Patience and myself. Respectively, Fannie wore a burgundy dress with grey reticule; Patience a grey dress with burgundy reticule; and I a gold dress with burgundy reticule. When I completed my work, Patience had insisted on overpaying me even for my own. I had told her such extravagance was absurd, but she had dismissed my complaint with, "Indulge me. I have always wanted to pretend we are related."

Seamstress that I am I was impressed by Douglass' navy-blue suit and silver brocade waistcoat. To the consternation of several men, women whispered about how striking he appeared, but at the time I thought he was no more than a man, handsome yes. My Charles was a paler but more comely and well muscled man.

Douglass scanned the crowd with supreme confidence, touched his powder blue bow tie as though tempted to straighten what was already perfectly straight, smiled at catching himself in a vain moment, then more fully at the crowd. When we quieted our applause, he removed his top hat, handing it to his associate. His mane was like a lion's, combed back, bushy and thick. He used his magnificent baritone voice to set the tone for the day. I was forced to change my opinion of the man. He was an Adonis made flesh.

As a tease, he stopped perhaps ten minutes into his talk. Cued, although the end was false, we responded with applause. His magnificent words encouraging freedom for the slaves certainly deserved the accolades. From a stern face, he segued graciously into a smile. It felt as though he were only on earth to be together with we villagers. Recharged by the spectators, he continued speaking for forty-five enthralling minutes before stopping almost in mid-sentence. Robbing us of an opportunity to call for more with a spin toward his associate.

"Now for a few words from my faithful secretary, Luther Duncan, a man born in Culpeper, Virginia on a plantation that had the ironically delightful name 'Fruits of the Spirit'. Slavers often attest their Christian sincerity not by turning water to wine but Truth on its head. I suppose the chief fruits, although left unspoken and dishonored, were the captives bound and beaten. Luther, would you address the crowd for a moment?"

"Ask them, how can they shrink from agitating against oppression. Proceed to lay before them the right cause. In the loftiest eloquence, demonstrate how a black man's mind can develop despite the lie that we are not human. Sprinkle your English with salient Latin phrases. Be a pattern for aspiring children and men on the rise."

As soon as Fruits of the Spirit had been named, Fannie and I were as focused as I had been when fleeing slavery. Without realizing he had relatives present, Luther rose his seat. His black suit with matching tie had no waist coat, but his shoes showed the son of a cobbler's respect for polish. He was not scheduled to speak but any good Baptist minister realizes he may at any time be required to sermonize. Luther was prepared but for an entirely different message than the one outlined by Douglass.

Luther ended his short, employer-scripted speech with, "'Arduum sane munus,' Life is a truly arduous task. However, we will overcome slavery pari passu, moving together. Fiat lux! Let there be light.'"

It was Douglass' plan to close out the gathering with part two of his oration. I am certain it was guaranteed to move us to a still higher level. In the pause between our Luther's ending and Douglass's reprise, my brother was nearly knocked off his feet by Fannie and I running up to embrace our long-lost sibling. We were in his arms when he asked the nearest person on the speaker's platform, "Who are these wild women?"

"We are your sisters, Sarah and Fannie!"

Douglass who was slightly younger than all three of us, clapped his hands, bowed and, trying to reclaim the spotlight, said, "This is obviously a cunning arrangement to entrap the defenseless." Many in the crowd were already shedding tears of joy as though they themselves were being reunited with lost relatives. As one the audience roared with laughter at Douglass words. Feeding the mood, he said, "If a few words of Latin brings forth blandishments from such beauties, I must learn the arcane properties of the Caesars."

Only a small portion of the crowd immediately returned their attention to the great man. Here was entertainment in the hinterland. This day was as much Luther's as any other in his life.

Before his employer grew impatient, Luther said, "Can we speak privately? I feel we're making a spectacle of a dream."

With Fannie and me leading him several yards away, under a buckeye tree, Luther missed Douglass' finale. Later I considered that without my brother's presence as bodyguard, had we been in a place like Cincinnati, his absence may have led to a bully boy attack. Our community was founded by Quakers but the brutish live where they will or may. At the time of the day's reunion, to the House of Esi, Douglass was a forgotten man.

"My Jehovah, sisters!" said Luther wiping the tears of joy from his eyes. "All these years, traveling from Florida to the Indian Country, Canada to Philadelphia and not finding one of you and now here are two!"

"It feels like love returned," I said.

"Are there more nearby? Are you alone?"

"Dan and Robin were here," I said.

"They've both gone to join mother in the other world," said Fannie. "Had you come a few weeks earlier a slew of us were gathered together."

As though he had not heard about the living, our brother honed in on the one he loved most. "Mama's dead? Oh no!"

"Yes, we learned of her death through a friend of ours, Patience Starbuck."

"Patience Starbuck the abolitionist?"

"Yes, Patience Starbuck, the abolitionist," said a voice from behind.

"Why, we've been acquainted with each other for years," said Luther turning to her. "Why didn't you tell me you knew my family?"

"We have not exchanged twenty words," she paused, and he remembered that as Douglass' employee it had always been his job to remain to the rear. "And if I'd thought for a minute that thee is who I now know thee to be, I would not have hesitated. Why did thee never mention Fruits of the Spirit?"

"It wasn't me who mentioned it today," said Luther. "I try to live in the now and the future, never resurrecting places where I was disgraced."

"Fruits of the Spirit doesn't exist anymore," said Fannie.

"What?"

"Soon after Sarah escaped with Robin and Dan and sold

the rest of us apart, Anne Prescott sold the plantation and freed the remaining slaves," said Fannie.

"Anne Prescott...that witch an emancipator? When?"

"Did thee not hear, Fannie? Our family had been broken up only a short while," I said softly. "She freed the others."

"Jehovah!" said Luther starting to cry in earnest. "Jehovah, why did you forsake us?"

The silence was both brief and awkward. Patience said, "I am told that there are those who call thee 'Reverend. The True Revered One never forsakes His lambs."

"Thee may be right, Patience," I said, "but thee does not have the right to say this to those of us who have been slaves."

"Perhaps I am not as much a relative as I dreamed," said Patience.

"This is not about you, Patience," said Fannie.

At that moment Luther saw Douglass approach and quickly dried his eyes. Douglass must have seen Luther's recomposing but addressed Patience instead, "I see the notorious Patience Starbuck is also here. I thought I saw you almost in Quaker grey and tripleting with these beauties. Your health remains good, Patience?"

"As always, my health suffices, Fred."

"I had forgotten that you live near this hamlet. "Before she could reply to his description of her chosen home area, Douglass turned to Fannie and me. "Now if you would be so kind, Luther, indulge my interest by introducing these out-of-the-common-way women."

"Frederick Douglass, these are my older sisters—"

"Sisters will do," I interrupted.

"Fannie and Sarah, this is the esteemed Frederick Douglass."

"Fred," said Patience. "I know thee and thy party are scheduled to stay at a local house, but be my guest for dinner.

My cook, Mandy, is the best thee is likely to see for some time."

"Yes, of course you are right, Patience," said Douglass. "These siblings deserve time to themselves. I too have long lost siblings who I would love to see. Perchance have you ever come across any Bailey women by the names of Sarah, Eliza, Kitty or Arianna? My brother's name was Perry. I have not seen any of them in almost twenty years."

"I'm afraid I don't know any Baileys," I said.

He turned to Fannie who said, "I wish I could help."

"I thought not, but if one man can be fortunate, why not two?" asked Douglass. He noticed a well-dressed black man wringing his hands and guessed the problem.

Douglass turned to Patience. "It seems my esteemed host is here. Through the controversy over refusing to integrate the academy, Harveysburg has made its colored population suffer sufficiently. I will pass on your invitation and dine where I have already promised to hear the concerns of the colored populace."

"Thank you, Mr. Douglass," said his host. "My name is Asa Pratt, sir, and my women folk have been cooking for days. They would have died or killed me, one or the other, had I returned without you."

"I am honored to be your guest, Mr. Pratt," said Douglass extending his hand in greeting. "And following the repast would you or your good wife care to introduce me before I speak at the Zion Baptist African-American Church? Luther has had his day in the sun and perhaps may be otherwise occupied."

The host was speechless.

"I will host thee another day, Frederick," Patience said.

"I will not let you off so lightly," said Douglass. "If the

esteemed Mandy is still on duty come breakfast time...you may complete the sentence."

"Oh, Fred, you are a dear. The northbound train leaves at noon and 3pm. Which is thee scheduled to ride?"

"Our tickets say noon, but judging from today's empty seats and Luther's new interests," he stopped to laugh and gesture with both palms open to the three of us, "tickets can be changed easier than we can change this lost nation."

"For now, come with us, Patience," I said. "I may not be in Mandy's class as a cook, but I believe I can bring joy to my brother's palate and have satisfied yours countless times over the years."

"Forgive me, Sarah," said Patience. "I have overstepped too many boundaries in one afternoon. I will not intrude on a sibling gathering."

* * *

That night, I made an easily put-together meal of favorite dishes including fried chicken, collard greens seasoned with pork, and Maryland biscuits, that I learned to prepare after our escape. I topped off everything with Mama's sweet potato cobbler. Fannie helped while Luther sat asking about our dead brothers and everyone's children. We also informed him that several family members were probably in Cincinnati.

"If so, how could I have recognized them?"

"They would have been with Dan's wife Zephyrine," said Fannie.

"So he did marry her. He was certainly sweet enough on her back in Fruits of the Spirit. Is she still as beautiful as in her youth?"

"Who is?" said Fannie.

"You two." Fannie said, "You were born to flatter."

"Was I?"

I should have said something in follow up for it was clear he was carrying a burden. I let the moment pass by simply saying, "These are hard times."

Luther clearly prevented himself from introducing something. Instead he said something that was a difficult subject for each of us. "You can't know how much I've missed Mama. This year makes 25 years. Every time it rains, I think of her."

"We all remember when she prophesied our separation and said no matter where we might be, she would be in each shower's 99th drop'," said Fannie.

Luther told us the circumstances under which he had met our father in Philadelphia.

"I still marvel that he has returned to calling himself Kofi?" asked Fannie.

"It suits him better than the white man's Kenneth," said Luther. He recited the stories Daddy had shared with him, including many about Fante-land, a subject he refused to touch when we were growing up. He said that learning that once in Philadelphia, Daddy had set aside his dreams of being accepted as a full American were almost as sad as when he learned of Mama's death. "My pain comes not so much from the lost dream but that millions are suffering from the same disease."

Before leaving, Luther said, "I like it here amongst the Buckeyes, I shall return."

I said, "Should that much light be brought into my life, much will be restored."

18

THE HISTORIAN

The heart of this story belongs to my sister Fannie, but I freely admit that my love for both Fannie and, the now deceased, Patience Starbuck colors it.

* * *

In 1853 Patience Starbuck accepted a marriage proposal from a man who had loved the 55 year-old woman since the two were teenagers. I believe his love was so strong that he would have gone to Comancheria to exchange vows. When she accepted what may have been Thomas Hussey's fortieth proposal of marriage, she wrote back that she wished to be married in her native Nantucket where the unkissed fiancé still lived. No sane woman travels alone in America. With four children and a husband I was not available. The year before, for the second time in her life, Fannie's family had been decimated by cholera. She had left the Rocky Mountains and was living with me in Waynesville when Patience accepted the marriage proposal. It was my sister who accompanied Patience down the Ohio and Mississippi Rivers with the intention of traveling the same ocean that had been the seed of the Starbuck fortune. One of their stops was in New Orleans where they were guests of Patience's southern free-labor attorney David Dequindre.

Dequindre's home was a 17-room mansion, replete with high ceilings, a second equally crafted staircase, three parlors, eight crystal chandeliers, twelve fireplaces—each with matching imported marble mantles. Mahogany was used wherever wood was required and three different double-glass doors separated the well-appointed rooms which were also adorned, where appropriate, with marble. The house was maintained by a staff of seven white house servants who had come to their position in the same fashion as had the chef and his wife, bonded as indentured workers.

Dequindre had his associate, Louis Duchamps, give Patience a tour of the city with Fannie as an attendant. Duchamps arrived wearing a suit with a grey half-waisted coat, burgundy ascot and French cuffs sleeves adorned by diamond cuff links. The coachman, Jesse Cailloux, wore a top hat that had been discarded by an aristocrat who he had complimented and a black suit. Duchamps ordered Jesse to drive them through the French Quarter. In route occasionally Duchamps would point out something he felt certain would impress a Yankee. Patience was on amazingly well-mannered behavior. Not once did she inquire how the building or garden was tied to slave labor.

Upon arrival in the French Quarter, Duchamps asked Patience if she wanted to stroll down Rampart and Canal streets. She surprised him by asking, "Might Jesse drive us to the docks?"

"He knows the way but, may I ask why you might be interested in one of the least refined sections of this great city?"

"Before we go directly to the restaurant, I would like to say hello to a woman I met the first time I was here," said Patience.

Duchamp looked at his pocket watch. "We are running early for the mid-day meal. I suppose the detour is acceptable."

"Good," said Patience, "Jesse, doth thee by chance know Chimène Amelin?"

"Yes ma'am, I know her and all her peoples."

"Could thee find her for me. Unless Louis objects I would like for her to accompany Fannie while we dine."

The driver turned to look at Duchamp who said, "Proceed, Jesse."

Jesse drove them to the wharf, stopping a few yards from Chimène's cart. "There she is, Madame. Shall I fetch her?"

"If you would," said Duchamp.

Jesse released a deafening whistle that jarred both white passengers. A slightly wrinkled black woman in a billowing, faded green dress turned around disgusted, but when Jesse gestured with his hand to come forward she got a good look at the splendid carriage and approached.

"Doth thee remember me?" asked Patience.

"I remember the first man to pay me a dollar for a bushel," said Chimène smiling despite four missing front teeth. "How could I forget a woman who gave me $18 for a maracujá?"

"Perhaps I was too free on that scorchingly hot day!" said Patience.

"'Too free' don't exist, Madame."

"Might I purchase some of thy time?"

"I have sold many things, but never time. Perhaps you should rephrase your question."

Patience thought a moment. "Would thee be willing to show my servant around town? Jesse will drive."

"I have known Jesse since the old days, but I have never had the pleasure of sitting as he operated a fine carriage."

"Good. It is settled."

"I did not hear the amount, Madame," said Chimène. "A gentleman taught me the word mundane. As a business woman, I like mundane notions."

"As a Quaker I am not inclined to bartering. Would thee accept a double match of whatever thy employee earns in thy absence."

"That is à propos de my 'time'!"

Chimène climbed into the three-seat carriage next to Fannie and Duchamp said, "Take us to Antoine's, Jesse."

Once at the restaurant, Patience said to Fannie, "It embarrasses for me to admit neither thee nor Chimène can be seated here. The two of you may ride about town under Jesse's watchful eye or wait in the carriage." The blacks had already been apprised of the plan and did not comment. Feeling guilty, Patience added, "I suppose under the circumstance I should refuse to dine."

"Patience," said Fannie, "you've been talking about Antoine's since you decided to take this way home. Go on in; Chimène and I will be fine with the driver."

"Is thee certain?"

"Enjoy yourself," said Fannie.

"Jesse," said Patience, "We may be dining for two or more hours."

"Yes, ma'am," said Jesse, touching the brim of his hat.

"Good," said Patience. "That is an excellent compromise."

Duchamp had watched everything unfold before saying, "Madame, I advise you to keep your servant near. New Orleans is not always the benign place it appears to be."

"Thank thee for thy advice," said Patience curtly. "We enjoy our day: she enjoys hers."

"I have advised and will say no more."

Patience stared him down. When he took a bit too long to

cast his eyes aside Patience said, "One of us is an employee. The other is not." The two whites entered the restricted restaurant and Antoine Alciatore, the proprietor, seated them at the law firm's usual table. At Patience's request Duchamp ordered for the two of them. Their meal featured oysters in a rich buttery sauce, pommes de terre soufflés and pompano en papillote.

When they were well out of hearing Jesse said, "That woman use some words like Quaker ladies I met back a few years ago except they was both in grey and white bonnets. She be wearing blue."

"You must be color-blind Jesse, teal ain't blue," said Chimène. "And when she cares to she's about as bossy as my Grandma Bernie."

◊◊◊◊◊◊

To show the utmost respect to his visiting passenger, when pointing something out, Jesse always stopped the coach, allowed Fannie to see the site in its fullness. The first time she asked for a closer view, he escorted her onto the ground but let Chimène fend for herself. On the second such occasion, Fannie said, "Either help us both or neither. I am no lady."

"I am," said Chimène, waiting for her old friend to do his duty.

Although the heat and humidity surpassed anything Fannie had experienced, New Orleans in June was a beautiful city filled with weeping willows and flowering maple trees, hibiscus and red iris flowers, dancing ladybugs, and slow-moving well-dressed strollers. Occasionally Chimène pointed out a distinguished man accompanied by a light brown belle. "It is not his wife but she gets the better part of him" or "That's my cousin's cousin although she stopped claiming me when he claimed her."

A scream pierced the air. The three blacks stopped in their tracks. "I know that sound," said Fannie. It was a cat-o' nine-tails repeatedly striking flesh causing a response for mercy that was too late in coming.

"The beating is a couple blocks away," said Jesse. "Whoever the poor man is he got the wrong idea. Them folk don't stop 'til they reach the paid for number of lashes."

"White folk send slaves there to be beat," added Chimène. "Even the good ones."

"That's just a lie, Chimène," said Jesse. "Good, white and slave owners don't go together no more than sugar, poop and love."

She did not argue. Jesse turned the carriage away from the sound of beating. He came upon a vacant, trapezoidal space on Saint Charles Street. "This used to be where the St. Charles Hotel stood," Jesse pointed. The massive entrance had been executed in Corinthian style. The courtyard was octagonal, and the hotel topped by a domed rotunda.

"It's got every shape but love," said Jesse under his breath. "One day I got took up to that dome by my master's half-wit son. You could see every which way outside of the city. If I was half the man my uncle was I would have pushed the little fool off."

"You talk a lot," said Chimène, "for a man who has come up short more times than not."

In its heyday, the St. Charles Hotel had featured four stories and 350 bedrooms, huge dining rooms, meeting rooms and parlors. In those days, the first floor buzzed with commercial shops, boutiques, bathing rooms, and even a wine cellar. But the most infamous space was the saloon and its immense bar. To keep the drinkers genial, it was well stocked with finger food that was free to the customers. Here deals were struck, duel challenges were made, and restraint was lost.

One woman was on each of Jesse's arms when he said, "Y'all believe in closing your eyes and seeing backwards? Even if you don't, do it today." While their eyes were closed Jesse said, "Inside that building, more slaves and cotton got sold than anywhere else in America."

"Hell, I know that," said Chimène. "I thought you was going shed some light on a subject."

"Just listen for a change. Jesse is trying to show y'all something that can't be seen with eyes." Then he lowered his voice. "I was sold there once myself. We had to bathe and shave—I liked my beard, but the wants of slaves don't get tolerated. Then us men got dressed in the cheapest shirts, pants, shoes, coats and even top hats. They put the women in calico dresses that showed everything they got and a tignon that was as cheap as master's smile. They had trained slaves show us how they wanted us to walk, stand, even smile. We had to stand tallest to smallest while the buyers felt anywhere on our bodies they took a mind to. One fool jiggled me in the whatchamacallits and said he reckoned I could produce product. Seven or eight looked in mouth like I was a horse. If they'd seen your missing teeth, Chimene, they would've walked on by."

"They ain't always been missing and if they was still here I'd bite you in your scrawny ass."

Jesse laughed. "And a li'l while ago, she tried to claim she's a lady."

"A lady can bite a gentleman and still be prim and proper," said Chimène.

"Ain't that what Jesse just said?" When he saw that Chimène missed the joke he added, "You can't even bite a maracujá so you ain't hardly no lady."

She opened her eyes and picked up a street stone. She

hurled it so close to Jesse's head that if it had been a book he might have read the title. Then she closed her eyes again as though nothing had happened.

"This woman is crazy as a gator frying a potater!" said Jesse.

"Please, you two," said Fannie. "Continue your story, Jesse."

"They put men on one side, women on the other. They sold us like whiskey right on the bar top. One of the most meanest slavers, Deacon Daniel Whitfield, used to celebrate each slave he bought saying 'This wench is for Jesus' or 'This coon is for Jesus'. Then he'd dance a jig grinning with his corn cob toofethes shining like dirty gold and his breath smelling like a unwashed mule's hole."

Jesse stopped and his breathing became labored.

Fannie opened her eyes, reached out and touched his arm. "Jesse, what's wrong!"

After a moment he calmed himself. "That's when it happened."

"What happened?"

"My brother Matty just snapped like a dry branch stepped on by a king-sized brogan. He grabbed one of them captain's guns and pointed it at this white fool who done pawed his wife. He barely had time to pull the trigger and send that devil to Hell before they was on him like white on rice. He shoulda known he couldn't stop the sell."

""I see why he snapped," said Fannie. "Your brother did not care what happened to him."

"I did. They lynched him right in that far corner. I heard tell they let the body stink til even white folks couldn't stand the smell." He paused. "Y'all can open your eyes now."

They resumed their walk. "You should have seen the fire

when the St. Charles burned down," said Chimène. "I thought that's what Jesse was going to talk about."

"For all you know I might be the one who set it," said Jesse in a whisper.

"You say that loud enough and, kidding or not, you'll be swinging like Matty." She waited for a response that never came then continued, "It burned down not long ago."

"On January 18, 1851," said Jesse almost shouting. "Oughtta be a damn holiday."

"This fool is trying to get us all lynched!" said Chimène, looking around to see if any angry whites were coming their way. In a hushed voice she said, "Except for them that had Yankee-wrote insurance policies, fortunes got lost just like that." She snapped her fingers.

"Thank God, old Deacon Whitfield was inside," said Jesse. "Jehovah burnt him crispy as charcoal. I hope he like breaking hot bricks in Hell. Be the only black man there."

"God don't like ugly," said Chimène.

"God didn't like pretty when it come to the Saint Charles," said Jesse. "It weren't the first time God rose up against this ugly down here. When my mama was a little girl, about 500 slaves rose up like the children of Israel in Egypt."

"I like reading," said Fannie, "but I never heard of this."

"Who the ones writing books wrote after the Bible? Ain't no white preacher going compare black slaves with Jewish slaves, and why would they want you to know we need our Exodus or that Charles Deslondes tried to play Moses and lead us outta Louisiana?" said Jesse. "Mama said back in 1811 Deslondes figured the regular militia was out east fighting the Injins. He got together some men and his warriors almost took New Orleans. Miss Fannie, I do believe they was going bring another Haiti. Black rule for black folk, make everybody white be the slaves or suspected slaves."

"I don't believe that for a second," said Chimène. "We ain't low down like them. Them rebels would have killed some and freed the rest."

"Freed?" said Jesse shocked.

"Freed them from fearing us," said Chimène.

Jesse dismissed her words with a wave. "Mama saw 'em. And she heard 'em. Slave and freedmen marching like Justice. 'Such a collection of Bambara drums ain't nobody heard in these parts,' was how Mama put it. Problem was most of the slaves was too afraid to help. Some even helped the white folk."

"Some folk ain't got the sense to know that they is slaves," said Chimène. "My guess is they commenced to counting guns and figured dead was worse than slavery. My granddaddy was one of 'em that fought. He was a mighty man."

"How did it end?" asked Fannie.

"Granddaddy was one of the hung but it ain't ended," said Chimène in a whisper. "Grandma Bernie told me when I was a girl, 'Don't think we lost just because we ain't won yet'."

"The whites brought out troops and the militia," said Jesse. "Like Chimène said, better arms, more fighting men. Her granddaddy was one of the lucky ones. They caught and cut off the heads of fifty or so. One of 'em was Mama's Uncle Smillett who was a officer of Deslondes'. White folk put they heads up on pikes for the crows to eat and scare black folk back to being docile."

"Did it work?" asked Fannie.

"Do Jesse act docile?" asked Jesse. "Let me say it loud and clear, I'm the one burned down the St. Charles!"

Chimène looked around quickly. Satisfied that no one was within earshot she said in her normal voice, "My man ain't docile either."

"I taught him everything he know," said Jesse, pinching her arm.

"You just a lie and the truth ain't in you! You didn't even know what a kiss was 'til I showed you how to pucker up, even then you missed my lips and hit my nose."

They both laughed. The trio walked arm-in-arm a little further and Jesse said, "You know white folk don't know what they want. Come War of 1812 and the battle of New Orleans, they needed as many colored fighters as they could get. My God-daddy, James Roberts was one of 'em. Before he got sold down here, he'd fought with Washington in the War for Independence, so when Andrew Jackson asked for help, he was ready to show folk he was a true man. He figured Washington had lied about freeing the slave fighters but no two high and mighty white men would tell the same lie. Fooled him! Hundreds of slaves and a couple of troops of freed colored men fought on the promise the slaves would be set free. There was even a couple hundred Haitians that come over to help out, and you know how white folk hate them—'til they need something from 'em. And Injins! They was in the process of seeing the white men steal everything but they toenails still they helped too and ain't one white man said, 'You boys can just stand over there on the sidelines and watch while we get killed'."

Fannie said, "You sounded surprised that Haitians volunteered to help fight the British. "

"Ain't nobody on earth American white folk hate more than Haitians. Them Haitians had already fought and got they self free. Kicked Napoleon's ass worse than Luke's daddy ever kicked his."

Chimène added, "White folk's scared Haitians might bring their magic up in here. Annick, my daughter back there watching the cart, she keep enough gris gris in her bag to make sure no one does the Amelin family a bad." She stopped and whispered, "I got enough hidden in my house to turn out half Louisiana and all of Mississippi, that hateful state where I was sold once. Sneaked out and come back here where your mistress' lawyer, Dequindre put me to work for five years as a maid then got me a free paper."

"I'd say that was good of 'em," said Jesse, "but the world know how he just use the down and out and pretend to be a saint. The man is lower than a sure enough slaver. They don't pretend nothing except that they're Christians."

"Don't the thought of gris gris scare you, Fannie?" asked Chimène.

Fannie had known her share of mystic healers out west. After two fights with cholera, being owned by two different depraved slaveholders, encounters with Blackfeet and Comanches, nothing in Louisiana would make her blink. "How did the fighting go with that mixed army?"

"From what my God-daddy said, Jackson ordered the slaves to make a parapet wall of dirt and wood and a deep moat around it. Some of the Tennessee volunteers got mad because they was against working in the first place, and now here come some slaves right along side of 'em. They thought that meant they could quit and go home. Them boys had been raised to believe they might be poor but least ways they ain't slaves and here they was being ordered to work beside colored men. They tried to desert but Jackson said, 'Hell no! Don't Go! All caught deserters will be shot and skinned like Creeks.'

"Four days and nights, with li'l rest, all them boys worked with Jackson shouting and cussing at 'em to hurry up. They built up a fine eight-foot high fort and filled in that moat. Once they was finished, Jackson sent my God-daddy to help the pirates who was working a few miles away. He used to say, 'I was shoveling them cannon balls to them pirates faster than master shoved biscuits into his big mouth'."

"You make it sound almost like a party," said Fannie.

"It wasn't a party. The Brits got cut to pieces, but a lot of slaves didn't make it out alive neither," his voice grew quiet. "Fact is, when they counted the dead on both sides, the dead slaves didn't even count like three-fifths a man. They didn't count 'em at all."

"They fought for no reason except to be forgot," said Chimène.

"My God-daddy lived but that damned Jackson told the same lie Washington did."

"You mean they beat the British and still the ones that helped went back into slavery?"

"You asked that like you surprised," said Chimène. "I see your white mistress treat you like you got some worth, but you can go a year of Sundays and not find another one knows a thing about justice."

"Sure as the President's wife don't mistake chittlin' juice for fine wine," said Jesse. "God-daddy woulda died a slave if I hadn't won big at the Metarie Race track and bought his freedom. That was the first time I ever made big money. I'll be doggone if it didn't take me two years to do it again. It really ain't no way to come out ahead on them ponies, but for me it's like whiskey is for some folk. I may not drink whiskey, but Jesse just can't get enough of racing."

"So you are a gambling man?" asked Fannie.

"Guilty, your honor."

Chimène said, "Jesse is not a man to give up on much. I ain't never been 'round him when he didn't find a way to work in that stale joke. Giving up on betting ain't hardly going happen either."

Jesse smiled. "Thank you kindly, Chimène. I see you still got a sweet spot for Jesse."

"What I got is some gris gris to freeze your scrawny--"

Jesse laughed. "Neither the horses, my wife or the coming

Jubilee, is likely to make me quit doing what I love doing till I can't do what I'm doing no more."

"Jesse is hopeless. It's his son, Andre, that I worry about," said Chimène. "My niece has two children by that scamp."

"Don't boil over, Chimène. I'm keeping Andre away from the races and concentrating on boxing, and I'm biding my time in this here 'redemption time' 'til I get enough money to risk betting big again and praying hard for the last two years. Yes, Sunday will make two years I been preaching on Glavier Street—"

"I did not realize you're a preacher, Jesse," said Fannie.

"I preach in parables that slavery must end. If I couldn't use the Bible, I'd find something else. It ain't the book going save us; it's the message. Just don't call me Reverend Cailloux and we'll get along fine," he said laughing.

During their tour, Fannie saw numerous slaves who were lighter in skin than Patience. "Chimène," she said, "I thought white folk can't be slaves."

"They can't," she said.

"But some of these slaves look like white."

"Whatever they look like, they ain't classified as white," said Jesse.

"Classified?"

"Let me tell you classifications New Orleans style," said Jesse. "You got Sacatra, Griffe, Marabon, Mulatto, Quadroon, Metif, Meamelouc, Quarteron, and Sang-mele. A Sacatra is half Griffe and half Black. A Griffe is half Black and half Mulatto. A Marabon is half Mulatto and half Griffe. A Mulatto is half White and half Black. A Quadroon is half White and half Mulatto. A Metif is half White and half Quadroon. A Meamelouc is half White and half Metif. A Quarteron is half White and half Meamelouc. A Sang-mele is half White and half Quarteron."

"My children got three different mamas and ain't nary one of my children classified the same as me or they mama. My daughter-in-law Felicie so white it took her babies awhile to know she wasn't colored, but Felicie know who she is."

"Down here everybody has to know their place," said Chimène.

Fannie was unconvinced so Jesse added, "I was sitting in the back of the courtroom when Mr. Duchamp was lawyering. He had a client who claimed to be white. The child was whiter than a picture of snow in Harper's magazine. Mr. Duchamp pointed out her thin nose and stringy blond hair and blue eyes. The other lawyer made her show her shoulder and brought up a doctor who claimed if she was white her skin 'oughtta been more creamy'. The judge scratched his head and hemmed and hawed."

"Who won the case?"

"Mr. Duchamp won, but the judge used to be Mr. Dequindre's partner. To this day, I don't believe if I was Jesus Christ I could tell if she was white or a Sang-mele. She coulda even been a Meamelouc like the other lawyer claimed." Almost as an afterthought he added, "You got all of that?"

"I let it go in one ear and out the other," said Fannie.

"I wish some of the rest of us had as much sense as you," said Chimène. "That's what broke us up. My mama thought Jesse was too dark."

"That's the first I heard that tale!" said Jesse.

"After she kept saying it," said Chimène, "I checked and there was more wrong with you than the color of your skin."

"Don't get me started," said Jesse. "I'll tell everything I know. "

"Please, Jesse," said Fannie. "Keep to the histories and way from bickering."

Jesse bit his lip before continuing. "I can't prove it, but I think all of them classifications was made up to set us against each other, so we would be less likely to rise up against the ones on top. One way or the other, I'm a Griffe, more black than anything. Chimène's mother was right. A black man is a mighty man. Too much for a Quadroon like her to handle."

"Meamelouc and you know it!" said Chimène.

"Pleassse!" said Jesse.

"Don't ask me what I really am," said Chimène. "Only my mother knows and she did not tell."

Jesse laughed with her.

"Do you know where your people came from in Africa, Jesse?"

"My father was mostly Ovimbundu; my mother all Fante," said Jesse.

"Both my parents were Fante."

"We could be cousins."

"We probably are cousins."

"Let me tell you a bit about the Akan in the New World, Miss Fannie. The rebellion down here wasn't the only one them Akans been in. Akans was leaders in a good many revolts. You wanna hear me call roll?"

"I would love to."

"Before he does, my mama's mama's mama's was a true Wolof, salt water from Sierre Leone," said Chimène. "They ain't no docile folk neither."

"Them Wolofs some good people too. As I recall, taste like chocolate, though some parts is more like chicken," said Jesse smiling.

"If you don't let me alone, Jesse, I'll tell my husband to use his Bowie knife to cut you where you don't want no steel."

He laughed. "Let me shed some light on the Akan. New York City in 1736, Antigua and Guyana in 1763, Grenada in 1795, here in 1811, South Carolina in 1822, Jamaica 1831.

Them's our revolutions. Each one was led by Akans. I don't know where some of those places is but I know they happened. Our men is mighty men, never meant to be slaves."

"The only way to become a slave is if Eshu tricks you," said Chimène.

"Eshu reminds me of my mother's Anansi," said Fannie.

"I have heard about that foolish trickster," said Chimène. "I would castrate them both more clean than I pare fruit."

When Jesse stopped laughing Fannie said, "How do you know this history?"

"A man don't know his history don't know hisself."

"Sounds good," said Chimène, "but that ain't no answer."

"Stand still and be taught," said Jesse. "I was taught to remember stuff because I come from griots. Mama's master fancied hisself a history man. One day while she was fanning to keep the mosquites and flies off him, he was talking with a friend and they got to wondering why except for them few rebels, most slaves seem harmless. He talked 'round Mama as if she was too stupid to care. She'd get a teenchy bit here and a speck there, tell me anything she thought was worth remembering. I'll bet there's more. At least there was enough for her master to write the governor to put more patrollers on the road."

"With all you say you know," said Fannie, "how could it be, Jesse, you never said a single thing about women warriors?"

"Warriors are men," said Jesse with certainty.

"That foolishness is why you only got to touch me a couple of times," said Chimène.

"Whose arm you on now?" asked Jesse.

"Arm touching is all a fool like you is likely to get from me or any sensible woman."

"Old age is not agreeable to your rememory."

"Cold in hand wasn't agreeable to your wishes was it?" asked Chimène bitterly.

"Yeh, you left me," said Jesse, "but that was the mistake of your life."

"Funny it ain't never felt like one."

Ignoring banter turned edgy, Fannie said, "My mother was a warrior although I never saw her with a gun."

"I am a warrior too," said Chimène. "I'd kick Jesse's ass right here except it would embarrass him in front of white folk on the street."

"Jesse," said Fannie, "stop laughing and answer me this: did the women who loved the rebels approve of revolting and what happened to them after the men lost in that revolt you spoke of?"

"They ain't in the story," said Jesse.

"How can we get stuck with peacemaking and healing what has been wounded or lost and then be left out of the story?"

Jesse shrugged. "Ask Chimène. She thinks she knows so much."

"I know a woman who knows the whole," said Chimène, "but her name ain't Chimène."

"What's her name?" asked Jesse. "I need to talk to her."

"When you feel a lightning bolt in your pants you'll learn her name."

They climbed back into the carriage. "We have been away for some time," said Fannie.

"I suppose you're right, Miss Fannie," said Jesse. "We better get back to Antoine's before they come out. I'd hate to be sent back to the sugar fields for being late."

"You're a slave, Jesse? I thought you were a free man."

"I was born free but I lost my freedom at the Metarie race

course a while back. I was drunk and bet myself against five of Duchamp's slaves."

"Jesse, how could you?" asked Fannie.

"It wasn't the first time," he said. "The other two times I won. Sold 'em right back to their masters and pocketed my money. With a little luck and a lot of tips I'll be free again soon."

"Can't you see that by selling them back into slavery you were little better than white masters or P.C. Richards?" asked Fannie.

"Don't compare me to that colored man! He's a disgrace to the race."

"You also sadden me," said Fannie.

"Me too," said Chimène. "Why does he make you sad?"

"His gambling and selling those people back instead of freeing them."

"I heard tell Injins gamble as much or more than the black man," said Jesse. "Wasn't you married to an Injin?"

"That's your excuse for gambling away your freedom? I never knew an Indian who would even think of that."

"I didn't mean to sadden nobody," said Jesse sincerely apologizing. "Aside from the races and being with my kinfolk, Louisiana ain't nothing but misery tea. You been out and about. You seen a place where a colored man can be happy?"

Fannie thought briefly and said wistfully, "Not in the States."

19

TURNING

My dear friend, Patience Starbuck, had a suitor who waited more than forty years for her to say, "I will." He may have been the most surprised person on earth when she at last both consented to marry him and said she would come to him for a wedding on the island of Nantucket. After spending decades without visiting once, she wanted to return to their birth place from which he had never left.

I had known Patience since my escape from slavery in 1827, when she not yet 30. We had even traveled together incognito as mistress and slave in a glorious 1832 rescue of one of my brothers. I knew that in most endeavors she was motivated by her desire for freedom. I judged first in her heart the to be an extreme passion to be unencumbered with slavery. Empowering friends ranked just behind freedom to be herself.

The day after she made the decision to marry—even before Thomas Hussey had returned his acceptance of her acceptance —she came to visit me. She told me of her change of mind. While I was trying to make sense of it all she handed me two bookmarked catalogs and showed me dresses that she wanted me to make for her trousseau. I would suppose, had Quakers claimed saints some of them were blushing in their grave. As I studied them in the catalog she said, "After I make a fresh pot of coffee I will tell thee of my itinerary."

I was working on a particularly stressful section of another customer's dress and welcomed her offer. She returned carrying on a tray that she had given me a few years before when she wished to purchase a new one. On it were cups, the pot and the last two slices of short cake, I did not have the heart to explain the sweets were intended for my husband and I when he took his mid-morning break from the fields. This usually solemn woman was acting so giddy over the turn of events that asking her to cease and desist seemed unjust. She did not seem to notice when I set aside my husband's slice and sipped my coffee.

Once the decision to marry had been made she had set down and planned how best to honor her roots as a one who had been orphaned when her father and brothers had gone down at some unknown place as whalers. Instead of overland, she had planned to take steamships down the Ohio and Mississippi Rivers, across the Gulf of Mexico, around the tip of Florida and up the country's coast.

"I have been living land-locked but water is in my veins. I will make several convenient stops to visit friends in Louisville, New Orleans, Charleston..." she paused before continuing. "Matters become more complicated. I must keep my promise and see the Grimkes in Philadelphia but I wanted to gift myself with a stop in New York City then on to Nantucket."

"I don't see the problem. Surely such a voyage will take weeks. There must be a day or two to please thy desire."

She wiped an unseen crumb from her lips and said, "Removing the nut from the shell: I should not skip over making a call on Johns Hopkins in Baltimore. I must free him."

It had never occurred to me that one of the richest men in America needed freeing. Patience had often spoken of the fact that the wealth he had made for her with his railroad corporation nearly matched the combined income from all of her other businesses.

Seeing my perplexed face, she said, "The man is nearly as much a slave to false notions of the Religious Society of Friends as I was to believing marrying Thomas Hussey would limit my own freedom."

"There is still something missing in this cloth."

She laughed and said, "Following Thomas's last letter—he writes quarterly, propose on his birthday and my own-- I privately promised myself that if he asked me one more time I would consent. Moreover, I had secured steamship schedules. Thus I know that there is no way to see other friends and see Johns unless I miss my excursions in New York! What shall I do?"

"What would thy mother do?"

"My mother? My biological mother died young and my second was sickly before she too died. I hardly knew either."

"Thee often criticizes men who claim to be self-made. Was there not a woman whose decision making has helped guide thee?"

I knew the answer before posing my query. She had spoken so often of Jane Boston, the colored servant who had "watched over" her while the Starbuck menfolk were out to sea that I assumed she realized, the woman had actually reared her.

She went into a period of silence and I continued working on my customer's dress. Several minutes later, Patience said, "Jane would cancel the trip to New York and stop in Baltimore to rescue Johns." She took the last sip from her third cup of coffee, smiled and said while standing, "I do make a good cup, if I must say so myself." She laughed again and said, "But thee did make the extraordinary cake. Thee must share the recipe."

She kissed my forehead which was bent to needle and thread and said, "But I have never pretended to be as faithful as Jane. I will only postpone my trip to New York to the return trip from fulfilling my own happiness. Outbound I will stop in Baltimore."

Patience believed she needed a traveling companion. My recently widowed sister Fannie served in that capacity. Sadly, from the outset Fannie had to pose as Patience's slave in order to keep herself from being kidnapped and sold as one. I am dependent on Fannie's testimony for this story. I firmly believe that she should be the one who writes it but she is a reluctant author and has given me leave to retell her experiences. To her budding glory, she has insisted, for once, that she sign off before publication. Does this mean that she found some small concerns with previous stories of hers that I have told? If so, she is too much a middle sister to say so. Bless her and her love.

From Cincinnati they stopped in Louisville, New Orleans and Charleston, South Carolina before docking in the Patapsco River at Baltimore's intersection of Light and Pratt Street.

The sensation of a cooling sea breeze was left behind on the water. The new dominance was a mixture of smells from fish, crab, coffee, tea, peanuts, and rum. It was mid-morning. The hawkers screamed out what they had for shoppers and the prostitutes displayed their offerings.

"This is where our friend, Fred Douglass was enslaved

when he ran away. Is it not exciting being where history was made?" asked Patience.

"My mother taught that history is wherever there are people," said Fannie.

"Come with me and I will make memorable moments with a new dress. She already wore an emerald colored dress that I had designed for her that would make Quakers blush. She had insisted I cut the neckline lower than my preference. Fannie a much more modestly designed ivory colored dress. Patience noticed that most street walkers dresses closer in their ability to catch eyes than was Fannie's.

"Must thee always dress in so plain a fashion?" asked Patience.

"My spirit is not like yours."

"Then I will indulge my own once more."

Patience sent their bags to her hotel as she led them in shopping for a new dress. Fannie told her employer she needed no more than the three dresses with her and was thankful Patience did not press her into the embarrassing position of having to explain colored women were not allowed to try on garments even in Cincinnati shops.

Leaving the boutique behind, they passed a grand slave mart kept by Austin Woolfolk at the head of Pratt Street. A sign on the building read, "300 slaves desired between 13-25 years of age. Cash and highest prices paid."

"I thought we were too far north for this," said Fannie.

"Really?" asked Patience. "In some nations north may be a direction. In America, north is a state of mind. Our north can be a haven, but it is far from any person of color's heaven."

"But I thought you said slaves are no longer sold in the District of Columbia and we are miles north."

"That is true," said Patience. "They are not dealt openly, but there remain hundreds of slaves in the nation's capital. For most Americans the land of the free does not include thee or thy people. A white woman is barely better respected."

"And yet," said Fannie, "even without voting privileges and lacking most property rights, I could see from the way Miss Anne, my slave mistresses, and her friends lived their lives that they were benefitting from their husbands' rule."

"I cannot dispute what is clear truth. They had privilege. So do I even though I have never kept slaves. This guilt galls but I can only set my heart and actions to correcting these hateful rifts. I would escape accepting these ill-gotten privileges but where do I begin?"

On the second day in Baltimore, Patience and Fannie were strolling the city when a policeman addressed the white woman, "Ma'am, in about an hour we will be lighting the gas lights." Patience thanked him and he walked past Fannie without acknowledging her presence.

Patience missed the significance of the shunning and hailed a coach to where they were scheduled to spend the night, the Quaker businessman Johns Hopkins' summer home in the suburb of Clifton Park. Hopkins's mother was a Janney. Thus, he was a cousin to many of the Quakers who lived in Patience's community. He was also a frequent correspondent and a co-investor in the Baltimore and Ohio Railroad Line.

In route, Patience talked about the estate. "I have yet to see what is 330 acres acquired quite reasonably when one of our

partners, Captain Henry Thompson was in distress over business misfortunes."

"Do you mean he took advantage of a friend?" asked
Fannie.

Patience thought a while before saying, "I suppose one
could make that argument, but Johns is a bachelor and he did
not require a second home. Paying top dollar would have been
unnecessary. The captain owned several transport ships traveling from Boston to New Orleans. No doubt a few of those
were also purchased during some downturn or other. That is
the nature of business."

"Dare I ask if given the Captain's route he also dealt in
slave goods and perhaps slaves themselves?"

"Oh, Fannie, I have no idea but thee may well be correct.
Since I personally purchase only slave-free merchandise and
only was united with the captain as investors in the railroad I
cannot say for certain."

They arrived when dusk was just gathering. There were
only a few lights shining in the windows of the great house on
the hill, "This is a bachelor's house?" asked Fannie.

"It is more of a mansion with an estate. He does entertain a
great deal and the Hopkins are a large family. Thee should
know, however, although this is a slave state, Johns is an abolitionist who employee no slaves to tend his orchards, gardens,
glass house and grounds. There are also none working in his
home. He employees quite a number and writes lovingly of
them in the letters we exchange.

"What say thee of the tower? It reminds me of
Nantucket."

"The craftsmanship appears to be as fine as the one you
have on your house."

"If we are blessed, perhaps at sunrise, he will allow us to see
the view to the harbor. I would so love to see the sun rise from

the water. Later we may walk in his extensive gardens. We do not have to leave until the rise of the mid-day meal."

* * *

A servant met Patience and Fannie at the door. "Welcome to Clifton Hills Estate. We are expecting a Miss Patience Starbuck and guest. Judging by the newspaper rendition I was shown, you are her."

"I am," said Patience surprised. "And which Newspaper might that have been?"

"A Mr, Brandeis from Louisville, Kentucky sent it recently. I believe it was The Daily Journal. We only receive progressive newspapers from all over the south, it is the only one we receive from that city. Your bags arrived from the hotel an hour ago and are in the hall between your rooms. For now, walk this way."

He led them a few steps and silently paused so that they could admire a huge wall mural of a view of Naples. Watching Patience's eyes closely, when she had contented herself in drinking in the beauty, he said, "My employer does not have the time to bother with traveling. Bits of the world are brought to us."

Fannie noticed how his pride in his employer's possessions mirrored that of slaves she had known.

He led Patience and Fannie into a huge room where they found a long-legged man with thinning dark hair dressed in such bedraggled Quaker clothing that those unfamiliar with the religion might have thought he was a vagabond.

"I am pleased to host thee, Patience Starbuck," said Hopkins with a smile and twinkling sea-blue eyes. "Welcome to my little villa."

"Some in Ohio say that my house is too large for a single woman," said Patience. "Whatever would they say of this dwelling? There are those among us who do love quiet elegance. Are there not, Friend?" He smiled and she added, "We thank thee for thy kindness, Johns Hopkins, may I introduce thee to my good friend and traveling companion, Fannie Swift?"

"Swift Eagle is her full surname as I recall," said Johns Hopkins. "So, this is the illustrious woman of whom thee have written so eloquently, Patience."

"Yes," said Patience.

Hopkins took Fannie's hand and said, "And thee lived out among the Bannocks and Shoshone?"

"Yes, sir," said Fannie.

"I am no 'sir,' but I am an avid reader of the travels of Lewis and Clark and they speak often and well of those esteemed Indians."

"She also lived for a season among the Comanche."

"That must have been a fearsome experience!" When Fannie failed to comment, Hopkins said, "Fannie, thee will spend the night in the same room that the Marquis de Lafayette used. Gilbert was a committed abolitionist you know."

"Yes, I have heard as much. I appreciate the honor…"

"Johnsie." He returned his gaze to Patience. "Considering the many letters that we have exchanged, here at my home you both may call me by my more intimate name, 'Johnsie'."

"What an honor," said Patience.

"Is that what it is?" He smiled and escorted them into a luxurious parlor with polished wood everywhere. The windows were floor to ceiling, looking out on a gracious porch with well-trimmed grounds in the foreground. He motioned for them to sit on a loveseat and asked, "Will you have something to drink?"

"I have been known to have a small cordial on rare occasions but surely will not imbibe of your 'Hopkins Best Whiskey'."

"Will I never live that down?" Hopkins laughed. "Moving grain by Conestoga over hilly, nearly mountainous terrain, forced me to have my customers liquify their corn and place the product in easily transportable barrels. What made it my 'best' was it was my only whiskey and it formed much of my early income. Those co-joined facts would have made what some connoisseurs refer to as 'rot-gut' my 'best'."

"I will pass on 'swigs' of any aged brew thee may still have stored. Should thee have a tiny cherry or peach cordial I might have a few sips."

They all laughed, and Hopkins said, "Better yet, in honor of your visit I have a special passion fruit cordial. Patience and passion do have the same root."

"I speak no Latin but Fannie's sister Sarah does. She informed me years ago that thy understanding is correct."

Hopkins waited for Fannie to announce her preference.

"Sir, few things satisfy me more than clear water."

Patience reached into a huge bag that she had brought with her. "Here, friend, is a knitted stole from thy Springboro cousins. I am instructed to say, 'Perhaps this will keep the chill from thy legs while reading in winter'."

Hopkins bounced the scarlet and gray stole's up and down in his hands. "What heft! I shall use this sturdy garment to keep warm during the cool evenings. It's almost as thick as a blanket. Only a pioneer woman could have transported such beyond the mountains. Was it also in a barrel? Give them my heart filled thanks."

Patience laughed. "I have only carried it the short distance from the city to thy estate. As thee well knows, we came by sea and there were men a plenty willing to assist with moving our 'produce'."

Hopkins motioned and handed the stole to a second servant standing duty in a far corner. Then he said to Patience, "Although Quaker politics in Ohio are warm, the state must be cooler than I thought."

"Thee is certainly right about the politics," said Patience. "Those of us who have joined Indiana Yearly Meeting of Anti-Slavery Friends have been nearly isolated from the rest of the Religious Society."

"Times have long been much hotter here. As I recall, you have never lived in a state where slavery is legal. Years ago the grandfather for whom I was named was friends with the grandfather of Supreme Court Chief Justice Taney."

"Taney was born into a Quaker family?" asked Patience surprised.

"Yes and no. His mother's father, Roger Brooke, was a Quaker who owned slaves. When in 1781 the meeting discussed making it a requirement for all who own slaves to release those poor souls, he refused. Roger was 3 years old at the time. No Quaker has he been as an adult and I fear more bad decisions will be forthcoming from him than ever his grandfather dreamed."

"May I ask if your grandfather owned slaves?" asked Fannie.

"Thee may and he did," said Hopkins. "At the Yearly Meeting's decision, almost immediately he began the process of freeing his without seeking compensation. Because of the infirm who could not fend for themselves in this cruel world, it took him years before he was slave-free. In the interim he cared for those who had cared for him. As for the hale and hearty, I am told that even before the emancipation they were all treated well." He read skepticism in Fannie's eyes. "I'm sure thee hast heard that tale many times. Would thee care to comment?"

Fannie hesitated only a moment before saying, "Stealing

people's labor and confining them to live at a human's mercy can never be proper treatment."

Patience added her agreement and then informed Hopkins that she had visited the Brandeis family in Louisville. They had asked her to thank John Tyson for speaking out in favor of Jewish rights.

"The Brandeis family are beacons in that part of the world. We write each other from time to time. As for my cousin John, when I see him, I will convey your words. That it took until 1825 for my Jewish neighbors to win their rights here is almost as great a stain as the state's continuance of slavery."

Patience blurted out, "Johnsie, I stopped over in Baltimore to personally tell thee that, Elizabeth should be thy wife."

Hopkins blinked at the abrupt change in the course of an evening that he had assumed he was controlling. Readjusting with a sigh, he said, "I'm afraid, Patience, that train has left the station."

"Why?"

"We're too old."

"Johnsie, we are nearly the same age, and yet here I am traveling to pledge my troth'."

"I thought," he said smiling, "that among other restrictions, we Quakers are not to pledge."

"I spoke metaphorically and will not be distracted by thy wit. Now I speak plain: marry Elizabeth."

"Thee knows it's been forbidden because we are first cousins," said Hopkins.

"How close were Adam and Eve?"

Hopkins stood and without excusing himself walked over to one of the windows. He stared off into the distance for several minutes. Meanwhile Patience closed her eyes and went into silent prayer.

Upon his return, Hopkins resumed his seat.

"Patience, the world knows all of thy life thee hast defied decorum. Hence, thee wears a dress worthy of Godey's Magazine instead of London Yearly Meeting business sessions. I have always been a conservative man, one who lived by the laws of both the land and the Religious Society."

"Enough of thy strength has been conserved in bachelorhood. Release some in a liberal marriage to the love of thy life."

"Perhaps in the other world," said Hopkins soberly.

"Thee is about as obdurate as any man I have known."

"It is that stubbornness that has made thee rich through B&O stock," he said with his eyes twinkling.

"Perhaps I should add self-deceived to thy known characteristics. I was more than comfortable before trains touched rail. It is Nantucket and her love for whale hunting that formed my fortune and stole my beloved father and brothers."

"Perhaps that is why they say thee does not care for wealth."

"If 'they' say it, 'they' slander," said Patience. "I give away freely, but I have grown, not reduced what I inherited. That said, I do not worship wealth. My heart belongs to Truth."

"What say you to all this Quaker banter, Mrs. Swift Eagle?" asked Hopkins.

"I don't know what to say in the face of monied people who turn away from love, in one case for decades, in the other for a lifetime," said Fannie.

"That was put rather plainly."

"Excuse me, sir. Talk of turning away love to a widow who has lost two good men seems like disrespecting Nyame, the one you call the Lord."

Once more Hopkins stood and went to the window. He watched the sun set and came back. "Well, Patience, thee and thy good friend here have caused quite a disturbance."

"How so?" asked Patience.

"After all these years, I came very close to reconsidering my decision not to defy tradition and ask for Elizabeth's hand."

"What prevented thee?"

"I was prevented by believing the setting sun was a metaphor."

"Wait a bit," said Fannie, "and the moon will rise. Will that also be a metaphor."

He looked at Patience and said, "Some say wrongly that coloreds are not an intelligent people. Fannie here and Frederick Douglass prove otherwise."

He turned his eyes again on Fannie "Elizabeth and I have spent decades convincing ourselves that our desires are misled. How could we ever curse a decision that we have embraced longer than the lifespan of most of my grandfather's slaves?" There was a deep silence. "What say thee now, my friend?"

Fannie was still thinking the matter through when Johns resumed his seat. Fannie startled the room by taking his hand. He almost jerked it away but thought better of what might have been interpreted as an insult. She calmed him with the other on top with a touch as gentle as the one she used to settle jumpy stallions. Looking steadily into his eyes she said, "If my mother was here, she'd say, 'Re-memory' the first time you said to yourself, 'I love Elizabeth'." She paused. "Was sleeping cold alone what you had in mind?"

He gently removed his hand, patted hers and stood, "You have turned from pleasant guest into a dangerous woman."

She also stood and placed her hands, palms mirroring each other and nearly touching each other in prayer position. "No, watching love grow cold is dangerous. When two people have the power to turn on its head a decision that keeps hearts from soaring and such a turn will hurt no one, wouldn't it be generous to turn, turn, turn."

A servant wearing a large pocketed apron came into the

room. She silently waited to be acknowledged. "Dinner is prepared. Shall I cover it for a while, sir?"

* * *

All people cannot be rescued. As I write in 1860, both Johns Hopkins and Elizabeth Hopkins remain united in surname but unmarried. Each time the calendar turns a page my sister Fannie and I pray that they will change their positions.

2 0

THE SHAWL

I had chanced upon my brother Luther Duncan in 1852. At the time he said he would consider moving to Ohio where he could both be with family and live on the frontier. I did not have the heart to tell him, except for a few in hiding or who had amalgamated, the Indians had nearly all been removed from the state. The frontier had long since moved west. Of course, his family was living in the metropolis of Philadelphia where my children's Quaker forebears had been instrumental in removing the Indians over 150 years earlier. While living with the Seminoles in Florida he had been part of yet another Indian removal.

* * *

Angelica, Luther's wife, was a member of the Philadelphia black aristocracy. Her family had lived there in freedom so long that all stories of their enslavement had been relegated to the stuff of rumor. She had never dreamed of coming to a place even within a week's ride of wildness. Ignoring his wife's feelings, Luther convinced several members of his congregation to move with him. As a committed Baptist minister's wife, Angelica had come with her children and husband. Faithfulness to her wedding vows did not prevent her from complaining all the way from Philadelphia.

They arrived in June of 1853. Within a week she who had lived a life surrounded by her own relatives, complained about Luther's. They chose a place a respectable distance between her family and my own. We both considered the other overbearing, so I had not stooped to protest when they located in Middletown. Although larger than nearby Waynesville, when Angelica saw the village's small colored section and ascertained that there was neither public library nor museums, she switched from brooding to verbally attacking Luther. After a veiled hint that she might leave him, Luther worked to make the Miami Valley seem more like a land of milk and honey. He and his Philadelphia transplants established the First Baptist African Church and the Angelica Duncan School which eventually counted twenty-five African-American regular students between the ages of five and eighteen and a handful of illiterate adults who sporadically attended.

By 1855 the church had grown from the original twenty-two to eighty adult members. On the First-Sunday communion days, when he assured parishioners without partaking Hell fire waited, the gatherings of the House of Esi who came from both Waynesville and Cincinnati pushed the church numbers almost to 300. If Luther was as great a preacher on the other Sundays, he was indeed more gifted than Angelica declared. On those communion days, "Amens" abounded except from her mouth. Even my Quaker-reared little ones cheered on Uncle Luther.

The money that Luther and Angelica made together, pastoring and teaching, did not bring in enough to sustain what

she deemed an acceptable lifestyle. As well, the Ohio abolitionist movement lacked the strength to free Luther to supplement his income to deliver visiting sermons where "love
offerings" and "release money" could supplement income as it
did for leading eastern abolitionists.

Angelica saw the end of their savings was approaching.
"More money is what we need."

"My passion is for preaching and studying," said Luther.
"They've yet to pay much here but—"

"Passion has never purchased sustenance," interrupted
Angelica. "My father taught me that nothing buys groceries but
work, yours or another's."

Luther found odd jobs to assist with supporting his family.
He did almost anything from painting and carpentry to helping
local farmers plant, cultivate and harvest. He also swept down-
town sidewalks and stables. Still it was not enough. "We left
with $500 in savings," said Angelica. "Because moving to this
God-forsaken town cost so much, in two years we are only back
to $437 saved. How much did you say your father saved to free
his family from Virginia's slavery?"

Luther overlooked her comparison of Ohio living to his life
in a slave state. He was also happy to learn that they had made
so much progress. Since his days on the road with Frederick
Douglass, Angelica had been the family treasurer. Seeming to
revel in making him ask for an accounting, she only gave him
one when the whim struck her. Alas, an unexpected expendi-
ture forced the savings to dip below $200.

One day Deacon Addison Cooper reported to Angelica
that he had, "seen Reverend Duncan shining shoes on a street
corner."

That evening Luther walked in smiling bravely and
carrying a bag of groceries that he had earned by serving as a
bootblack and charging two illiterate locals a penny each for

taking dictation for letters. "Look what I have, Angelica." He handed her the fresh food.

"I heard that you were out on Main Street and Central disgracing the family by shining the boots of white men!"

"Even a broken clock is right twice a day, Angelica," said Luther. "You make me feel like I'm never right."

He had spent his formative years as a slave and rarely verbalized his complaints or even furrowed his brow. She recalled to herself, "I guess I haven't been a good preacher's wife."

He was shocked. On average, Angelica offered less than an apology a year, stepped on toe or burnt pan toast. Luther found his tongue. "Please, darling, forget that now you're a small-town preacher's wife and grew up as a daughter to a preacher of the biggest black church in Philadelphia. Just think of me as a man tonight, a man who set aside a chance at fame for the chance to make you happy."

* * *

In the morning Angelica asked, "Was I better to you last night?"

He wanted to ask, 'Better than what?' Discretion got the better part of vindictiveness. "You were this man's dream." Peace in the house is better than peace in the mind.

"Now with your new earnings, I suppose you can buy me that shawl you promised last month."

Luther recognized the trap too late. A few days later, he heard that the owners of J. and J.M. Johnston's Ice Chests were looking for someone to dig the earth for a new double-stall outhouse behind their shop. He offered his services for two dollars a day and a new personal ice chest. He did not reveal the assignment until he and Angelica went to the commercial district to purchase the shawl.

"What?" she said. "How can a professional woman have a husband who welcomes degrading himself?"

"Angelica, how can a professional woman wants a new shawl when her husband has just put his little money in groceries?"

"I am Head Mistress of my own school. I deserve this shawl."

"I don't question what you deserve. If I did question, I would not be purchasing it."

"Still, Luther, I'm disappointed in you yet again." When he did not respond she lowered her voice. "Am I wrong? Didn't we have something called love once upon a time?"

He felt the knife twisting in his rib cage just beneath his heart. "While you make your purchase, if you finish before I return, wait for me, I'm going in Mosley's to buy a new sledgehammer."

Luther ran into a parishioner who asked for counseling and was delayed in arriving at his rendezvous. Angelica finished early and stood in front of Samuel Barnes' carriage making shop pretending she was the first colored model for Godey's Magazine. Her new scarlet scarf set off her pink dress with matching bonnet just right. She was daydreaming when suddenly a voice said, "How much and where?"

She was recalled to the present. "Excuse me?"

A man took her arm. "Dense wenches starve. I repeat: how much and where?"

"Why, I am not a common... common..."

"I could not care less if you're common or elite," said the man slightly tightening his grip on her arm. "But it will not do for a good Christian gentleman to linger long on a corner with the likes of you."

"Come on Simon," said a second man. "I don't think this nigger is in the trade."

For the first time Simon allowed his eyes to meet Angelica's directly. She was terrified and wilting like a rose held too close to a flame.

The two men left quickly. When she regained her composure, she immediately surveyed the dusty streets. There was no evidence of witnesses. Luther came out braced for more complaining. Instead Angelica broke down crying and ran into his arms. He dropped the sledgehammer and held on tight.

"What's happened?" he whispered repeatedly as he kissed her hair and stroked her back.

"I've been insulted by a white man."

"Insulted?"

"A white man propositioned me."

Although he recognized the danger of his chosen path, Luther coldly asked, "Do you know his name?"

Missing the cue that would have protected him as her mother had taught her that colored women must, Angelica answered, "A second man—I believe his brother—called him Simon."

In the small town only one man met the description, Captain Simon Karsten, retired Mexican War hero. The second man was his younger brother Abe. A strange calm came over Luther. He picked up his wife's hat, handed it to her, and bent down again for the sledgehammer. "Let's go home, dear," he said.

They climbed into the wagon. Half-way home it dawned on Angelica why her husband was so calm. Fearing the direction in which they seemed headed she said, "Please don't, Luther."

He lacked interest in playing a game. "You have been insulted, and so has every black woman in this country. In the name of Esi, I won't wander outside while your honor is being stolen."

She did not understand that the reference was to his parents and all the times that Nathan Prescott had displaced Father while raping Mother. When she asked him to clarify his meaning, for the first time she learned what for years he had attempted to hide from all who knew him. They arrived home, and Luther left the driver's seat to walk around the wagon and help Angelica climb down.

"I teach my students that holding grudges is like carrying a canteen full of poison and taking a sip whenever the memory crosses your mind. Luther, please."

"Believe me darling, I won't hold this grudge long." Usually he would have simply walked beside her into their small frame house. Instead, he offered and she accepted his arm as though she were being escorted to a high seat in a mythological court. At the door, he kissed her softly, went to the bedroom, retrieved his pistol from the top drawer on his side of the bed, put it in his pants, covered it with his coat, and went back to town.

The two Karsten brothers shared a house just off Main Street on Second Avenue.

Luther knocked politely. A man came to the door. "Yes?"

"In front of Mosley's General Store, you insulted my wife today."

"Unless you're married to a mule, nigger you came to the wrong place."

"Step aside, Abe," said a second man. "I suppose you're referring to me, boy," said the next man. "My name is Captain Simon Karsten."

"I accuse you and I demand satisfaction," said Luther.

"Demand?" spat out Abe.

"This is my affair, brother." Simon held out his arm to restrain his brother.

"A nigger comes to our home and makes demands—"

"I'll handle this," Simon turned back, "I apologize."

Although Luther was surprised at how easy this was unfolding, he said without hesitating, "I accept."

He turned to leave but Simon said, "If you don't want your bitches to be mistaken for mongrels, keep them in kennels."

Outnumbered and aware that if things escalated, by state law, blacks could not testify against whites, Luther thought quickly and said in a clear, soft voice, "If you are one, I will have a gentleman's satisfaction."

"You will get satisfaction, boy. Choose your poison, anything from fists to shotguns."

A recent article in the local newspaper had claimed, "Captain Simon Karsten could outbox any sergeant, outshoot any marksman."

"I've read about you," said Luther.

"I'm impressed that you can read," said Simon. "Now you can choose a possibility of living here in Middletown's colored heaven or the certainty of an early Hell. If you 'demand' satisfaction choose which fate will bring you ecstasy."

Luther's exploits had not been lionized in the newspaper. That did not make them less worthy. "I choose axe handles at dusk by the riverside parallel to Seventh Avenue. Be there at dusk today and bring a second."

Luther turned to leave. "And, boy? What is your name?"

"Reverend Luther Duncan."

"No 'sir?'" asked the Captain with a smile.

"No 'sir', boy."

"Well, Lucy Duncan, you have my word as an officer and a gentleman, that should you survive you'll not be lynched."

"Do your words have a second or are you your own character witness?"

"A second?" said Abe Karsten as outraged now as Luther had been over his wife's insult.

"Second my words, Abe," said Simon.

"To a nigger?"

"Second I say," said Simon.

"I second," said Abe. "Enjoy the rest of your life, preacher boy. It's almost over."

Our nephew, Diego Perez, was the son of our brother Dan and our one-time slave mistress, Anne Prescott, came early to Luther's house. Anne had given birth to Diego in Cuba and had him reared an orphan slave in a nunnery. When he reached his majority, he was given a fortune. Upon learning his parentage, he had relocated and purchased a farm on the Middletown section of the Miami River.

"Uncle, this is so primitive," said Diego to Luther. "Is it really necessary?"

"I have no idea how honor is practiced in Cuba. In the States we cannot let the whites simultaneously put their women on a pedestal and denigrate ours."

"But you can be killed. How will it look for a preacher to be killed fighting?"

"Diego, I have an anger—no a rage—so thick that it could be sliced into six large pieces and there would still be a lifetime worth of leftovers."

The sun was going down above the western tree line when Luther and Diego arrived at the riverside sight of the duel. A few minutes later, wearing his dress uniform and a double line of metals, Simon Karsten arrived with his brother. Silently, the captain took off his hat and decorated coat. He handed them to Abe, smiling slightly. He rolled up his sleeves. "Luther Duncan, I trust you've had time for prayer?"

Luther started to assume a wide stance. Before his first step was planted, Simon swung at his head. Luther slipped left, swung his left axe handle at the spot behind the Captain's right knee and, before he hit the earth, his right handle across his right shoulder. Simon attempted to stagger up but Luther came down with handles on both of his opponent's shoulders. The sound of cracking bones was almost as loud as Abe's shocked scream.

Simon fell unconscious face first into the muck.

Abe stood with his mouth still agape. Unless Luther intended to kill the captain, the fight was over in less than five seconds.

Luther looked at Abe. "I don't believe your brother is any shape to speak. As his second, do you want to say 'Quarter' in his place or shall I send him to 'white folk's Hell'?"

Luther raised his right arm.

"Quarter," said Abe.

"Perhaps you should receive a Riverside Medal for saving a life," said Luther.

* * *

That night Luther returned home tight-lipped. Angelica quietly fed him a humble meal of pinto beans, cornbread and a single pork chop. Other than, "Please, pass the salt and pepper," few words were spoken. The children realized something was amiss but their father's mind was far off and their mother fighting to maintain her composure, shielding the children, shielding herself. The parents put the children to bed early and retired to their bedroom.

Luther was undressing when she said, "You came back unscathed."

"I did?"

"Then you called it off?"

"No. I have not been manacled, so I also did not kill him. He lives, I suspect in hiding until healed, but he lives."

Angelica sat down heavily on the bed as Luther finished undressing. "No more questions?"

"At long last I have an answer."

He turned to face her. "What might that be?"

"Thinking of losing you clarified my world. I have been cheating myself and us. I do love you."

He took her hand. "I cannot remember the last time you said so."

"Neither can I." He kissed her hand as though she were royalty. She hesitated, then said, "For so long I have believed you could not see me."

"How so? Have I gone blind without my knowing it?"

"There is the flesh and there is the soul. It took white insults for you to see my soul."

Luther was stunned. After several seconds, he said, "If all my thoughts have been in response to their actions, I have been no more free than was my father on Fruits of the Spirit."

A tear came to her left eye. She wiped it. "Step out of the room and I will show off my shawl to its best advantage." He looked confused. She stood and gave him a gentle shove.

In his underwear he retreated to the darkened dining area. A few moments later she said, "I am prepared for you to enter."

He opened the door. Standing before him was Angelica wearing nothing but a purple shawl and a radiant smile.

"Not exactly the school marm look."

"No and the thoughts we two own this moment have nothing to do with a white man."

THE KISSING GAME

My last dream of the night was about my parents. Although I grew up considering myself a Daddy's girl, as usual, the dream featured Esi. My mother was a granddaughter of the Fante Queen Mother and reared in the royal compound. Mother spoke of Fante-land often but never of her high birth. Daddy, a Fante commoner, wanted to be an American and never spoke of Fante-land except the few times he told me who Mother should have been. Sometimes he expressed rage or grief over her treatment. Always he ended with a proud sigh because she had chosen him as husband. The books that I read made it appear that proposing was a man's job. Some of my siblings have said that he did ask the initial question but she was the one who accepted. That is a symbol of how much power she exerted even as a teenager.

One of the blessings of my parents' lives was the fact that although they were captured along with their parents, the Queen Mother and her husband were not. I suppose that somewhere in Africa one of my relatives is esteemed.

Dream over, I could feel the sunrise trying to break the dark night. I rolled over in bed and a wave of guilt washed over me. Lying next to me was my Scots-Irish Quaker husband. He had defied both the laws of the state of Ohio and Quaker discipline by marrying me, a woman of another race and without membership in the Religious Society of Friends. His family had expected him to be expelled from the local congregation. Instead, mysteriously, he was given a letter of condemnation. I was grateful but not so much that I wanted to be the first colored person to join Caesar's Creek Meeting. So long as they were not moved to pick up arms and fight to end slavery, I was not moved to write a letter requesting membership.

While growing up on Fruits of the Spirit Plantation, I never asked my long-suffering slave mother how she was feeling or said, "Good morning." I could see in her eyes that, with the exception of a devoted husband and children, Mother was oppressed in every way. As first-sight greeting, I always said something like, "Hello, Mother." She replied with "Hello, Oseye," which was the name she had given me at birth. Daddy had changed my name to Sarah because the overlords hated everything African except the use of our bodies.

In my Ohio home, I dressed as quietly and quickly as I was able and turned around when I heard Charles stretching in a huge morning yawn. I was happy that I had beaten the sun and he had not seen my nakedness. Neither of us was modest, but with so much work ahead I could not afford to return to bed to please desires that would be better gratified later. Once relaxed he displayed the loving eyes and smile of a free man. I said, "Good morning husband. Is thee feeling well?"

He quoted a line he had heard my scampish brother Dan use, "I'm not sleepy but I do feel like lying down." I laughed and threw his shirt at him before quickly leaving the room to prepare breakfast for the family and help with the big day.

* * *

The local Quakers hosted the area's quarterly business meeting for the surrounding local meetings for worship. People had traveled up to a day's drive away for this gathering time where the older people concentrated on matters peculiar to the faith and many youngsters looked for possible lifetime mates as well as rare opportunities to flirt with someone who at least had a chance to not bring a scolding. Mary Crispin, my mother-in-law, once had served as Presiding Clerk. Now she was too tired to attend more than the first business session. However, she was blessed to have daughters and daughters-in-law to help with serving meals.

Men and older children had set the many borrowed tables in Mary Crispin's and Clark's yard. My nine year-old twins, William and Henry, had been taught that American lies claim that although we do nearly all of the work in slave territory, and most of the lowest level work in the north, blacks are indolent. With guests scrutinizing our every move, I refused to let the twins run around playing with their white cousins and neighbors. Without me needing to encourage them, they were helping with the set ups along with much sturdier children.

There were places for 240 people with host committee members' dinnerware gleaming in the early autumn sun. Arrayed in serving dishes were such dishes as bacon dumplings, chicken stewed with fresh picked corn, Dutch oven loaf, Maryland biscuits, peaches in cider, fricasseed tomatoes and various greens, including collards, my favorite. Inside was an array of desserts featuring a sweet potato cobbler that my mother had taught me to make, and what was to be the last Black Cake that Mary Crispin would bake.

I stopped helping the others at around 10am and left to bring hearty plates of food and drink to Charles and three black workers from nearby Middletown who were helping him complete the corn harvest.

From afar I heard singing.

"No more peck of corn for me
No more, no more.
No more peck of corn for me."

"No more overseer's whip for me,
No more."

"No more pinch of salt for me,
No more."

"Got my freedom and my woman
Come rain or hot son
this is the day we won."

I thought back to variations on this song when I was enslaved on Fruits of the Spirit and thanked God that these good men would be fed well and paid fairly for their labor.

Charles accepted the plate. "What of the water?"

"Thee usually wants to eat first."

"Not that in the jug. That which is inside thy mouth."

I kissed the flirt and turned to leave. He squeezed my elbow and then my rear.

"What am I going to do with thee?" I asked.

"If thee has not solved the riddle yet, for shame!"

We both laughed and I went over to bring food to the hired workers. They stood at my approach and I said, "You men look healthy and well."

"Life is good," said Jed .

Far removed from even the best parts of my former life,

nostalgia momentarily grasped me and I said, "Jed, could I ask thee to play juba before I head back to help the others prepare for our guests?"

"Why sure, ma'am," said Jed.

He patted rhythmic time to a tune on a leg with his right hand. After a moment the other two men danced buck and wing steps. I laughed with them as Charles sneaked up behind me and grabbed my hand and whirled me around. To my amazement they had taught the Quaker lad to dance. He could almost keep up with me!

I broke off my amusement and rushed back to my chores. Life is good when love is strong.

The morning business meeting had ended at the meetinghouse which was a few miles up the road. The congregants were coming for the midday meal. Many of the guests had heard the rumor that I was married to Mary Crispin's most headstrong son but had never seen me because we rarely traveled. I suppose most thought my daughters Susan and Eva and I were merely servants. I busied myself helping my girls, sisters-in-laws, and committee members with making certain all was well on the tables. From the corner of my eye I saw a man wearing a pair of calf skin shoes that were above average in workmanship, though not as fine as those my father and brother Robin had made. I dismissed the shoes but the longing for the lost lingered a second before I dismissed it. The man was a widower named Andrew Hinshaw who had recently relocated to Ohio. My work took me near. Apparently, he was staring at me when I overheard someone stage whisper, "They say she married one of the wild sons."

I felt eyes as Andrew studied me closer. When he was sure

of his assessment he said, "Why Sarah." I turned to look at him. "Thee is Mary Pool Hoge's Sarah?"

I recognized the name of the beloved Quaker with whom I had lived for a time in Virginia but not the bearded man who was speaking.

"Yes, I lived with Mary Pool Hoge and her husband Tyler, but I never belonged to her. Who might thee be, Friend?"

"Why I'm Andy Hinshaw." I searched vainly to remember such a name. "We were schoolmates with the Negro Bill Coleman."

"I remember Bill well. A friend told me he is a steamship steward."

"Do you recall the day I beat you in the spelling bee?"

"Should I?" I asked disingenuously. I had beaten him more times than I could remember if given a thousand dollars for each, but yes, I did remember the lone loss because of a silly mistake.

"Does thee recall once we—" He caught himself before scandalizing us both by sharing a story of the only time he had won the spelling bee and my penalty was to take the far end of a string with my mouth as his teeth clinched the other end. I was forced to inch along until my lips touched his. I think I obeyed the rules long enough to make contact. I know I spit an imagined taste out immediately. "We must talk later. Perhaps this evening."

"That is quite impossible," I said more loudly than intended or necessary.

A sister-in-law heard the exchange. I had nothing to hide, following the meal, I stood openly with my former acquaintance. To make certain no one thought I was being unfaithful, I stage-laughed at unearthed memories. Suddenly Andrew said, "If I had known that all that might happen if I had pursued thee might be a letter of condemnation such as was served on thy husband, I would have taken the risk."

A misguided person or a fool may believe myriad notions but Andrew had not crossed my mind once in decades. That we had played a kissing game once at age 12 was as irrelevant to me as the longitudinal placement of the afternoon's clouds in the Berlin sky. As I was turning to walk away from what had become an uncomfortable conversation, Charles ambled over. I stopped my retreat and waited for my husband to join us. "Charles Ferguson, my husband, meet Andrew Hinshaw an old schoolmate from nearly thirty years ago."

The two men shook hands. The crush of a seriously pressurized thumb on the spot between Andrew's thumb and forefinger and something in Charles's eyes reminded the visitor that another business meeting session was due to start soon. He excused himself.

Charles said, "I know thee, Sarah. Something is amiss. I know thee!"

"Do not ever deceive thyself that thee hast mastered my thoughts. A woman tells what a woman tells and very little more."

"What is that supposed to mean?"

"It does mean there are always what my father called arcana imperii, the secrets of the empire, and I am the Empress of my own mind." I caught myself. Perhaps the years spent in slavery made me too sensitive. Charles was only showing his untamed self to a foolish old acquaintance. Softening my voice, I said, "The gentleman was addled by memories: his, mine and his alone."

"What is that supposed to mean?"

"It means we shared certain memories of youth and he has nursed fantasies that are beyond foolish." Charles was taken aback that I was so frank. "Out of the blue he indicated that he felt an attraction that at age 12 I could not have felt if he had been thee. As soon as I was aware of the water's depth I was turning to leave before I would have been forced to watch a man drown in his own shame. Then thee came and he turned like a white-tailed deer."

"He insulted thee?"

In my mind, regardless of a yard full of Quaker witnesses I feared Charles might thrash poor Andrew. I said as casually as I could, "Of course, he was not so forward."

"Then what did thee mean by saying thee 'could not have felt' what he was suggesting?"

"Aside from my father and brothers I have never loved— or even dreamed of any man—not named Charles Ferguson." By this time, I had noticed standing near was the sister-in-law who I believe had alerted Charles to my conversation with Andrew. She was observing what she might from twenty yards away. Knowing that Quaker etiquette forbid such public tenderness, I reached out and touched his face and spoke so that more than my sister-in-law heard the borrowed line that he had used that morning, "I am not sleepy but I feel like lying down."

Hand in hand, scandalizing all afraid-to-publicly-touch Quakers, we walked to our house. Silently we went into our bedroom where I said, "Help me remove my corset, please?"

"Have I ever failed to do so?" He gently nibbled at my neck

.

"Thee is not the only wild Ferguson."

22
BROWN'S BRIGADE

This story was related to me by Jeremy Baker, my nephew through my brother Dan Crispin and my younger brother, Luther Duncan. Because of the way circumstances unfolded during that unforgettable incident, as in any combat, as historian, I have been required to stitch together what is more a quilt than a curtain.

* * *

In May of 1859 John Brown, my nephew Jeremy, brother Luther and Aaron Stevens, one of the highest-ranking officers in Brown's brigade of slave freers, took a train from Cleveland to Ashtabula, Ohio. The rumply dressed hard men walked the short distance from the station and spied a sea of chickens from the road.

"I haven't seen this many chickens since I left Rock Island," said Jeremy.

"Then you've seen less of the world than I thought," said Luther.

Brown led the small group of men up the walk to a two-story, 11-room brick house above Lake Erie. On the porch, the motley crew of men were greeted by William Hubbard a wealthy underground railroad conductor. In league with his commercial schooner-owning brother, Henry who often helped fugitives make the 40-mile trip across Lake Erie into Canadian freedom. The Hubbards' work did not always go undetected. At a time when colored men fortunate enough to be paid for their labor might be happy with $2 a day, the Hubbards were caught and fined three times, totaling $5000. Instead of being deterred, they continued their commitment to fight for freedom. They stated publicly that they had no right to complain. Others were jailed. A white abolitionist named Elijah Lovejoy was murdered for his work. The deacon and his brother also never stopped serving The Lord.

Brown said, "Sir, I know your given name is William, but don't know whether to call you Mister or Colonel."

"Deacon will do," said Hubbard. "I take my religion seriously. Do I call you Mister, General, Old Man or Captain?"

The group laughed. "John will do just fine."

Jeremy stepped forward and gave the Deacon a container of crystallized maple syrup sent by a slave family who the Hubbard family had sheltered and helped cross into Canada years before. He thanked Jeremy and said to Brown, "Sir, I would love to host you men both for dinner and breakfast at which time we might have some of what I am sure will be fine syrup on hot cakes."

Brown possessed enigmatic concepts of time. What others considered early or late had no effect on his actions. His men were divided, most wanting to push on south and east. General Brown accepted the invitation. Hubbard said, "I have a delightful surprise. After-dinner we will have a small concert for our entertainment."

The Deacon believed in eating well. Helped by her cook, his wife Katherine served the men Seneca style chicken stewed with new corn, broiled chicken, chicken cooked in a batter, walleye fish, rice, potatoes, field green salad, green beans, fresh baked bread, lemon pudding and gingerbread.

"Please forgive me. There are those who say that I am too fond of chicken," said Katherine.

"Ma'am, if you knew how we eat in the field you would call this a feast," said Brown.

Over dinner, Brown and the Deacon kept the conversation on experiences in Northeast Ohio where the guest had spent his formative years. Afterwards, together with several guests from town, the men walked upstairs to the ballroom.

When Luther noticed the room had dividers, he prayed that it did not signal there would be a division of races. We were startled when Katherine placed her arm in his and said, "Come Reverend, we would like for you to sit in the front row."

"Thank you kindly, ma'am."

From the wings, Virginia-born Justin Holland came out with his Spanish guitar. Seeing Luther on the arm of the hostess he called out, "Why Luther Duncan! Imagine two Virginians who are not on the run being together here on Lake Erie!"

"You know our guest performer?" asked Katherine.

"Yes, ma'am. Mrs. Katherine Hubbard, meet Mr. Justin Holland. We are both native Virginians."

"One born free, the other born a slave, both dedicated to abolition," said Holland.

Hubbard left Alex Fobes and his wife Eunica and joined them. "You know each other?"

"Our paths have crossed many times," said Holland.

"I was secretary to Frederick Douglass for years before I became a minister," said Luther.

"And a soldier," said the deacon.

"It takes one to know one," said Brown.

The group laughed. The Hubbards assumed their seats with the deacon sitting between Luther and Katherine with Eunica on her side with Alex sitting between her and Brown, forming the first row.

Beginning with a variation on The Magic Flute, the entire program was devoted to Holland's arrangements of music that had been introduced to him in Europe by the Spaniard Fernando Sor. Asked for an encore, Holland said, "I have played guitar tonight but I am at heart an abolitionist and a teacher as well as a musician. I play for you Sor's Hercule et Omphale because tonight we are blessed with heroes including black ones. As the world should know, the hero Hercules was a descendant of the Ethiopian princess Andromeda, she of the stars and her husband Perseus. May John Brown and friends lead our people to the stars and in doing so, imitate Perseus by slaying all monsters in their path.

Holland ended the concert with unbridled passion.

* * *

Brown, his men, and Holland spent the night sleeping on the ballroom floor where the concert had been held. The Fobes were given the first floor suite that had once been used by the deacon's parents.

After a simple breakfast of bacon, eggs, cream muffins and coffee, Charles Garlick arrived to drive Brown and his men to Jefferson. Garlick said to Luther and Jeremy, "I would suppose you two men are on 'French leave'."

Neither knew the phrase. "He thinks," said Brown, "that you are runaways."

"I was never a slave," said Jeremy, "but freeing them is what my life's about."

"I knew you were never a field hand."

"How so?" asked Brown.

"His hands is as soft as a chicken's throat. The other man here picked cotton. I know that by the thick pad under his thumb when he shook my hand."

"I picked more than my share of cotton but I have a legal free paper," said Luther. "I got it when the Americans stole Florida from the Seminoles. They took my dreams and gave me a passport."

"You're a Black Seminole?" asked Garlick in shock. "Never met one so I couldn't rightly size you up." He slowed the carriage, reached back and shook Luther's hand again. "You didn't spend near as much time as my friend Eddie picked cotton."

"I picked tobacco before then but ran away when I was young and joined the Seminole. That's where I became a man."

"Once y'all were the baddest men on God's good earth."

"I am also a minister," said Luther.

Garlick was quiet for several miles before he said, "Reverend Luther or is it Mr. Luther?"

"You may call me by my first name."

"I been wrong on some of my guesses about you, but I expect to be right on this one. My guess is you was called to preach."

"I was and I am."

"How come it seems like the Lord took back His call or did the people kick you out?"

"Neither," said Luther. "I'm a fighting preacher even as there are slave master preachers."

"You can't be a Christian and be a slave master," said Garlick.

"I did not say those preachers are Christians. From where I sit, The Lord sent me to tear down the walls of slavery like Joshua fought the battle of Jericho."

"I always liked that song," said Garlick. He remembered something. "You are that man who used to be Douglass' body guard then secretary."

"Yes," said Luther.

"When Douglass came this way in '47 I followed him all over northern Ohio. He was the prettiest man and best speaker I ever heard."

"He still is."

"Everywhere he went he told us to get an education and that's what I did."

Garlick told the story of his own escape from slavery, bragging about many of his experiences during the year that he had spent as a student at Oberlin College.

"My good sister studied there too," said Brown.

"As did my sister," said Jeremy.

They exchanged names. Garlick had not overlapped with either but there had been a few instructors that Garlick named and either Jeremy or Brown had a vague remembrance of. "Rememory is the salt of the earth," said Garlic.

"I still can't get over the foresight to let both races and genders study together," said Stevens.

"There are more than two races," said Luther and Jeremy at the same time. One had been a Seminole, the other had grown up with close Sac and Fox friends and lived for a while with the Bannock.

"Too often I forget that," said Stevens.

"I'd like to see The Almighty only sees one," said Brown.

The trip had almost ended when Brown said to Garlick, "How would you like to go back into Hell and impale a few devils as we free thousands of your people."

Garlick said, "I've heard that out in Kansas you all proved you are stone cold killers. I'm a man of peace unless I'm attacked."

"What is a life sentence of slavery but a never-ending attack?" asked Brown.

No argument could move Garlick to join Brown's brigade.

* * *

At 6'2" and weighing over 200 pounds, Joshua Giddings was physically imposing. The white-haired man was also almost as self-taught as our Frederick Douglass. Unlike the men I knew well, Giddings often used violent language and did not hesitate to encourage bloodshed. What I personally loved most about what newspapers said of him was his attempt to end the hated Ohio Black Laws, give blacks the vote everywhere, overturn the Federal Fugitive Slave Act of 1850, and recognize the nation of Haiti, the pride of all black people. He was such a champion for our cause that someone in my birth state of Virginia had placed a $10,000 reward for his arrest and $5000 should his decapitated head be delivered on a plate, as was that of John the Baptist. I will never understand how the so-called Christians missed the fact that John the Baptist was said to be both the cousin to and forerunner of the Messiah. Brown was in town to see how far Giddings was willing to be his own forerunner.

At Giddings' office John Brown began the conversation, "Since we both agree that slavery and freedom are by nature at war, it's fitting the two of us talk. Congressman what I have to say to you is undercover, intended only for the ears of the faithful."

"Those in Washington have outraged our Constitution," said Giddings. "A system based on torture and coercion will never fit my idea of God's Higher Law. I would revise the Constitution and restructure society to fit the Golden Rule. But I am no longer a congressman."

"We agree on almost everything political, but I was expecting your party to put forth Chase or Steward for President. Instead from what I hear this new upstart Abraham Lincoln is 'a slavehound'."

"I once lived in the same Washington rooming house with Lincoln. He's not so new and you are correct. He is not an abolitionist. He is hardly even anti-slavery. I have chided him for everything from going to see minstrel shows with capering fools in black face, to failing to see how accepting Texas as a slave state weakened freedom, and backing slave owning Taylor for President."

"Yet we have read you are backing him," said Luther.

"You obviously do not understand politics. Lincoln is the best man we can find who has a chance of victory. Jesus or Moses would be better candidates but neither could win."

"And both are dead," said Jeremy. "One didn't get to see the promised land and the other was killed because he did."

"We are here to make what Jesus saw become reality," said Brown.

"I admit that sometimes I personally seek more than the votes can deliver," said Giddings, "but this is a nation where votes count."

"What of Chase?" said Brown.

"He's a curious man. I love him but I cannot say that I trust him. Ambition has been known to blind more men than King Herod and Napoleon Bonaparte."

"Sir," said Jeremy. "What I know best about you is not about your ambition but the many times the papers say you have defended the rights of slaves to take up arms. Is that the grapevine or the truth?"

"The grapevine quotes a certain famous man as saying, 'I cannot tell a lie'. I am not that man, but I am one who has argued for the human rights of all men. Yes, even slaves have a right to defend their freedom. You have heard the tale of a sinking ship in which the passengers overlooked the life boats and clung to the anchor?"

"That's a good one," said Jeremy.

"I've heard it before," said Stevens. "It sums up where this country is today."

Giddings nodded slightly and addressed Jeremy. "I would guess that for you and your uncle here the Dred Scott decision denying all rights for colored people was the last straw."

"No," said Luther. "The last straw was the first kidnapping in Africa."

Giddings said, "Well stated."

"Sometimes," said Jeremy, "white abolitionists act as though, left alone, we blacks were too stupid to come up with the idea of freedom."

Brown waited a moment for Giddings to respond. When he hesitated, Brown said, "Talk is good, sir: ours and yours. What we need, sir, is more action."

"I understand that, Mr. Brown, but my words are used to spur those in power to act. Policy is the pudding's proof."

"Policy from haters," said Stevens, "begets hateful policy."

"Well stated," said Brown. "The way I read things, those controlling the slave states will never consider the evil they do until moral persuasion learns to bite more than how to bow wow."

Luther tried to ease the tense air by thanking Giddings for his words during the Seminole War. In his eyes and those of many of his best friends, Giddings was their best friend among those in power.

"In which newspaper did you read them?"

"I was there."

"The United States military will not permit blacks as soldiers. As a cook or baggage carrier?"

"As a Seminole warrior."

"If you were reading my words while fighting against our soldiers, some would say I was giving aid to the enemy."

"Excuse me sir, I read your words on many subjects before coming here. As for being 'the enemy', as you so aptly pointed out in a 3-hour Congressional speech that nearly caused a riot in Congress, the Black Seminoles were free citizens living in Spanish controlled land. We were being invaded. The Federal government was mainly in Florida searching for runaways who had stolen themselves from kidnappers and their descendants who were born free. I also read that you called Robey's Slave Emporium in Washington an 'infernal Hell.' As a child in 1827 I was sold there and experienced first-hand what you observed from the outside."

"And into which state were you sold?"

"To South Carolina. It was from there that I escaped, finding my way to Florida."

"You were an exile from what should have been your country." The statement was too obvious to win a response. "Obviously you passed through Georgia, a state sworn for a short period only to uphold freedom."

"In the minds of both Black and Red Seminoles 'liberty and justice' should have been ours from before Columbus and at least since 1776."

Giddings appeared stunned that colored people fully understood the logical extension of the Revolutionary words.

"The past must not be forgotten," said John Brown, "but I'm here to get you to step forward."

"You have vengeance in your aspect," said Giddings.

"Vengeance is the Lord's and I am His tool, one ready to purge this guilty land."

"Vengeance too is based on the past," said Giddings.

"For some," said Jeremy. "From our viewpoint vengeance is about preventing future wrongs."

"It would please us greatly, Attorney Giddings," said Luther, "if you would move a little further than saying slavery is a states' right issue."

"Instead of controlling it where it is," said Brown, "and keeping the Federal government out of it—which is impossible with the Fugitive Slave Law being enforced by Washington— why don't you do like Reverend Duncan here tells his congregation, 'Come on up!'"

"Have you worshipped with colored people, sir?" asked Aaron Stevens.

"I have heard that they are quite spirited in their practices," said Giddings.

"Spirit is good," said Stevens. "Physical is better."

"Aaron," said Luther, "one of my sisters is a seamstress. She often says, 'beware of going too far when you measure the cloth'. There is more to the black race than even we can always see."

"Forgive me," said Stevens.

John Brown rubbed his thick beard. "We need your help Mr. Giddings."

"I am with you heart and soul."

"I'm afraid we need a bit more."

Giddings gave a long discourse on his theory that by nature slavery and freedom have always been at war with each other. His visitors listened politely, hoping he would come to the logical conclusion that violence now was the only worthy road. He stopped at the brink of the inevitable. Brown said that it was necessary to reach as many supporters of freedom as possible.

"I own," said Giddings, "what I have stated publicly for years: the Federal government has been subsidizing slavery. It is time to subsidize the slaves."

"I knew you had it in you," said Brown. "Who might help with the proper subsidizing?"

Giddings recognized the trap his own words had set for him. In silent surrender, he reached for his pen and wrote both a letter of introduction and, without commentary, a list of potential patrons. Brown accepted the gifts, looked over the list, but did not disclose that he was already in contact with most men on it. Then to the surprise of everyone in the room, Giddings reached into his own wallet and gave a modest contribution that Brown chose not to count in front of witnesses, folding it up into the small stash in his pocket.

Brown led the visitors in standing. Giddings was shaken by what he had just done. "Sir," said Brown, "you may no longer be a congressman, and the road may have been long, but you just became a statesman."

ABOUT THE AUTHOR

Dwight L. Wilson is father to four sons and grandfather to two grandsons and two granddaughters. He lives in Ann Arbor with his wife Diane, an attorney.

He spent 41 years as a school professional including serving as Headmaster and Dean at various independent Quaker schools, Founding CEO of New Jersey SEEDS, as well as Assistant Chaplain at Oberlin College and Associate Dean at Marshall University. He is also the only person of color to serve as General Secretary of the oldest Quaker denomination in North America, Friends General Conference.

He has published historical fiction including *The Kidnapped: A Collection of Stories, The Resistors: A Collection of Stories* and six books in the series *Esi Was My Mother*. He also writes modern psalms. Current books include *Modern Psalms in Search of Peace and Justice, Modern Psalms for Solace and Resistance* and *Modern Psalms for Change Agents and Activists* are fed by his Quaker faith and a lifetime of social activism. His haiku and essays on Japanese Poetry have been published in periodicals spanning the globe.

OTHER TITLES BY RUNNING WILD

Open My Eyes by Tommy Hahn
Legendary by Amelia Kibbie
Christine, Released by E. Burke
Running Wild Stories Anthology, Volume 4
Tough Love at Mystic Bay by Elizabeth Sowden
The Faith Machine by Tone Milazzo
The Newly Tattooed's Guide to Aftercare by Aliza Dube
American Cycle by Larry Beckett
Magpie's Return by Curtis Smith
Gaijin by Sarah Z. Sleeper
Recon: The Trilogy + 1 by Ben White
Sodom & Gomorrah on a Saturday Night by Christa Miller

Upcoming Titles
Running Wild Novella Anthology, Volume 4
Antlers of Bone by Taylor Sowden
Blue Woman/Burning Woman by Lale Davidson
Something Is Better than Nothing by Alicia Barksdale
Take Me With You By Vanessa Carlisle
Mickey: Surviving Salvation by Robert Shafer
Running Wild Anthology of Stories, Volume 5 by Various
Running Wild Novella Anthology, Volume 5 by Various
Whales Swim Naked by Eric Gethers
Stargazing in Solitude by Suzanne Samples
American Cycle by Larry Beckett

Running Wild Press publishes stories that cross genres with great stories and writing. Our team consists of:

Lisa Diane Kastner, Founder and Executive Editor
Barbara Lockwood, Editor
Peter A. Wright, Editor
Rebecca Dimyan, Editor
Benjamin White, Editor
Andrew DiPrinzio, Editor
Lisa Montagne, Director

Learn more about us and our stories at www.runningwildpress.com

Loved this story and want more? Follow us at www.runningwildpress.com, www.facebook/runningwildpress, on Twitter @lisadkastner @RunWildBooks